Melville

Melville

Timothy R. Rice

To my wife Marcy, my love for 43 years and counting.

Table of Contents

Chapter One

As I came through the door, I knew something was amiss. What better way to begin a mystery with amiss? Maybe not. The new Jack Higgins book, *Day of Judgement*, which I'd been reading the night before, was falling off the table near the back door of my house. I have my "reading chair" and table near the back door for natural light from the afternoon sun.

When I entered, my leg brushed along the table, knocking the book to the floor. I saw the book hanging on the table's edge at that moment. I remember putting the book directly in the middle of the table. I do not have to remember this because it has become a habit. I placed things, intentionally, on the center of the table to prevent me from knocking things off it, which was precisely what had just occurred. Again, I knew something was amiss. My friends, especially my best friend, will tell you I am orderly to a fault. Okay, obsessive. I knew the book was in the wrong place.

Switching on the light near the back door, I see my small filing cabinet open. Strange. I do not leave it open haphazardly. I keep things in order, especially about my house. It is a special place. More about that later.

On top of my particularity of being a neat freak regarding the organization, I have a memory as good as they come. So, I will not likely forget to put my book in the correct place in my neat home or close a cabinet drawer.

In the three-drawer cabinet, the first two drawers were opened. The first consisted of my things and no interest in anyone. The second drawer was different. The second was full of solved criminal cases, which I will explain later. The opened drawers certainly explained the book on the floor. Someone had been in my house. And the reason was obvious. They were searching for my cases.

The cases I am referring to are the criminal cases I have solved in the last five years with help from my friends in my town. The characters range from my closest friend, a character, to other close friends. One was a tall slim factory worker, another a disabled researcher/CB radio guy, and a policeman.

The other assortment of characters in town, some who have helped me in cases in the past and some who will later, include Burt, the garbage man, an Ava Gardner lookalike, a widowed librarian, and Ethel and Myrtle May, the town gossips.

The two sisters seem to know everything happening in our little hamlet and what will soon happen. The easiest way to have the two old maids, dear as they can be, not know what is going on in your life is to stay in your house, close all the curtains, and never leave it. If you get your morning paper at 6:30, your neighbor on the other side of town would call and tell you at 7:00 that they heard you got it at 6:30 that morning. The old girls are that good. Don't get me wrong. They are sweet as they can be, but how they love to talk!

These characters and I live in a small town in North Carolina. Those cases would not be solved without them. I get everyone else involved with my nosing around and getting personally involved in those criminal cases in the first place. And I am seen as the leader. If troubles occur, my friends will look to me. I am the leader since I get them involved, whether they like it or not. I'm just that kind of guy.

The local police department would get credit if they deserved it. They do not. More about that fine group later.

People might say that I am an amateur sleuth. Some have done just that. I like to think that my friends and I are better than amateurs. Those friends, who are all different, help me solve all kinds of crimes in our small community. The greatest help comes from my best friend.

My name is Humphrey Larsen, and the only child of Gilbert and Virginia Larsen. My parents were English professors at nearby Wake Forest University in Winston Salem, North Carolina, a two-hour round trip by car from our small town. Being professors of English and lovers of books, my parents decided to name me from a Jack London novel. One of my dad's favorite London stories was "The Sea Wolf". The antagonist in London's story is Captain Wolf Larsen, and the protagonist is Humphrey van Weyden. My dad thought it would be cool to name me Humphrey while having the same last name as Wolf Larsen. Go figure. Sometimes my dad would tell me, "Aren't you glad we didn't name you Wolf?" I was glad they had not named me Wolf. Even though they named me Humphrey, I have been forever called Hump.

Our story takes place in the small town in which I live. And the same small town I was raised in. The small community has not grown very much in my last twenty-nine years. I was away for some time but returned several years ago. The small town is Melville, in the western Piedmont of North Carolina. In 1979 and the year of my story, the population numbered exactly 3,550. It is a nice small town, as people would say, and like those quiet towns, there is gossip, domestic problems, troublesome teenagers, and even murder.

Our town is in the northwestern part of the state. The mountains are in the northwest part of the state, as well as the foothills. Most of Melville is in the foothills. But it depends on who you talk to. Much debate is on whether Melville is a foothill or a mountain town.

In 1963 when I was thirteen years old, my parents were killed in an automobile accident that changed my life forever. My dad drove his 1962 Ford Fairlane from Winston-Salem on Highway 52. Their car collided with a drunk driving the wrong way. My parents and the driver were killed instantly. My dad never drove over fifty miles per hour. It seemed unfair that a man so careful on the highway could die in such a way.

My mom's sister Janice and husband Bill took me in soon after and adopted me as their own when I was fifteen. They raised me as if I was their son. It was in my parents' will that my aunt and uncle would care for me. They could not have children of their own and were excited to have me a part of their lives. The transition was easy since they were already a big part of my life. I did not go into a rebellious teenager phase, even though those years were still tough without the presence of my parents. I never went into a shell or rebelled against them or anyone. I know this was due to my upbringing by my parents and the continuation of that by Bill and Janice.

My father was not a big sports guy like I am today. I played sports growing up, and I am an avid football fan. This gene I did not get from my dad. He was a writer and English professor. Not that English professors cannot follow sports or be fans. He was never interested in too much athletic unless you called angling an athletic event. My father would go fishing any free time he had. He would go to ponds, lakes, and oceans. It did not matter.

Besides fishing, my father, an intellectual and college professor, introduced me to the world of literature. I should say here, my mom as well. Like my parents, I am an avid reader and will read anything I can get my hands on. But there is something about mysteries. I have read Agatha Christie, Conan Doyle, and mystery writers most people have never heard of.

The major reason for an easy transition to a new way of life was one thing. I was raised right for the first thirteen years of my life. I grew up in a strict but loving household. Schoolwork had to be done on time. Housework had to be finished before any play. Always show respect to people, be thankful, and treat every person the same. Even though it was a strict household, it was a loving one.

Aunt Janice and Uncle Bill are patient, kind, and loving. They are as down to earth as they come and as genuine as any two people can be. There is no pretension in them at all. Their idea of a wild time is at the church's Harvest Festival in October. My Aunt Janice has been known to go so over the top that she brings not one but two of her famous Carrot cakes. These cakes sold for thirty dollars at the festival's auction. Somehow Uncle Bill finds a way to bring one home every year. Janice is now thinking of making three cakes for the auction—one for Bill and the other two for the congregation.

Uncle Bill is 6'2 ft and 195 lbs. Aunt Janice is 5'4 ft and 130 lbs. Even though I know women do not like it when you announce their weight to the world. My explanation of my estimating people's weight comes later. Bill works at the local furniture factory, and Janice is a bank teller at one of Melville's two banks. While my mother grew up in Melville, left for college, and stayed away several years, Janice never left. Janice is one of the few people who call me Humphrey but calls me Hump too.

I graduated in 1971 from Wake Forest University and earned my master's degree from the University of North

Carolina in Chapel Hill in 1973. With the advanced degree, I could study in England at Oxford University—a small-town boy doing good. But a small-town boy returned. I lived in England for a year and traveled to many parts of the world. After having the traveling bug out of me, I returned to America, having not decided exactly what I would do with my life. I wanted to teach but not for thirty years. I had always been my own man and wanted independence without being tied down. I was an English major but did not want to be a college professor. I thought teaching part-time would be okay, and doing research and writing as well. I wanted to return to Melville. Unlike in Melville, I had made many friends during college and worldly adventures. I was twenty-four years old, with a turning point in my life. I did not know how big that turning point was until I returned. It was bigger than I imagined, and it changed my life forever.

Chapter Two

After returning to Melville in 1974, Janice and Bill told me they had something to discuss with me. I lived with them until I found my place, never thinking or dreaming a week later that I would be in my own, outright home. That home would not be mine from the small income I would soon receive from my new part-time job teaching at the local community college. I was searching in the Melville Gazette for a rental home when they walked into their den, and Janice said, "Humphrey, we have to talk."

I said, "Wow, you guys must be up to something. You're calling me Humphrey, and we must talk on top of it." My Aunt Janice would always say we had to talk when something was serious, or I had done something to displease them when I was growing up. Me making light of it did not make them smile. They did not have disappointed, unhappy frowns like when I threw eggs with my buddies one Halloween night—an old-fashioned small-town egg fight.

Hey, I didn't know it was an unmarked police car that we bombed! Thankfully, the only repercussions from that unfortunate event and the only serious thing I erred in were washing police cars on Saturday. Since I did not call my old friends to catch up by bombing a police car with eggs, I knew something else was happening.

Bill began because Janice had suddenly got choked up for a second. I knew she would not get the words out. She cries at Hallmark card commercials, so I did not think much of it. Bill said, "We must go to Greensboro to meet your parents' attorney."

"What?" I said. I'm not hard of hearing. I didn't understand why or what this was about. People seem to always reply with a what when clearly, they heard what was said.

Bill said, "Your mom and dad's attorney called yesterday. It's about their last will and testament."

"What do you mean by last will and testament? I didn't think they had one. I never thought about it all. I guessed their will had you as my parents."

Bill replied, "Hump, we know no more than you. A secretary from the law office of Mr. Philip Fitizberger called. That was the name, right, hon?"

My aunt could only respond with a slight shake of her head, getting almost despondent as if she had just watched a marathon of Hallmark commercials.

Bill continued, "Yes, that was it. We were told that Janice and I had to be present for the will to be read."

On the day I met my parents' attorney, and now mine, I had no idea that when I left the attorney's office, I would leave a very wealthy man. It was exactly one week after my twenty-fourth birthday. Through saving and my dad's inheritance, my parents left me 3 million dollars. A lot of money. A lot of money in 1974. A lot of money any time. And certainly, a lot of money for a person who has just turned twenty-four years old.

I learned the money came from my dad and grandfather's frugalness. I also learned that day my father never spent a cent that was left to him by his father. I always knew that money was never an important thing to him. He never talked about it. It never seemed to be a priority in his life. He only said, "Humphrey, we are college professors, we don't make the income like some folks, but we have everything we need right here."

The money that my dad received from his father and never spent originated from my grandfather's business. My grandfather, Harry Larsen, owned and ran the local dairy. He started it in 1914, and even though it was called Melville Dairy, it served the county.

In the early days of business, milk and other dairy products were delivered to homes. Then as the supermarkets grew, the company slowly adapted to the times. Harry Larsen was more frugal than my father and saved enough to accommodate the times and invest in expanding his business and putting the product in grocery stores. He might not have been able if he had not saved most of his money. The saying around Melville was Ole Harry probably still has the first nickel he ever earned. My dad used to tell me, "Don't laugh; it's probably true."

My father hired people to run the business after my grandfather's passing in 1958. Then my dad sold it in 1960. Since I was only ten years old, I never thought about it too much until now. The attorney told me that my father never used a cent from the sale of it. He would invest the money, and the investments paid off big time.

And now, I have 3 million dollars. There were three stipulations to the will. If I never accomplished all three, the will would never be read to me until I was 40. And then I would have found out I would receive nothing. The first stipulation was that I had to be 24 years old. Second, I would be a college graduate. And third, I would have a full-time job. When I turned twenty-four the week before, I had achieved the other two. I did my undergraduate work for three years, got a master's degree, and studied at Oxford. I had the education requirement covered. I had just begun a full-time job at the local community college. Every stipulation was taken care of for the inheritance.

Aunt Janice and Uncle Bill knew these stipulations. They did not know about the inheritance. They told me later that when I was about 8 or 9 years old, my parents had told them about the requirements of the will. And that my parents wanted them to take care of me if something happened to them.

So, I learned all this the day we drove to Greensboro and the attorney's office. It was a quiet ride to Greensboro. None of us knew what to expect. Janice and Bill had forgotten the stipulations to the will. It all came back; old memories long forgotten came back to them. The attorney, Mr. Philip Fitizberger, had a downtown office that looked like it was built in the 1920s. It was on the third floor, with Fitizberger's name etched on the glass door. A door was reminiscent of the one Humphrey Bogart had in The Maltese Falcon. I half expected to enter the office and see Bogie sitting down with his feet propped on his desk with a cigarette dangling from his mouth, saying sweetheart and kid to his secretary. Instead of Bogie, we were greeted by a secretary who looked to have been born in the 1920s. She looked to be about 55 years old. I am not as good at estimating people's ages as I am at their weight. Her hairstyle was that of the 1950s. She looked thin, and like Bogie, she had a cigarette dangling from her mouth. Sitting down, she looked as if she was about 5'6 and 100 pounds, soaking wet, as some may say. The cigarette looked freshly lit, even though a butt was still smoldering in the ashtray. A chain smoker. Aka Bogie. After a brief introduction, she called back to the attorney in the next room and permitted us to go back.

We were met by Philp Fitizberger, esquire. He was around 5'8 ft and 220 lbs.

"Hello, hello, come on in. Glad to see ya," the barrister said it cartoonishly on one level and all business on another. "Hey, Bill, Janice," the attorney added. Seeing astonishment on my face, unaware that my aunt and uncle had already known him, Fitizberger said, "I've known Bill and Janice for years. I first met them when you were seven or eight, Humphrey. If you do not mind, your parents wanted me to call you Humphrey immediately, not Mr. Larsen or anything else. Only your parents and I know what is in the will. Bill and Janice know the requirements for your inheritance, which I will read in a moment. I would meet with them periodically to see about your progress, that is, as a person. You have achieved, Humphrey, all the stipulations for your inheritance. We would not be having this conversation if you did not have a good head on your shoulder. You met the requirements without knowing you had to. Your parents did not want you to know anything about it. They wanted you to achieve those with your discipline and ambition. They laid a great foundation for you. If they ever thought about their last will and testament, they knew you would not have a problem with your life. And with your aunt and uncle's love and encouragement, they continued like your parents. I don't think there are any finer people than those sitting here with you today. I'm sure you already knew that."

"Yes, sir," I replied. Thinking of all that Janice and Bill have done for me all these years, I was on the verge of getting more emotional than I needed to be. Looking at my aunt had already gotten a Kleenex out of her purse.

Fitizberger continued, "They wanted you to have stability and hoped you would have that when you became twenty-four. Let's face it; some people are not mature even at that age. They felt you could manage this inheritance if you're educated and have a job. Also, your parents knew you would be well cared for with Bill and Janice."

When Fitizberger read the will, leaving me 3 million dollars and what it entails, I was so stunned I was speechless. I said nothing for what seemed like a minute. I felt as if my jaw was dropping to the floor. Fitizberger saw my shock. "Don't look so surprised, Humphrey. Your parents wanted you to have a life of no worries. Your dad said he didn't need his father's inheritance. They were happy with what they had, no more and no less. The only thing they treasured was you. They loved you more than anything, Humphrey." I began to feel tears forming and knew I had to keep it together, especially for my Aunt Janice, who was about to lose control. Fitizberger concluded that his parents loved their work, and they gave, especially to less fortunate people. "They had a charitable heart, no doubt about that. I do not think we will ever know how much they gave to people. Of course, there were gifts to organizations, non-profits, and the like, but I've seen your dad give people money right out of his pocket."

With that, I just put my head down, with my hands over my eyes, and cried like never before in my twenty-four years. Then I felt Aunt Janice over me, hugging and sobbing. Bill came up behind us and hugged us both. Oh, what good people my parents were! What good, loving people! How could I ever live up to them? And how much I missed them.

After being comforted by Janice and Bill and getting over the shock of the inheritance amount, we left to go back to Melville.

I didn't leave Philip Fitizberg's office a new man but slightly different. What am I going to do with 3 million dollars? 3,285,450, to be exact. I knew I might spend some; I am twenty-four, after all. But I also knew that my parents had instilled in me early on the importance of saving money. Going out and buying a yacht, a penthouse in Manhattan, or a mansion was not in the cards. As we left Fitizbergers' office that day, he handed me an envelope. It contained a letter handwritten by my dad. When I returned to Melville, I opened it as soon as I stepped in the back door. It was written two months before my parents' accident.

"February 18, 1963

Humphrey, we hope you spend some of this, but we know you will save most of it. We know we taught you that. Also, find a group, charitable organization, or anything that captures your heart. Give to them. Invest the money wisely. Your mother and I are so proud of you. I don't know when this letter will reach you. We wanted to leave you as much as we could. But we want you, hopeful that you have become

what we wanted you to become, to help people. We know the
future is bright for you.

Love, Dad"

Almost losing control again, I rushed to the bedroom where I spent my teenage years. My dad knew I would have the ability and fortitude to save and invest, no matter the amount of money. And he had probably felt that Bill and Janice would ensure I was levelheaded enough to manage my new windfall. I hoped I would be as confident as my parents were about me being disciplined enough not to go on a spending spree. Since then, even five years later now, I have invested wisely.

It didn't take me too long after we got back from Greensboro that day to realize I did not want Melville to know I was now a multi-millionaire. Bill and Janice would keep it a secret. I would, if I chose, tell others in time. The only stress Janice and Bill had with my inheritance was when I brought up the subject of giving them some. I was ready to provide them with half, even two-thirds of it. I felt I could never repay them for what they had done for me in the last eleven years. But I knew they would never accept anything. However, I tried convincing them I would feel better if they accepted. They refuse profusely. Janice said, "Humphrey, what in the world would we do with all that money?" I knew it was a lost cause. I do leave them cash from time to time. They got upset the first time I did it. But now, five years later, I slip into their house and leave some in Janice's cookie jar, which usually contains her homemade peanut butter cookies. They don't ask about it. We don't discuss it.

Since then, I have saved, given some, and invested wisely. Saving was easy, and the giving was from the heart. And from good raising. I had to learn to invest and use my head. I studied the stock market and have a great financial advisor. The 3 million dollars from 1974 have now grown to 4.5 million dollars in 1979. That is good growth on my money, considering that I have given some away and have spent some of it.

The big spending did not come until almost three years after I learned of my inheritance, except for buying a house. I wanted the money to grow before I spent too much. I bought something just for me, not a need but a dream I had had for some time. In 1977, I found a car identical to the one Steve McQueen drove in Bullitt. A 1967 Ford Mustang Fastback. My dream car. Maybe that is an investment as well. Not that I would ever sell it. I keep it locked in my small garage at the back of my property. I drive it sparely to show it off. I can't help it.

My latest investment is in a new company. My "money man," even though he is from New York and close to the financial district of the Big Apple, keeps track of things in my neck of the woods. He has advised me to invest in this company. Small as it is, he believes it will take off and grow. I hope he is right. I have invested in several well-known companies. But for this one, I have decided to put 30,000 dollars into it. I think it is because they are based in Winston-Salem. I trust my advisor explicitly, but it may be too much for a new company with only one product, and of all things, it is doughnuts. The new company is called Krispy Kreme.

Now, in 1979 and five years after receiving my inheritance, I work part-time at the community college. I work two days a week at nearby Northwest Community College, teaching English. With my investments, I do not have to have a job. But I enjoy what I do but choose to do it part-time. Besides, when would I have time to solve crimes? I am busy with my other activities in the metropolis of Melville. I volunteer at our local library, helping local historian Clara White twice weekly. The rest of my time is spent tutoring at the elementary school one day a week and harassing our local police department. The police think so, anyway.

My inquisitiveness is a big part of my life in Melville. I am not seen in high regard by the Melville Police Department. They do not like my inquisitive nature and detest it when I get involved, especially in things below their intelligence or when I prove how inept and incompetent they are as civil servants. But that's just my opinion. Unfortunately, many people in Melville would agree with me. The cases in my filing cabinet are the ones the police could not solve. And some are not major crimes but small, petty crimes. There are cases in which the police department did not want to put effort into solving. If it wasn't for one officer who happens to be a good friend and is included in my assortment of characters, I'm not sure if any police work would get done.

The police chief has told me, "You and ya friend may think you're Sherlock and that other fella (Watson, genius.) but my department is the expert round here boy and don't you fer git it! Let me solve da crimes here in Mel - vil. Ya hear me, boy."

My usual retort is, "Only if you could, Chief. Only if you could."

For now, back to my house. This is the house I bought a few weeks after receiving my inheritance. I had always liked the brick ranch in the heart of town on the corner of David and Eighth Street. Built in 1938, it is a two-bedroom, one-bath house perfect for me. It has small bedrooms and baths but spans over 1680 square feet. It has a living room and a den that flows with the kitchen and a small room off the kitchen in the back. It is a roomy house, perfect for guests, mostly my friends/cohorts in detective work.

The rest of the house was undisturbed except for the kitchen. I saw proof that someone had been in my place. Cans of Minute Maid Lemonade were lying empty in the middle of the kitchen floor. The people who came into my home took the time to get the ones out of the refrigerator and the two cases I had stored. I knew at this moment that this was personal. They had to know about me and probably knew why I had so many blasted cans of lemonade in my house. I keep them for Quirt, my best friend. Quirt is also the major cohort in our case-solving. I guess you could say that he is my Watson. He often calls me Sherlock, so I reckon that makes him Watson, Even if he calls me Sherlock uncomplimentary. One might think Quirt Eastman would be much nicer since I have a lemonade store in my house for him, which I never drink. But he lives on the stuff, drinking about three cans a day. Now I must clean up the mess on the kitchen floor, no thanks to my best friend. The burglar must have slammed some cans down hard on the floor. Half are busted from just that, splattering soda all over the sides of the cabinet, countertops, and oven door. Either he did not find anything in his search and slammed the cans down out of frustration, or he didn't like me very much. Or Quirt. Or both of us?

Nothing else in the house was touched. The house was not broken into, with no shattered window glass or sign of forced entry. There was no need because I did not lock my door. Who closed their doors in little ole Melville in 1979? Even though Quirt has said to me on numerous occasions, "Hey Sherlock, don't you think it's time you started locking your doors when you step out?" He may have a good point after solving seven cases and gradually getting a reputation around the area. So, the burglar knew about me and Quirt. They had to. And they knew about Quirt's lemonade addition. The destruction of the lemonade was not a happenstance. They made it personal. The main purpose for coming to my house was to search for my files.

Everything else in the house was undisturbed. If my Chock full o'Nuts coffee were all over the floor, someone would pay! No one messes with my coffee. I drink about two cups in the morning when I get up at 6:30, at 11:30 before lunch, and again at 5:00 PM. I do my best work at night. That is when I work on my cases. Or my writing. If my coffee and

I usually say my Chock, was destroyed, then I would be on the culprit like Quirt's namesake. His parents are huge John Wayne fans. They like the name Quirt Evans from Wayne's movie Angel and the Badman so much that they named their son Quirt.

Quirt and I have been friends since we were big enough to walk. He was always my protector, even when I did not need one. I could then and can now hold my own. Today, I am 6'1 and 170 lbs. I don't go looking for bar room brawls, mind you, but I won't back down. I have always used my brain. Quirt is the brawn and has always been big. Today, he is 6'3 ft and 235 lbs. And at twenty-nine, it's still mostly muscle. He was a major football star at Melville High School. He went on to play at nearby Appalachian State University and made All-Conference in his senior year. He was not good enough to get drafted to play in the pros, nor did he want to play after college. He decided to return to Melville and help his father at the grocery store that his dad started in 1950. It's not that Quirt didn't have ambitions; he just wanted to come back and live a quiet life in Melville. I can relate to him because I wanted the same thing. We could have had careers in other places, but we like the serene life here in Melville. Well, it was that way for a while, but not recently. And certainly not as of today. We have had seven cases in five years. Nor did we know that this burglary would lead us to our most dangerous case.

The seven cases we solved are the ones the fine local police department could not solve or did not want to solve. The police chief says, "Don't put your nose where it doesn't belong." Whatever that means. I have never put my nose in places it doesn't belong, like bear traps or alligators. I do interfere when I see the police do nothing. Quirt calls the police department the Barney Fifes of law enforcement. I like to refer to them as the Keystone Cops. I say that because they bumble into each other, thinking they are competent and top-notch when they aren't either of those. Arrogance and stupidity get in the way of each other, and that's a bad combination. You would think that our small town would not be too difficult for the Barney Fifes of the world. No offense, Barney.

It is also the lack of effort in the department. The police chief thinks we are lucky in solving the cases. The department does not try to solve crimes in Melville. Quirt believes it's just their stupidity. I may have to agree. He says that I have a knack for solving those cases. He says, "You just have it, the knack or whatever it is. You must have watched every detective show, like Joe Mannix or Columbo." Quirt flatters me much more than he should.

Organizations that are corrupt or inept usually begin at the top. Melville begins with Chief Stanley Wilson and assistant police chief Jim Lucas. Unfortunately, they are the most experienced. There is at least one good cop on the force, probably a great cop. Another one is young and decent and tries to do a good job. The one good cop is a good friend of mine. Without him in the force, it would be difficult for us to solve those criminal cases. He is Adam Eastman and a cousin to Quirt. He is invaluable in all our cases. He does everything he can to make the department positive and to help Chief Wilson, mostly to no avail. Adam is also a native of Melville. He has been here his entire life. I do not believe he would live anywhere else, even though he could be a good policeman in a bigger department and city.

The decent cop is one young Bobby Matthews. He is naive and has not been in the force for very long. Adam tries to influence Bobby as much as possible and steer him away from the incompetent Wilson and Lucas. The worst police officer on the force would be, hands down, Dave Smith. Most people call him Dummy Smith. The dummy moniker originated from Quirt.

Chief Stanley Wilson is 55 years old and has been police chief for too long, according to most people in Melville. I calculate that Wilson is close to 5'11 ft tall and a whopping

260 lbs. Describing people, I always size people up literally and figuratively. I can get remarkably close to my estimate of their height and weight. It is just something I have always done. I don't know why. Maybe, it's some form of obsession. Sometimes I can get it right on the money. I can tell if Quirt loses or gains some of his huge mass. "How do you do that?" He says to me.

Chief Wilson spends his day in his office drinking coffee and stuffing down the ever-present sugar doughnut. He always keeps a bag on his desk. If anyone does not see any sugar on his uniform would assume he has been on a diet for an hour. He has been a police chief in Melville for 15 years. Before that, he was a county deputy. It helped greatly that when he was selected as Chief of Police, his uncle was the Mayor. Wilson can retire in seven years if he chooses, but with the support of other idiots and all the time to eat doughnuts, why would he?

The Assistant Police Chief, Jim Lucas, is slightly under 6 feet, sandwiched between 5:10 and 5:11. He is 160 pounds. His head does not measure the size of his body because it would be more fitting for Goliath. Lucas is not a native of Melville. He came to town three years ago and missed our first few cases. Had he been here, he would have told us that we don't know what we are doing, that he has been doing this kind of work his entire life. Because it is exactly what he has been telling us for three years. He tells us often that he will get us someday. Since my friends and I are law-abiding citizens, I don't know what he is referring to when he says he will get us. What is he going to get us for? Quirt drinking too much lemonade?

The best officer on the force is Quirt's cousin Adam Eastman. He is young but eager to learn, even though someone would think Adam is a 20-year veteran. At 27, he is the second youngest in the department and the smartest. In that department, one does not have to be that smart to be seen as highly intelligent. But Adam is smart as they come. He is levelheaded, steady, and fearless. Adam, two years behind Quirt and me in school, was the star quarterback on our Melville high school team. He was an all-conference selectee for three consecutive years. He is fit, 6'1 ft 190 lbs, and could suit up today. Unlike Quirt, Adam chose not to play football in college. Instead, he chose law enforcement. It was something he always wanted to do, and he started early.

Bobby Matthews, at 21 years old and 5'10 ft, and 160 lbs, is the youngest officer on the force. However, he may be the most diligent and hardest-working one there. He tries extremely hard to be a good cop. Except for Adam, the other officers give him a hard time in the workspace and outside. He is too sweet of a guy to be in law enforcement. He does not stand out with his physique and looks more adept at helping old ladies cross the street. But Adam insists that Bobby will be a fine police officer one day. Bobby got his associate degree at Northwest Community College, and the position at the police department was the first to come along. He is from a neighboring county, and most people here immediately took to Bobby. He is so gentle and has an easy-going manner. He is easy to like. Think Jimmy Stewart playing George Bailey in "It's a wonderful life."

The last and the least of all the police officers in Melville is the notorious and annoyingly incompetent Dave "Dummy" Smith. With his 5'10 ft 250 lbs frame, he spends most of his time promoting himself. When he is not doing that, he sneaks the Chief's sugar donuts off his desk. I'm not sure why he does that because he stops at the local Melville general store to get two Twinkies every morning at 8:00. Quirt and I are still trying to find a clue on how Dummy Smith got on the force. I'm not sure Joe Mannix could figure this one out.

Let's get back to my home invasion. Again, this intruder violated my filing cabinet and Quirt's lemonade. It didn't take me long to search the house. Quirt is the only person besides my aunt and uncle who knows about my 3 million dollar inheritance. When I used to stay in my small place, The Cottage, Quirt implored me, "Hump, with your instant richness, why don't you get something bigger?"

I always answered, "Why? Do you need more space for your lemonade?"

I go now back to the filing cabinet. I turn on the lamp at the table near my back door. It was the time of dusk. I looked over the patio at the setting sun with a beautiful apple blossom sky of red and purple. It was almost five in the evening. The autumn days were getting shorter. It was a Wednesday, and I had just returned from the library, gone since 10:00 in the morning. I stopped at Quirt's dad's grocery store today to get some things around 4:30. I talked to Quirt for almost 15 minutes and then walked home. So, my house was invaded between 9:30 this morning. When I arrived home around 5, I called Quirt at the store. "Hey, big guy, can you come by after work?' Quirt said, "Sure, what's up?"

Sensing the tribulation and tension in my voice, he said, "You okay, buddy?" I responded, "Sure, just come by."

Quirt came in at 6:15. "Holy Moly, Hump, what happened?"

"Holy Moly?"

He replied, "I can say an expletive if you want." Quirt said.

"No, I don't. Look at my cabinet. The top two drawers were open, but not the last one. It was as if they knew it was empty."

"But maybe they opened it and then closed it."

"No, why take that time? Quirt, why would they leave the first two open? To tease me?"

"I think you could be right, Hump. Maybe, that's exactly what they did."

"Precisely. A file is missing."

I keep the Manila folders of the cases we have worked on alphabetically. A few were easy to solve and not major crimes, but I keep a record of all.

"What file, Hump?" asked Quirt.

"The H file. Our first case. Is it a coincidence?"

"Or they opened the drawer, reached in, and just happened to grab the H file," Quirt countered.

"Has anyone told you you're smarter than you look, Quirt? You could be right."

"I guess that's a compliment, the part about looking smart." He replied.

"But Quirt, I think that it is not a coincidence. It may have been if the H file was our third case."

"Maybe you're right, Hump, but why that one. Besides being our first. That case may have been the easiest one."

"You may have just said it."

"Said what?"

"About it being the easiest. On that one, we had help from Miss Clara White at the library, Slim, and even Burt. Burt sees and hears everything, so it is easy for him. Not to mention your football skills came in handy at the right time. Everything fell right in place for us to capture the Howards."

Quirt responded, "But you had to put the pieces together, Hump."

"The person or persons who grabbed it must be interested in the Howards. There is only one explanation for it."

Quirt, taken aback, said, "You mean–?"

"Yes."

Taken aback even more, Quirt said, "You mean—"

Hump interjects, "Yes, I mean *The Shadow*."

Chapter Three

The Howard case was our first case, five years ago in 1974. The Howard case was easy but more dangerous than our other cases. It was easy, but we did try to put the clues together. Well, I did. Quirt was working late at the store doing inventory. But when I needed the big guy, he came through just like he has done on our other cases.

Quirt made a game-saving tackle on the two guys behind the crime. It was a simple bank robbery or an attempted bank robbery. It was a failed attempt by the Howard boys, as they were known. The Howard twins, John and Jake, were 33 years old at the time, jobless, and in no hurry to look for steady employment. They were known for many things, but working was not one of them.

The two masterminds stood right at 6 ft tall and weighed 185 lbs. They grew up just north of town and lived in an old house. The Howards, or "The Boys" as they were known around town, grew up poor and mean. The twins had no ambition to become less needy and nicer. Townspeople would say they got in a fight every week. If Chief Stanley Wilson did anything, he rounded up either John, Jake, or both once a week, kept them overnight, and released them the next day. Wilson released them so much that people called him "Chief Catch-and-Release."

The Howards decided to rob the other Melville bank, the First Union Bank. They planned to rob the bank early, right after it opened at 9:00 in the morning. Their reasoning for robbing the bank soon after opening was, "thar wussint goin be minny people thar."

Planning to rob the bank early with few people present was not a bad idea. The two rocket scientists didn't know that some people waited eagerly for the bank to open on certain days. Another time would not have been much better for the dynamic duo. Another snag for the boys was the day of their attempt. It was a Friday. Everyone in Melville knows that on certain Friday mornings (except for the Howard Boys, obviously), a certain someone comes into the bank at 9:05 sharp. That person would be Odie Jackson. Farmer Jackson, as he is known, drove up to the bank in his big red Ford truck, loaded with farm hands in the back of it. He brings those tobacco workers on Fridays to cash their checks. The Howard boys did not know that or didn't care either way. But they soon found themselves in for a shocking surprise.

The twins did not expect Ms. Juanita Everhart's third-grade class on a field trip. So, with her class and Farmer Jackson's workers, approximately thirty more people were in the bank lobby beside the Howards. With peas for brains, they were also not quick on their feet. They were unable to adapt to what lay before them. The two Howards came busting in at 9:15. Never on time for anything. They stopped at the Melville general store for Jake to get his morning Dr. Pepper, delaying their quest for riches. They busted into the bank wearing clown masks, which for the Howards is fitting. They came in yelling, "Dis is a holdup." To their dismay and shock, they saw Miss Everhart and her class, the farmhands, and the most formidable obstacle in their way. That obstacle was all of Farmer Odie Jackson at 6'4 ft and 240 lbs. At 54, in 1974, most of those pounds were muscle. Jackson was seen all around Melville as one of the nicest people. Also, a person you did not want to cross or do anything stupid around like the Howards did that morning.

Mr. Odie Jackson was a World War II veteran and a war hero. People in Melville always said he had more medals than one could think of but also ones that no one would ever see. Quirt has often told me, "Hump, I'm telling you, the man is like John Wayne. There were two things that Mr. Jackson could not tolerate in a person. One was lying, and the other was stealing. "If you're a liar or a thief, you're capable of doing anything," he would say often.

Since the Howard boys knew Mr. Jackson as everyone else did, their plans changed drastically. When they saw him, they ran out of the bank as fast as they came in. Having no escape car (another dumb idea The Boys had), they ran toward the railroad tracks across from the bank. The town of Melville is divided by those railroad tracks. The First Union Bank was on the north side of town, and the Melville Bank was on the South side. The Melville Police Department was located on the South side of the city. The Howard brain trust planned to rob the bank and escape north and away from the police station. Why the Dillinger wannabes ran South across the tracks and about 300 yards from the police department is anyone's guess. Later, Quirt would say, "Any law enforcement officer worth their salt would have seen the two clowns cross the tracks." So, sometime between 9:15 and 9:20, when the Howards were crossing the tracks, the police department was busy.

Doris Friday (5'1 ft 160 lbs), secretary, receptionist, and dispatcher of the Melville Police Department, was on the phone with Dummy Smith, telling him he needed to get his hind parts in the office right now. She did not say hind parts, but I keep it clean here. Assistant Police Chief Jim Lucas was in the station restroom trying to recuperate from a late night at one of Melville's finest drinking establishments, The Stumbling Pig. Yes, that is the correct name. While that was happening, the esteemed Chief of Police was working on his fitness by finishing off his third jelly donut. When Mrs. Friday got off the phone with Dummy Smith, she got on another line and got word from the bank. By that time, the Howards were about 3 minutes running time past the police station. Take away the police department's extracurricular activities of the morning. They may have caught the robbers crossing the railroad tracks since you can see the bank from Doris Friday's desk and through the big pane-glass window.

I live on the South side of town and a few blocks from the police station. As it so happened, the boys were headed in my direction. Two minutes after Doris Friday got the call from the bank, I received a call. This was my day off from teaching, tutoring, and volunteering at the library. I spent time writing the night before—a late night into the wee morning hours of 2:00 AM. I write about two days a week. Please do not ask me what I am writing. I don't know myself. I will write things about the town and the people of the town, and those criminal cases that have been solved. So, I slept in later than usual. I was on my second cup of coffee when my neighbor across the street called me. He is more than a neighbor because he is one of my best friends and my other "Watson" in solving crimes. Sherlock Holmes had his Baker Street irregulars. I have Quirt, Adam, Robert D, and Slim. More about Slim later. Robert D is the guy across the street from me.

My neighbor and good friend, Robert David, is known as Robert D around town, but my buddies and I call him D. He is the local "I keep up with everything that goes on in Melville," kinda guy. He has a police scanner, a ham radio, a collection of World Book encyclopedias going back fifteen years, and a National Geographic collection that needs to be stored in a library. I don't think Miss Clara has space for them in our little local library. Robert D is one of the Davids of David furniture factory. Established in 1885, the company built Melville into what it is today and has expanded to four other towns. Robert David has no financial worries since his family set him up long ago. The Davids gave him his house, and Robert D receives a hundred thousand dollars a year. On top of that, he is the sole heir of his family. D says he only needs this house, his collections, and his friends. I am honored to be included as one. However, with all that, his life has not been a bed of roses. He was born with cerebral palsy and has been in a wheelchair since he was eighteen. Quirt and I built a ramp for him at his house so he could glide right to the sidewalk and then onto the street where we live, which happens to be called David Street. We built the ramp one summer in 1972, long before things were handicapped accessible. In 1979, Robert D was 37, 5'9 ft, and 220 lbs. The muscle built in his arms using crutches for 18 years had slowly turned fat.

Back in 1974, D called me the morning the Howards were running. "Hump, we have got something going on. Two guys just tried to rob the First Union, and they're headed our way!" We were four blocks from Center Street, where the bank was located. The runners could have been near my house or in the vicinity. D and I live on the corner of David and Eighth Street. The runners (at that time, I did not know it was the Howards) could have been running right up Eighth Street. I ran out my front door and looked to my right toward Eighth Street and saw nothing. However, when I looked left, I saw two men wearing what looked like clown masks at the corner of David Street and Seventh Street, running away from the direction of the bank and up Seventh Street. Being inquisitive or putting my nose where it did not belong, I ran toward them. It was not a smart thing to do since I knew they were bank robbers. I could hear Quirt saying, "For heaven's sake Hump, the guys could have been carrying guns, machetes, or a bazooka." I did think the runners might have weapons. If I had known it was the Howard idiots, I would have run faster, even though I knew how mean the boys could be. When I reached Seventh, where they were seconds before, I saw a clown mask. I looked up Seventh Street and saw them at the top of the hill. I had no chance to catch them. I saw only their backs, but something about them looked familiar.

I grabbed the mask and ran back down David Street to D's. I knew this was obstructing justice by holding the mask because it may have belonged to two bank robbers. I did it anyway. I wanted to investigate because I knew Chief Wilson, Jim Lucas, and the other Keystone Cops at Melville Police Department could not do it. I see D coming from his house in his wheelchair, and he meets me on the sidewalk in front of his house across from mine.

"Hump, what you got?" D asks.

"A mask," I replied. I hand it to him and explain about the two men running up Seventh Street. We go into this house to discuss it and try to find out more about the robbery. His house, one of the largest in town and much too large for D since he lives alone, is a five-bedroom, at one time, a 3-bathroom Victorian built in 1890. It is now a one-bath house since D converted two bathrooms into labs. One is a photo lab, and the other is a science/whatever-he-wants-it-to-be lab. If one did not know our friend D, one might think he was a mad scientist.

We are now in that big lab looking at the clown mask.

"You know we are messing with evidence, don't you, Hump," D says with a big grin that he likes getting under Stanley Wilson's skin more than anyone I know.

"Yes, I do. But they don't know its evidence yet, do they? It might not even be evidence. We are just two people interested in clown masks. Someone must use a lab to look at these masks. Do you think Chief Wilson has a lab like yours? And do you think he would have enough sense or the gumption to do anything with it?"

"I know that, Hump, but we are still messing with evidence." He asks in concern.

"Are you going to tell? No, you're not. We will find something; the police will not." I reassure him.

It took little time for D to find that the fibers were red. Therefore, it was easy to conclude who the red hair fibers belonged to, even though it would not hold up in a court of law (this was before DNA analysis became prevalent). It was easy to decide who the perpetrators could have been, at least those wearing clown masks and running up the hill on Seventh Street.

D said, "What other clowns, pun intended, can you think of trying to pull this off, Hump?"

"With red hair?"

"Yeah, with flaming red hair, almost orange," D replied.

In his spare time, Robert D researches hair fibers, hair colors, or anything else that may fascinate him. He is more of a Sherlock Holmes than me. I wonder if he can distinguish distinct types of pipe tobacco like Conan Doyle's 19th-century sleuth. Since there are different shades of red, D put the fiber under his largest microscope for a better look. D had seen very few people in Melville with bright orange hair. It could only be one of two people.

"Well?" asked D.

I said, "The Howard boys."

"You got it, Sherlock."

What? I thought only Quirt called me that.

At least one of them," D added.

"Both. They would have done it together. They are not working with anyone else. Who else could it have been? There is no one else who would wear clown masks. Put two and two together, and you get the Howards."

D and I decided to keep this discovery between us for now. We knew it would be a waste of time to tell Chief Wilson. I chose not to tell my best friend Quirt, not wanting him to be pressured to stay quiet and keep it from his cousin Adam. At that time, in 1974, Adam had not been on the police force long. D and I decided keeping things like this away from Adam would be best—for his own sake.

The attempted bank robbery was on a Friday. It was the talk of the town over the weekend. Throughout neighborhoods, people would repeatedly say, "Did you hear what happened at the bank?" And one might hear something like, "I hear there was a robbery in Mount Airy and one in Winston that was the same, that two men ran away." There was no bank robbery in Mount Airy or Winston-Salem for some time. Rumors were flying.

It was difficult for D and I to keep it from our good friends Quirt and Adam. We saw them most weekends. I saw Quirt every Sunday at church and most Saturdays. D and I had to keep quiet about what we suspected until we learned something new. Hopefully, that hope was fulfilled that Monday when I went to the Melville Library.

Miss Clara White, Melville Library's librarian, called me early Monday morning at 7:30. I had not been out of bed due to another long night of writing.

"Humphrey dear?" she said when I answered her call. Mostly, she addresses me as Humphrey, but sometimes I guess she can't help herself because she occasionally adds a dear. That morning she was apparently in a "dear" mood.

"Good morning, Miss Clara," I replied sluggishly. I was still trying to get my bearings together. After all, I was not even halfway through my first cup of Chock. Now, Miss Clara White has been a widow for some time. But everyone in Melville had always addressed her as Miss Clara before and after she was widowed. I don't know why. That is the way it has always been. Odd, I know.

"How are you?" I added.

"Fine, thank you, Humphrey. Humphrey, dear, would you be able to come by this morning? I have something I would like to discuss with you."

"Sure. Is there anything wrong?" I asked, sensing an unsettled tone to her call.

"I do not want to discuss it on the phone. When can you come, Humphrey?"

Sensing a more stressful voice in Miss Clara and knowing she would want me to come immediately, I said, "Is 8:30 too early for you, Miss Clara?" I knew she arrived at the library at 8:30 sharp to prepare things for opening at 9:00.

"That would be fine, Humphrey dear. I will see you then."

Then I heard a click which I was not sure was a hang-up until I listened to a dial tone. Miss Clara was so distraught about something that she did not say goodbye as she normally would have done. I drained my half cup of Chock in the kitchen sink and dashed to the bathroom for a quick shower. My second cup of Java would have to wait.

Chapter Four

Taking the short three-minute walk to the Melville library, I thought about the bank robbery. If it was the Howard boys, how could they have been clever enough to get away? Yes, the Police Department helped with that. And where are the Howard boys now? I also thought about Miss Clara's phone call. She did not tell me what it was about, being discreet. I knew she would not tell me on the phone. Having a suspicious mind, Miss Clara thought people listened to other people's conversations on the telephone; she had told me more than once. Maybe she thought Melville had party lines. I wanted to say to her that it was 1974 and not 1934. She tells me often that the two town gossips, the May sisters, could be listening. Ethel and Myrtle May were not just the town spinsters but the town gossips as well. Maybe I should question them. Miss Clara thought others, like the Russians, serial killers, or Chief Wilson, might be listening. She has told me this more than once as if I would forget it one week after another. But she might be right about Wilson. I think she reads too many Miss Marple stories.

I reach the library and walk up the wide sidewalk bordered by blooming dogwood. As soon as I reached the double doors, I saw Miss Clara anxiously waiting for me.

"Good morning, Humphrey dear. How are you today?" Miss Clara greeted me as if she was not expecting me. She added, "I have that book for you."

Book? Pretending I am here to get a book? I almost looked around to see if anyone was hiding behind a dogwood or one of the boxwoods in front of the library. She could not have been more clandestine than Sean Connery as Agent Double-O Seven. "Let's go this way," she whispered as we walked from the lobby to her desk a short distance away.

I whispered back, for some reason, "Okay." What am I doing?

She leads me behind the desk, almost in the library's center. We step between two rows of books, and she looks toward the front door as if stormtroopers were on the verge of storming the library to intercede in our covert operation. We are now standing in the romance section of the library. I'm wondering if Miss Clara had planned this. I mean, no one would ever suspect Humphrey Larsen to be in the romance section of the Melville Library. So, what better place? Right? The Harlequin section no less.

I find myself still whispering, even though we are the only two people in the building. Looking down at her 5 ft 90 lbs frame, I asked, "Miss Clara, what is it?"

"Humphrey dear, I've got to tell you about those Howard boys."

"Yes," I replied. "What about them, Miss Clara?"

"Well, they came in here a few weeks ago asking about books on bank robberies. I told them that I did not believe we had such books. We have mysteries, and I—"

"Wait, Miss Clara. I'm sorry to interrupt. The Howard boys? The Howard boys came in here? The library?"

I felt that the boys could, at most, read on a third-grade level and, in all probability, the same likelihood that a flock of pigs would fly over Melville would enter a library. I guess I will need to watch overhead when I leave Miss Clara to see if there will be an air force of swine swarming down on our fine community. I hope Miss Clara got suspicious immediately when John and Jake Howard entered the Melville Library. It would be a good bet that neither one had ever read a book or got close to one.

"So, what did they do?" I asked her.

"Well, Humphrey, they went to the history section. My curiosity took me, so I hid behind some books a couple of rows from them. I knew I would be able to hear their conversation. They were talking louder than they should have been in a library. You know how I feel about that."

"Yes, ma'am." I thought about when Quirt sometimes stops by when I am here volunteering. We can get a little boisterous.

"So, I get as close as I can, Humphrey. I would have sworn on someone's grave that those boys, well, I would do no such thing."

"No, ma'am."

"But I could have sworn those boys were talking about robbing a bank. I did not think much of it then, mind you, but lord have mercy, it scares me to death now, Humphrey. I don't think I slept a wink the last two nights. What if the Howard boys tried to rob the First Union? As I said, I didn't think much of it when I heard them talking. I even thought I didn't hear it right. You know I have a hearing aid, don't you, Humphrey?"

"Yes, Miss Clara. I know you have one."

Sometimes I think Miss Clara forgets about the two famous gossip in Melville. They probably learned that Miss

Clara would get a hearing aid before she did. Hey, those girls are pros at gossiping. Besides that, Miss Clara reminds me often that she has a hearing aid even when I can see it in her ear. On top of all that, she tells many people who enter the library.

Miss Clara did not hear much more from the boys. She believes she listened to the end of their discussion because they left shortly after and did not check out any books. No surprise there. I told her that there was not anything to worry about and to forget it. I tried to convince her that someone else probably robbed the bank.

When I returned to my house, I thought I had picked up a key clue on the robbery. Unlike me trying to convince Miss Clara, the true me believed it was the Howards. It was not proof but a step in that direction. I decided to stop at Robert D's and inform him of my discovery. I passed Burt, the Garbageman, on the corner of Brown and Eighth Streets. It was trash day.

Burt Meacham was a stocky 5'10 ft and 215 lbs. He was called simply Burt, the Garbageman. Even though he had other job duties for the town, he did not seem to mind. I asked him once if he ever minded being labeled like that. He said, "I don't mind Hump. Someone must do it. Hey, that's what I am. Would Billy Graham mind if people called him "Billy the Preacher?" No, I don't think so."

I call him Burt. Burt was collecting Andersons' trash when he saw me. "Hey Hump, can you come here a sec?" As ordered, I approached Burt as he dumped a big trash can in the back of the truck. He had four more to go since he was at the Andersons'. Steve and Mary Anderson had six children and were expecting another one in October. Since Burt worked at his own pace and his bosses had no problem doing so, he had time to talk.

"Hey, Hump. I gotta tell ya something. Do you know those two clowns who tried to rob the bank? I saw em that day."

Like Miss Clara, Burt would tell me things from then on, all the way to 1979 and beyond. He would tell me if he saw something odd on the streets of Melville. She would inform me if Miss Clara saw the same in the library or elsewhere in town. Burt does not miss anything on his route of trash collecting. If it happens in Melville, Burt sees it.

I answered, "Who did you see, Burt?"

"Hump, I don't miss anything with these baby blues."

"Burt, you have brown eyes."

"I do?"

"Yeah, Burt, you do."

"But you know what I mean, right?"

"Yes, Burt. I know what you mean."

He said, "Well, I saw them running up Seventh Street. They ran while I threw Old Lady Johnson's trash in the truck. You know Old Lady Johnson, who lives on the corner of Seventh Street and Brown Street?"

"Yeah, I know, Mrs. Johnson."

It's not the one on the corner of Seventh and David Street. That's Miss Rebecca Johnson. She's a doll, that one. I can't see how some people get them mixed up. Old Lady Johnson is pushing eighty-five. She is a nice, sweet lady you never will meet, but she's not Rebecca Johnson. She is a fine-looking woman Rebecca Johnson is Hump, if you don't mind me saying so."

Why would I mind, Burt? The back of Ms. Imogene Johnson's house faced the back of Rebecca Johnson's house, which was on my Street, David Street. It was Rebecca Johnsons' house that I ran past when I raced toward the two clowns. Her house is also on the corner of David and Seventh Street. She would have seen me pick up the mask off the road if she was standing on her front porch. More about her later. Much more.

Burt continued, "Well, Hump. I heard a noise on the other side of the truck. I saw two guys running up the hill on Seventh Street. I guess they must have come around the corner from Brown Street. I didn't see them come around Brown Street, mind you. My back was turned, facing the truck. But when I turned, I saw them running. One guy was wearing an orange pair of high-top Chuck Taylors. Now, who else in Melville walks around wearing orange sneakers?"

I answered the obvious, "Jake Howard."

"Right as rain, Hump. That is exactly right. John wears purple. Everyone in town knows that. John wears purple ones while Jake wears orange ones. Where the two idiots get the money is anyone's guess. I mean, who wears colored Converse's Hump? Unless you're playing for the North Carolina Tarheels, right? Now their backs were to me so that I couldn't see their faces or anything else, but it must be them, right.?"

Even when Burt is correct, he will always ask, right? Or am I right? I think Burt is right on this one.

"You are right, Burt. I think you are exactly right."

Burt must have seen them a few seconds before me, which makes him an eyewitness. That is one piece of evidence, small as it is. I had seen the hair sample from D's super-duper microscope. I did not ask him where he got such a thing. The FBI? Miss Clara's testimonial about the Howards in the library. Another clue. I am no Joe Mannix, but I have seen enough TV shows to know we have no proof. We have circumstantial evidence. Miss Everhart and Farmer Jackson will say they saw two clowns/idiots wearing colored shoes.

I went to D's house after hearing from Miss Clara and Burt. I summed up my morning to him. D and I knew we had evidence, circumstantial, but better than nothing. Unfortunately, the police would not believe it. In 1974, it was too early in Adam's limited tenure in Melville to influence Chief Stanley Wilson. The Chief relied on the arrogance, grandiosity, and stupidity of Jim Lucas. It would take time for the Chief to realize the quality and value of one Adam Eastman. If I had walked into the station with Robert David of the David furniture factory, the Chief would have locked us up in the old clinker. The Chief has always detested the David family. I was not certain as to why. I can only guess that it was due to jealousy or envy of the David family. The Davids were not snobs but rather humble, down-to-earth people. There has always been talk since anyone can remember that the family gave half of their earnings away. Everyone in Melville knew the Davids were giving people.

In my experience, I have never known of an arrogant member of that family.

I know the Chief and D got along like oil and water. With D's intolerance toward incompetence, laziness, and stupidity, his words not mind, but I would also agree he didn't think too much of Chief Wilson either.

We needed more proof. Or I should say, absolute proof. Robert D and I knew who did it without a doubt. But it would not hold up in any court. So, we came up with a plan to get proof. This was our first case or the first time we encountered this situation. After this case, we were able to solve things a little smoother. It wasn't a complicated case. I mean, we are speaking of two idiots in the Howards. But it was our first one. Adam was the only experienced guy on the team. And he did not have much. It was my inquisitiveness, as well as D's, that got us started. He considered himself an amateur sleuth like me, and in ways more so. We both were tired of the police department's approach to anything. Okay, we saw ourselves as the Sherlock Holmes of Melville. We thought we could solve it.

The plan would not have Robert D, Adam, Quirt, or me getting the needed proof. D and I decided on using a person who would become the fifth "member" of our crew. He was already part of our social group and was the best friend of

Robert D. Jim Johnson would be the key guy in helping us get the Howards. We planned to count on John and Jake's stupidity to blabber about their attempted robbery. They were known for, along with that stupidity, being the biggest braggadocios in town. We planned to get them to tell all to a person that they wouldn't suspect. A person they would see, and, in a place, they would see them. Jim Johnson is the last one of my irregulars. I call Quirt, Adam, D, and Jim "Slim" Johnson my David Street irregulars. Unlike Sherlock Holmes's Baker Street irregulars of young ruffian boys, these were all grown men and good citizens. Well, I guess Quirt would be included as a good citizen most of the time.

D's best friend Jim Johnson was a slim 6'3 ft and 155 lbs. Therefore, the nickname of Slim. As far as I know, Slim has always been Slim. He was everyone's friend, a pleasant man you would never meet. Slim went to the same place as the Howards. We planned for Slim to get the boys talking about their attempted heist. They would never tell Police Officer Adam. They resented the overall brightness of D and would never spill it to him. Quirt would try to beat it out of them, so that would never work. They were friendly toward me but always looked at me peculiarly. As if they thought I could read their minds and think they were always up to something. Well, they were always up to something.

Slim, with his easygoing manner, was everyone's friend. He can talk to anyone and anyone about anything. He had something about him that everyone could trust. People didn't say anything harsh about Slim. He could relate to everyone; no matter the social class, Slim could talk to them. He could be seen at Robert D's house when he was not working at David's furniture factory. While D was researching, most of the time it was the Civil War, especially Robert E. Lee. Slim would be reading the World Book encyclopedia or one of the many magazines of D's. Like Robert D in 1974, Slim was thirty-two years old. They were classmates until Slim became sixteen years old and quit school to work in the furniture factory. Even though he ended his formal education early, Slim was intelligent and knowledgeable, maybe from reading most of Robert D's home library. He is comfortable in a local bar, a Country Club, or a church meeting. He would not show off his knowledge but might show it just for fun at my house. If my buddies are at my home watching Sunday football, as we do most Sundays, one of us would test him on his knowledge of things. Most of the time, Quirt would try to stump Slim, "Hey Slim, what year did Jackie Robinson enter their major leagues?"

"1947," Slim would answer.

We enjoy testing Slim's uniqueness at my house, but he doesn't tell people to ask him a question. Being a regular, likable, trustworthy guy, it was a good plan that D and I came up with to get the Howards to tell Slim about the holdup. Yes, they were dumb enough to do that. Quirt, D, Slim, and I met at my house to review our plan. D and I told Quirt and Slim about what Miss Clara heard, what Burt saw, and the hairs discovered on D's microscope. We would tell Adam afterward the results if they were worth sharing. Again, we did not want to put Adam in a position where he had to say something to the police department.

On Friday afternoons, Slim goes to a favorite "watering hole" in Melville after a day at the furniture factory. It is one of our well-known beer joints in town. Slim is a regular customer at "The Stumbling Pig". Though most people in Melville, especially the patrons of the fine drinking establishment, called it "The Pig". Most of those patrons come from The David Furniture Factory and Southern Yarns, a textile factory. It is a favorite for anyone else who enjoys loudmouths, cigarette smoke, and dim lights. The Howards fit right in at the bar.

Most factory workers would come in for a drink or two and proceed home. Slim was one of those guys. But the hard drinkers, ne'er do wells, and brawlers would come in later and stay until closing. And some of those people would come early and stay late. The Howards were that type. Slim would get there at 4:15 on Fridays. That would be the only day Slim would go to the bar. He was a creature of habit and some eccentricities. You could time Slim for a year and see that he got at the bar every Friday at 4:15. No sooner. No later. The bartender and owner of "The Pig", Wimpy Saunders, a beefy 5'10 ft and 250 lbs, would have the first of three Pabst Blue Ribbon beers waiting for Slim on the bar counter. Slim would nurse those beers until 5:45, then walk to D's house, arriving approximately at six o'clock. D would have six hot dogs on the kitchen table for him and Slim. Slim would have four hot dogs, always "all the way". This is the only way a person should have a hot dog in North Carolina: a good hot steamed Bun, Mustard, Chili, Slaw, and chopped Onions. No ketchup or anything else a person might dream of adding. With any add, you take away the "all the way". If you add bacon, you take it away. If you add cheese, you take it away. No add-ons. You can boil your dog, fry it, grill it, or roast it in an oven or a campfire. But you must have chili, slaw, and onions to have an all-the-way hot dog. I'm just saying. I am passionate about my hot dogs. Slim would have a sixteen-ounce Pepsi Cola to wash down his dogs. Every time. Not Coke or any other soda. Slim had to have Pepsi. I may be particular about my hot dogs, but I can wash my down with a Coke. I can have mine from The Grill, the best restaurant in Melville that serves hot dogs. After those hot dogs, Slim would spend a quiet evening reading or watching TV at D's. He would leave at ten o'clock on the dot. Not at 9:58 or 10:02. At ten. That was Slim's idea of a wild Friday night.

With our plan, Slim would have a different night at The Stumbling Pig. He wasn't very keen on the idea because he would have to stay at the Pig longer than usual. And he would not be eating his customary four hot dogs at Robert D's and reading a 1964 World Book encyclopedia or a National Geographic. After I talked him into it, I promised him four charbroiled hot dogs from my grill. I would charbroil them black like he likes them, even though his dogs on Friday night and from The Grill are boiled like many hot dogs in North Carolina restaurants. He often says, "Hump, you know I love the Grills' hot dogs, but they boil 'em, and I like my charbroiled." So, I promised him four black hot dogs that Sunday. The "gang", Quirt, Adam, D, Slim, and I, would get together most Sundays. We would meet every Sunday in the fall to watch our beloved Washington Redskins. Since it was May and there was no football that Sunday, I provided a lunch of hot dogs.

The plan of catching the Howard boys was to have Slim sit down with them. After a few drinks or many drinks, maybe the boys would start yapping about their mishap at the bank. I don't think the boys would take very long to tell Slim. By the time Slim got to the bar, the boys would most likely be inebriated. They would be there two hours before Slim, getting an early start on their drinking. Their favorite past times were bragging and drinking. With that mixture, Slim should have no problem getting information from them. Besides missing his normal Friday night supper, Slim had no trouble staying at the bar to talk with the Howards. He knew the boys would never speak to the rest of us. Besides, if D and I went there, the boys' mouths would be clammed shut. John and Jake might be dumb, but they aren't completely stupid. Well, maybe. But right or wrong and dangerous, we were using Slim.

The bar was already crowded as Slim came to The Stumbling Pig on Friday afternoon. The same usual crowd from Davids and Southern Yarns were there, relaxing after another week's work. And Slim saw a few people he had never seen before. As stated earlier, the owner was Wimpy Saunders. He was wiping the ancient, worn-down wood counter when Slim walked in. Wimpy had a week-old beard because he shaved only on Sundays and wore a flannel shirt all week. If it got too hot in the bar, and it often would, he would take his shirt off and have on the crispest white tee shirt anyone had ever seen. You wear the same shirt all week but have on starched white T-shirts? Go figure. Wimpy saw Slim come in at his usual time, popped open Slim's regular Blue Ribbon beer, and set it on the corner of the bar. Always on time. But tonight will be different.

"Hey, Slim," said Wimpy as Slim approached the bar counter.

"Hey, Wimp. I'm going to a table tonight."

Wimpy replied, "Okay, wait. What?" surprised by Slim's diversion. Slim never changed anything.

Slim walked toward the back of the bar, hoping to see the Howards. Most tables were full since the Southern Yarns' work shift ended at 3:30, beating the furniture factory workers by thirty minutes. John and Jake Howard were at a dimly lit and smoked-filled table in the back of the beer joint. They had been there since their usual time of 2:00. When someone is not employed, they can hit the bars early. They had no working shift time since they did not partake in any labor except for odd jobs around town, which gave them indulgence at the Pig. Slim sees them and walks toward the table. Before he reached them, he knew that getting something out of them would not be that difficult. He could tell that the Howard twins were on beer number four or five. It was Schlitz for John and Pabst Blue Ribbon for Jake.

"Hey, Slim, buddy! Come on over. What's going on?" said Jake.

Slim, tired, and weary from a tiresome day at the factory and a scorching day in May of ninety-two degrees. He wondered how he let Hump talk him into this encounter with the Howards. But why kid himself? He knew he would do it. He would help Hump with anything. And, of course, D, his best friend since he cannot remember when. The disabled but highly intelligent and sometimes brash-mannered Robert D always looked out for him. And likewise. With an Ichabod Crane build and an easygoing manner, Slim helped D deal with certain things. They were different but the same. Neither were misfits in society but not regular guys either. Each had certain eccentricities that brought them together. Slim learned through D's many books. He knows more now than when he was in school because of those books. Yes, he would help them. There was no question about that.

Slim responded to Jake with, "Well, a hot day for one. I just wanted to come in and have some cold ones. How have you guys been?"

In doing this job, Slim would have to slow his drinking down because he knew he might have to stay longer than his usual 5:45. He would never go past his three-beer limit. He decided not to leave early in case the Frank and Jesse James impersonators got suspicious. But the boys would not have noticed if Slim did leave because by then, they were about to stumble drunk from the Stumbling Pig. When Slim left later, the boys had nine or more beers in them, bragging to Slim about how many they had. Later, Quirt said they probably had more since the boys could not count past nine. It helped Slim that the Howards came early, around two o'clock. They were buzzing around five o'clock and had fewer inhibitions than usual. They would be drunk by eight o'clock at the rate they were going, thought Slim. By the time Slim left at 6:30, the Howard twins had revealed everything to him.

After the boys told Slim, he went to his regular spot at the bar. While sitting there, he tried to be his typical self but was anxious about telling D and the rest of us. Now sitting at his spot on the corner, Wimpy brought over Slim's third and final beer. Slim sat and sipped his beer, replaying the conversation by the Howards of the bank fiasco.

Jake says, "I told ya we never should worn dem masks."

John responds, "If ya had er on like I done told ya a million times ya wouldn't had it fall off ya stoop id face ya moron! We be rich now."

Jake annoyingly says, "I swear ya aint right in da head, Johnny. How could I done dat? It weren't near tight e nuff."

John said, "Ya aint got no sense, ya aint got no sense more than nuttin! No, sir re. Daddy always said ya a stoop id boy, stoop id as can be."

Jake complains, "It was too loose, Johnny."

John replies, "If ya were wearin' da hose over yer head, dat were my plan. But no, ya stoop id, had to cry bout it."

Jake says in concern, "I aint wearin no pantyhose. No Way!"

Relieving the conversation, Slim hoped he was calm, not showing he was prying for information. Again, his congeniality and demeanor helped us get that information. He remembered when he began to ask the boys about the bank.

Slim asks, "That was you, boys?"

Both Howards laughed simultaneously, loud enough for some people to look at them. The Howards and Slim were at a table far enough away for anyone to hear. The bar had gotten loud at that point, drowning out their conversation.

Jake says, "We git it next time."

After their laugh fest, the Howards generally spoke about the bank. But terms anyone could know thought Slim. But then they told him something big that he could hardly wait to tell me when he got to D's house. Moments later, the boys stopped discussing the bank and brought up a new topic. Slim figured they were done talking about the bank when the boys brought up another subject. Slim didn't know if that was by design. He just thought the boys were finished talking about the bank. Slim waited about fifteen minutes before he headed to the bar. And then stayed there and finished that last beer. Slim was on his last beer when he saw John Howard at the other end of the bar talking to a man with a hat and jacket. The man turned his back so Slim did not see him up close. But he felt that the man was a stranger in town. A few minutes later, Slim looked back at the other end of the bar and didn't see John. Slim wondered if he left or was in the back of the bar. Slim didn't look, finished his beer, and headed out the door.

When Slim got to D's, I was waiting for him and Quirt. He told us he had to sit for an hour with the Howards before they began talking about the bank. Quirt, perplexed, said, "Why so long?"

Giving Quirt a wary look, Slim said, "Because their mind wanders. And their attention span is shorter than an inchworm. It's difficult enough for them to concentrate when they are sober. I think they told me because of their never-ending and never-ceasing bravado. And the beers and whatever else they had in their system. On top of that, they are comfortable with me."

"But it may be them just bragging. We all know that they might brag about doing it and not even have been close to the bank. What do you think, Hump?" asked Quirt.

I replied. "Well, it may be just that, bragging. But I don't think so. I think they did it. But do we have proof?"

"We have enough," Slim said. "The boys said that Farmer Jackson was in the bank. They saw a school class there."

"Everyone knows that, Slim." Robert D said.

"I know, D. But wait. They gave a lot of details. You can check with the bank, but they sounded very precise in their description. They told me where the class was standing in the bank and where Farmer Jackson and his workers were in the bank. The Howards told me that Farmer Jackson was on the left side of the lobby with his workers. The class was headed toward the counter. Some students were going behind the counter. That's a lot of detail, guys."

I said, "Yeah, maybe so. That's good, but we need more, something better."

"We do," replied Slim.

After what seemed like a minute but was probably seconds, Slim had not replied. Quirt looked at Slim and shouted, "Well, What?!"

Now sensing our impatience and realizing he may have gone just a little too long with his exciting buildup, Slim said, "They are going to try it again."

I almost yelled out, "What? When?"

Slim replied, "Tonight."

Chapter Five

I think the three of us, Robert D, Quirt, and I was somewhat surprised that Slim did not tell us as soon as he walked in the door. But that was just Slim. Then D said, "Are you kidding? These two morons couldn't rob the First Union when it was opened. How are they going to do it when it is closed? I know they don't have the brains to break into it."

I knew we all were thinking the same thing. The two clowns couldn't finish it in the morning, so where will they get the smarts to do it at night? The First Union may have been a small bank in little, ole Melville, but it was a large corporation throughout the state. I think it would be more secure than the Melville Bank. A person may be unable to break in the front door, unlock the door, or open the vault easily. The Howards would need an accomplice, someone smarter than them, to reach their goal. Then Slim told us of their plan.

"They are going up over the top of the bank. There is a door on the roof that is to a storage room. According to John, you can break the flooring of the storage room, which is the ceiling of the bank vault. You know how close Jones Hardware is beside the bank, right?"

"Yes." D, Quirt, and I said in unison.

Slim went on. "They are so close to one another that it is not much of an alley. We all have been there, goofing off as kids. It's only about six to eight feet wide. In his brief stint working at Jones, John would jump from the roof at Jones onto the bank roof. Well, one day, when he was goofing off on the bank's top, he discovered the door that led to a storage room. While in there, he learns how easy it would be to bust through the ceiling. But more importantly, he hears voices. It's the bank manager, Mr. Griffith.

Then he says he sees a crack in the floor and bends down to see Mr. Griffith and one of the bank tellers in the vault. So now he's thinking that he and Jake could bust through the roof and be right in the vault."

"You mean he's been hatching this plan for over ten years?" said Quirt.

Slim responded, "I just think that he just now remembered it. The boys don't agree much but decide they should have done this instead of going into the bank in the morning."

I said, "Well, we are sitting here discussing it; it can't be close to this time, can it, Slim?"

He replied, "No, they're talking about midnight."

Quirt came up with what we were probably thinking, "Those idiots will be passed out by that time."

"No, they usually take a break from their libations. Sometimes, they even leave before me or at the same time. They might go to the Grill for an hour and then go home or back to the Pig."

"How do you know all of that, Slim?" Quirt asked.

"People talk Quirt. Tonight, it was from them. John told me just that. They would eat, go home, and then hit the bank."

"Did they leave before you tonight?" I asked.

"I don't know," Slim replied.

D said, "What do you mean '*I don't know*'? Didn't you see them?"

Slim said, "No. I focused on having my last beer and leaving as soon as possible to get back here. Maybe they did; I don't know."

I said, "We need to figure that they did leave before you, Slim. They may be smarter than we think, as difficult as that is to believe. But they may be setting you up, figuring they told you too much. They are dumb in their ways, but they are crazy and dangerous. Maybe they don't trust you as much as we want to believe. They know you are our friend and may think or even know we may come after them. Knowing you will tell D, they may put two and two together, and then it will get to us."

"I don't think so, Hump," said Slim. "I think they're too arrogant for that."

D added, "I think Slim is right, Hump. Arrogance and stupidity are a bad combination. They must be upset they screwed up the first time, angry they didn't think of this plan last Friday. I believe they will do it tonight."

I said, "Well, guys, we've got to devise a plan." Which we did.

Later that night, we all had our stations and specific jobs. Robert D would stay home and listen to the police scanner in case something that would foil the Howards' plan developed unexpectedly in town. Plus, D might hear something on the scanner about the Howards themselves, such as disturbing the peace, bar fighting, speeding down the streets of Melville, or drinking and driving. There were many times D heard on his scanner something about the Howards. Our plans could be a waste of time if John and Jake got into trouble before their heist. We had Slim stationed at a telephone booth near Center Street and Ninth Street near the bank. D would call Slim if he heard anything on the scanner. The telephone booth was located diagonally across from the bank. Through D's ingenuity, he knew the number at the phone booth because only D could.

Besides being on the roof like me, Quirt's job was to call Adam and tell him about our plan. We decided to take a chance and bring Adam in on our schedule. The problem was that Adam had the night off and was out with Sue Ann Daly. It so happened that Sue Ann was the prettiest girl in town. The town of Smithville that is. It was a call that Quirt did not want to make. Since Adam worked many hours at the Melville police station and sometimes at his uncle's grocery store, he valued his time with Sue Ann. Now Adam is a nice guy unless asked to shorten his time with his girlfriend, his only night of the week with her. Things worked out after that night's events, which Adam was an integral part of, because Adam married Sue Ann in 1976. Quirt was even his best man. Isn't forgiveness a wonderful thing? But in 1974, on a beautiful night, a great night to be on a date with a pretty girl, Quirt, called Adam.

"Hey, Adam buddy, how's it going?" said Quirt.

"Okay. Quirt, what do you want? I can hear the sugar and honey coming from your mouth."

"What do you mean by sugar and honey? Can't I call you to see how you are doing? Man, I can't believe my favorite cousin, and not just my favorite cousin but a good friend, would think I would be calling him only because I wanted something from him. I must tell you, Adam, that hurts a little bit. I mean—"

An impatient Adam said, "Quirt, you are not calling just for that. I'm with Sue Ann. Can't this wait?"

"Getting a little sugar, are we?"

'Quirt!"

"Okay, Okay. We need a favor. Well, help."

"Of course you do," said Adam.

"What do you mean? Of course, I do."

"You know what I mean, Quirt. Suppose I could count the times. There're too many to count."

"Hey, I've helped you a few times, pal. Remember that block I made for you so you could score against Smithville? That probably gave you an All-Conference selection and put you on the map."

"Quirt, I would have scored anyway. Besides, the guy you blocked was a hundred and twenty pounds."

Quirt is now laughing at the exchange, and the constant ribbing the cousins give one another. He also knew that Adam would help them. Adam knew it the instant Quirt told him he needed his help. But he also knew he must make it up to Sue Ann. Quirt said, "Yeah, but he was a mean hundred and twenty pounds."

After several minutes of serious talk and deliberations, Adam relented and agreed to help. He hoped it was not a wild goose chase. He knew his business, and that was just how it was. And he wanted the Howard boys, knowing they had been dodging the law for some time. Like the rest of us, he tried to get these guys.

The biggest problem for Adam would be Chief Wilson. If Adam informed Wilson, the Chief would go ballistic and keep us away, including Adam. So, we had to go without telling the head honcho of the Keystone Kops of Melville. We did not want to jeopardize Adam's job, but the Chief would be furious if we did tell him. I can hear him now. "What?! Are you crazy?! Who told you this? Larsen? Quirt Eastman? How about Robert David and Slim Johnson? I bet they are all in cahoots with one another. Are you kidding me?! I wish they would break the law. Just one time! I would put all of them under the jailhouse. That Larsen. He thinks he's so smart." Or something like that.

If we get the boys, Adam must explain it to the Chief. He would worry about that later. When we met Adam about our plan, he said, "Hey guys, he's not going to like it either way, so it's better to ask for forgiveness later if it does not work out. But we have got to get them. This must work."

Quirt and I knew this had to work, for Adam's sake. This was his job. We could cope and get by if it did not work. We were certainly okay if Adam got the credit for catching the Howards. We could not deal with him losing his job. I would blame myself instead of the others. This was my idea.

Going back to our stations, I would be on the roof of Jones's Hardware store. I would try to take photos of the Howards right before they enter the door to the storage room. The act of busting through the ceiling is a different story. We thought of having Quirt wait in the storage room, but that would not catch them with their hands in the cookie jar. A defense attorney would claim that the Howard boys were horsing around and did not intend to rob the First Union Bank. Their attorney would argue that the boys were stupid and doing something they should not have done. Every person in Melville could believe that.

We had Slim by the phone booth on the corner of Center Street. We told him to stay in the shadows so no one could see him. If the Howards saw Slim anywhere near the bank, it would be the end of our plan. But it might be the end of Slim. The boys might be friendly with Slim at a bar, but I believe they would hurt him. Quirt would be on the other side of the bank, on the roof of the Rexall Drug store. Like me, he would have a board that would lay on his roof, stretching across to the bank's top. We were lucky to find the needed panels this late at night. Thanks to the grocery store. We didn't want to jump from roof to roof, making too much noise. The last thing we needed was the Howards to hear us. After they dropped into the bank vault, we could make all the noise we wanted. Adam would be waiting for them in the bank. The two banks and other businesses in town gave access to the Police Department to have keys. That may not have been a good idea since the Police Department was untrustworthy.

Slim, Quirt and I left D's at 10:15. After a short walk to the bank, we arrived at 10:30 and got into our positions. We wanted to get there much earlier if the Howards decided to rob the bank earlier than planned. Adam told Quirt he would not arrive at the bank until 11 o'clock. He said that he would not hide in the bank for an hour and a half waiting for something that may not even happen. He was not sure about it, as we all were. Adam believed it was just the beer talking and the Howards' stupid bragging and nonsense.

I talked Quirt into having the long walk over the boards to the bank. His panel was about ten feet across, and mine was six feet. I figured if one of us had to jump, and that one was me, I wanted the shorter jump. D and I thought the Howard boys would climb to the bank's roof in the small alley on my side. It would be the darker alley. D told us, "You are not going to see that much in that alley that late at night, I can tell you. All the lights are on the street. It will be hard to see anything in there. If you do, it will be shadows. There is an old light in the back near a side door to Jones. But it probably needs to be replaced since it is so dim." Hump thinks to himself, *how does he know that?* John and Jake could see my board after climbing up to the roof in the back. They would have their ladder, we hoped, placed in the center of the alley, which would line it up across from the storage room. Were the boys smart enough to do that? We did not need the boys putting their ladder in the back and climbing up to my board's placement. After pulling up my ladder and getting in position, I would have to pull up my board quickly if the boys decided to come up in the same area.

We would hide on our respective roofs and cross over when I saw the Howards enter the storage room. Quirt would be able to see me cross. A tall streetlight across from the Hardware store would light me up when I began walking across the board or straddling the board.

I would place myself behind the chimney on the Hardware store's roof. The chimney was there for the woodstove in the store that seemingly burned nonstop on frigid winter days by Mr. Jones. The chimney was about four feet wide and extended to about five and a half feet. Not much room to hide. Before my hiding, though, I would keep a constant watch down below, and then when the boys began their ascent, I would hurry to the chimney. I was concerned that running back to the chimney would be too noisy, alerting the twin clowns, and they would abort their mission. I hoped their constant jabbering and the noise from climbing would drown out anything I did.

After waiting patiently at our places, John and Jake arrived at 11:45. I think a small part of me felt that Slim didn't hear it right, or the boys were just drunk and were running off their big mouths about robbing the bank. But there they were. Stupid, maybe, but daring and dangerous. I believe they would stop at nothing and hurt anyone they could that would get in their way. I hoped that Poe and

Conan Doyle had not gotten my friends and me into dangerous trouble by playing sleuth or reading too much. But here we are, in this situation. And there are the Howards.

Chapter Six

The Howards arrived at the bank fifteen minutes before midnight. I could not imagine the boys having the discipline to show up somewhere on time, much less fifteen minutes earlier. For the two would-be thieves, they were not too inconspicuous. They were as loud and brash as usual as if it were midafternoon. Lying on my stomach, I looked down into the narrow alley. as the Howards stopped and placed a ladder for the climb. I thought I saw movement behind them. Had Quirt come down from the Drug store's roof and decided to grab the boys early? He had to be smarter than that. If it were him, it would have messed up everything. Then I saw a shadow about 20 feet behind the boys. I was so startled by this new development; I jerked back away from the eve of the roof as quickly as I could. I feared I did it so suddenly that it was loud enough to alert the Howard twins.

I was hesitant to look a second time. My eyes could be playing tricks on me. There was no light in the alley. So maybe it was nothing. The only light was the streetlights on Center Street. They must have cast a shadow on the boys. I didn't hear a third voice. But what if it was a third person? I don't know who it would be. If it was a third person, who could it be, and why would it be a third person there? What if he was much smarter than the Howard boys? Okay, he would be smarter than them. And what if he was more dangerous? Adam is the only one of us who was armed. We did not anticipate him using it, but we didn't think a third party would exist if someone else were there.

I waited about thirty seconds before returning to the roof line to take another look down the alley. The few seconds felt like two minutes. Should I wait longer? Or not look down at all? Maybe I should wait until I hear the boys climbing up the ladder. That was the plan. When I listened to the boys going up the ladder, I would go as quickly to the chimney. Get behind it before the boys get to the roof. When I had jerked back from the roof's edge, I had returned almost a foot. To get back to the overhang, I would have to creep slowly. I couldn't just stand up and take a short step to look down. Did they hear me jerk back? I kept thinking over and over. Are they on their way to my roof as I lay here thinking about it? Do I take a chance for another look or wait until I hear them climbing the ladder? Was I getting paranoid?

Probably so. If I heard them climbing, would I be able to ascertain if they were going up the bank's roof or mine? Would I be able to tell if they were coming up to me?

I decided to go back to the edge. As I inched back, I thought I heard whispers from below. Did they hear me? The dynamic duo of John and Jake Howard have never whispered. A third person? Another person telling them to keep it down? Don't overthink, Hump! I started to the edge like a spider with my hands down on the asphalt surface and elbows up towards the sky. As I moved diligently and methodically, I listened for any changes below me.

I got to the edge, with sweat from my brow to my eye looked over the edge. To my astonishment, a third person was there. A dark figure was looking in my direction. I froze, which seemed mere ten seconds, but it was probably only two seconds. I jerked back as before but with a faster motion this time. I dropped my head down quickly, scraping my left cheek on the asphalt. I waited and heard nothing. Had the figure seen me? Then I listened to the boys babbling again, arguing with each other as they always do. "You hold the ladder!" shouted John Howard.

Then Jake replied. "No, you hold it!"

"I brung the ladder, Johnny."

Then I heard nothing. Did the boys shut up because the third person, the shadowing figure, told them to? Now, my panic intensified. I waited—nothing from below. Now I think the third person did see me. Do I get to the chimney, taking a chance the boys do not hear me? And wait there? Do I have to wait at the roof's edge? Hump, get behind the chimney. And that is exactly what I do.

Now I'm behind the chimney with new thoughts. I'm considering the third person and how he may come to my roof. He would go to the back of Jones's and see my ladder. Then I would be proverbial between a rock and a hard place. The boys may have been smart enough to bring some muscle. Or brains. I would have choices to make if he came on my roof. The best option was to forget about the board lying over the alley and jump over to the bank's roof. Unfortunately, that would no doubt alert the Howards and scare them off, ruining our plan to capture the Howards, notorious idiots of Melville. The large obstacle before me was when to conduct my leap if it came to that. If I waited for the dark figure, which I now call "The Shadow" to come up my ladder, I was risking that the Howards could be on the bank's roof. I did not fear a confrontation unless he was Dirty Harry bringing his 44 Magnum. Okay, I was afraid of a conflict. Since I was not in the mood to fall off a thirty feet roof, my options were limited. So, I decided to take one more look down. Maybe my imagination had gotten the best of me. I had time to think about my reaction if "The Shadow" was looking right at me.

I crept back once again. When I look down, my elbow knocks over an old bottle I had not seen. The bottle seems to roll forever on the asphalt, making enough noise to wake the dead. I turned back and looked in the alley to see "The Shadow" running away from the alley toward the back of the bank. Fleeing? This time I did not step back away from the edge as before. I looked down at the Howards. John was on the ladder's second rung, just beginning his climb. Instead of jerking back this time, I crawled gently on my knees to the chimney. On the way, I heard the boys discussing the noise of the rolling bottle.

I got behind the chimney and decided to wait there as I should have from the beginning. I ruled out "The Shadow" being a threat. I believed that he was aborting his mission, whatever that was, and leaving the Howards. Then my paranoia set back in, thinking the third man was going to Center Street, circling the bank, coming up the other side of the alley, and somehow getting up to my roof. Calm down, Hump! You are overthinking. As I sometimes did. After a few minutes, I calmed down and figured the dark figure had gone for good. Now I could hear the boys loud and clear with their consistent arguing.

Jake says, "Ya didn't hear dat noise?"

John replies, "What noise?"

Since my imagination was running rapidly, I knew Jake would respond with, "It sounded like a coke bottle rolling around on the roof of Jones's hardware" Instead, he said, "Ya didn't hear nuthin?"

"Did I say I heard somethin? I heard nuthin. Let's do what we came here fer. Let's go," replies John.

I heard the boys climbing and assumed it would be John first. A few seconds later, he reaches the top. He looks around as if he might see something. Then he calls down to Jake in a loud whisper, "Hurry up."

Then I heard Jake respond, "what da ya think I'm doing?"

"Looks like ya doin nuthin to me. Yer slow in the brain too," replied John.

"Johnny, when I git up thar, I goin to kick yer butt, ya just wait!" Then Jake stops abruptly and adds, "Wait, I heard somethin."

"No, ya aint Jake, just git up here."

" Im kickin yer butt Johnny."

Then Jake makes it to the top. They start on each other, slapping each other several times, with John getting the best of Jake as always. They were no longer in a whisper. I was afraid they would wake up all of Melville, even our Police Department, if possible. Then they would be captured on the bank's roof and not in the bank. And we would take what we could get. Now, this would be comical if it was not midnight and not on the roof of Jones's hardware and if the two clowns were not the Howards but Laurel and Hardy. This is another fine mess you have gotten me into.

Finally, after some more back and forth between the two brothers, they pulled the ladder up on the bank's roof. Then I hoped their eyes would be focused on the storage room at the center of the building and would not glance toward the back of the bank and see my board leaning over the alley. I was still thinking about the figure in the alley. Who was that guy? When the boys pulled the ladder to the top, it answered a question. It was how they would get out of the vault by using the ladder. But they would have to maneuver the ladder through the storage room door and the ceiling into the vault. Could they do that? Did they think of that?

When the boys were ascending the ladder, I had my eyes open for "The Shadow". Again, my paranoia. Who was that guy? I was not certain that he'd left. I was still trying to listen behind me while the Howards were blabbing, but nothing happened. When the boys had gotten to the roof, I felt assured that no one would be coming up from behind me. That their partner had indeed left. Was "The Shadow" my imagination? Maybe there was no shadow at all. No, I saw him. He was looking right in my direction.

The boys made it to the storage room. John went in first, again being the alpha male. Most people would assume that the first person through the room would bring the ladder into the room. But the Howards were not most people. I did not know how the boys would turn it around in this small space. Then Jake brought the ladder with him. Since it was Jake bringing in the ladder, he could not maneuver around John to put the ladder down through the bank's ceiling. I don't believe the boys thought this through. They worked that out a minute later when Jake came out with the ladder, and then John took the ladder from Jake and went back into the storage room. With the Howards, two brains are like one. I guess the boys would use the ladder to get up the roof, through the ceiling, and then use it to get out of the vault. Again, their two brains are like one.

I'm still behind the chimney, watching the boys enter the storage room. Before I cross, I must time it right to reasonably let the boys get established in the room. I did not need to be crossing over to the bank's roof and have either John or Jake come out and see me. Quirt and I were to jump into the vault after the Howards were there for about three minutes. Time enough for them to start raiding. Hopefully, they would be startled enough to run out the door of the bank vault and into the waiting arms of Adam. Adam was to sneak into the bank the second he saw the boys enter the alley.

When the boys re-entered the storage room, I waited a minute and began crossing. With a dim view of streetlights on Center Street, I could see Quirt crossing his board. I get to the storage room door about the same time as Quirt. It wasn't a stroll to get to the door but more stealth-like, so we would not make a racket. I was afraid that I might hit another soda bottle. We guessed by this time the Howards had busted through to the vault. They make it easy for us by leaving the storage room open, allowing a quiet entry.

We decided to peek, figuring we would not see them. We guessed wrong. Quirt looked and then stepped back. He pushed back as quietly as he could, away from the door. He said, "They are still there."

"What?!" I replied in a whisper, "No way."

"Way," replied Quirt.

"Jeez, I thought we gave them enough time. I—Quirt, what are you doing?"

"Taking another look-see. Maybe they're in."

"No. We just got here. We need to wait another minute or two. Those fools could be here all night. Probably trying to get the ladder through."

"What idiots!" Exclaimed Quirt.

Then Quirt and I saw lights come on in the room.

He said, "Hey, they must have gotten lucky. Bumped into a light switch. Or fell into it." He chuckled almost loud enough for them to hear him.

"Shh. Keep it down. John must have remembered that there was a light there. He worked at the hardware store. He must have remembered that it had a light."

We listened for another minute, and Quirt was about to take another look when we heard the boys.

"Hey Johnny, what ya doin with all yer money?"

"What ya mean yer money? It's our money," replied John Howard.

With that, we knew the Howards were still in the storage room.

"What do ya mean, what do I mean? What ya doin with yer money?" said Jake.

"Are yad dat stupid Jake?"

"I swear, Johnny. I'm goin a kill ya one of dem days. I swear."

"All by yourself, Jake?"

Then we heard the boys busting through. We knew it would not take long to get through the ceiling and into the vault. D said the ceiling was just old plaster and that there was no telling how old it was, and that you could go through it like it was paper. We heard a thud and guessed the boys were knocking through the ceiling. Then another thud. We were about to go in, and I had to brace myself, knowing there was no going back. We had them dead to rights, as they say.

Then we realized the boys were talking louder. We went from not making out what they were saying to hearing every word. Quirt took a quick peek around the door and then took a quick step back and turned to me with a surprised look.

He whispered, "Hump. They're already in the vault."

"What?!" I exclaimed. The thud we heard must have been them hitting the vault floor and not knocking out the ceiling.

Quirt said, "They had to come earlier and knocked the ceiling out. When they left the bar, do you think they might have been playing drunk for Slim?"

"I hope not. That would mean that they suspected Slim." They probably did come earlier. Out of their routine, they came here. If this doesn't work out, we have to keep an eye out for Slim.

"But the noise we heard?"

"Maybe they were finishing up crashing through the ceiling. Well, are you ready? Let's enter the room and do what we came here for."

Quirt said, "Ready to take your picture?"

I replied, "Yeah. Let's go. Let's do this."

Quirt and I came up with an addition to our plan. We decided that once the boys were in the vault, I would snap a picture of them. We had an excellent camera that D gave us. We hoped the flash would be so bright that it would blind the Howards briefly, making them look up to the ceiling. Most people's reaction is to look to the source. The Howards would be no different. When they looked up, I would take another photograph of them in the vault. And we would have two pictures. One took the money and whatever else they could get their hands on, and a second one looked directly into the camera, being caught red-handed. I think two photos would be enough evidence, along with Adam grabbing them as they come out. That should give the boys a nice sentence in the state penitentiary.

I go first, quietly, and see that the boys had knocked a hole about four feet wide. Quirt came in, and I saw the boys grabbing wads of money and tossing them in a bag. I put the camera strap around my neck and snap two quick pictures. I gave Quirt a thumbs up, my signal to get ready to pounce on The Boys from above. I take the first photograph, and the bright flash descends on the boys. I could hear one of them exclaim, "What the—" The Howards looked up, and I snapped another one. That was Quirt's cue to pounce. Before he goes down into the vault, Quirt yells out to them.

"Hello, boys." They look up in shock, and I take the second picture, and at the same time, Quirt decides to pull the ladder out of the vault, delaying his pouncing. He would tell me he hoped The Boys would get disoriented and unable to get out of the vault. And then The Boys would be trapped in the vault, making it much easier for us.

Quirt hauled up the ladder, and one of the boys was trying to grab it. We thought we had them trapped. With that, they had no choice but to run to the lobby and out the front door. They were desperately looking for a light switch in the vault. We did not think they would be smart enough to bring a flashlight, but they did. John switched on the flashlight and reached for the doorknob to the vault. The Howards did not know that Adam would be waiting for them in the lobby. The plan was for Quirt to jump down toward the bank robbers and chase them toward Adam. Now since I was the brain and not the brawn of this here outfit, I was smart enough to have the Howard boys trapped between Quirt, the formidable ex-linebacker of days gone by, and Adam Eastman, a good quarterback and a defensive player of the year. I had two guys on my side who could tackle if it came to that.

Adam was in a dark corner behind the teller's counter. He planned to step toward the vault as The Boys came out. By then, Quirt would have jumped down through the ceiling shortly behind the Howards. The Boys would be sandwiched between Adam and Quirt. Unfortunately, sometimes plans do go awry.

It was not so much the diet of Mae Edna Simpson that prevented our plans to capture the Howards but her disposal. She would eat three bananas a day. Through the bank teller's grapevine, it was well-known how Mae Edna got rid of her banana peels. She had an awful way of disposing of them during her work hours. I don't know what eating three bananas in a workday would do to a person's digestive system, but I have a good idea. She would eat a banana between waiting on customers, one at lunch, and her last one on her afternoon break. She would throw her banana peels in the trash can about ten feet from her counter. The same trash can that was right beside Adam in the dark corner of the bank. When the Head teller of the First Union Bank threw those peels in the trash, she would miss the can very often. The remains would be on the floor for hours before anyone would notice them. And on this day, about nine hours before we caught the Howards, Mae Edna had her last banana of the day. She threw the peel away and missed the trash can about two feet. It would not be in anyone's way, so she forgot about it. Since the bank would not be cleaned until Saturday morning, it was not a problem except for Adam Eastman. Mae Edna could not foresee that the peel was between the vault and where Adam now stood in the bank. Adam did not think about a banana peel on the floor near where he was hidden.

When the Howards dashed out of the vault, Adam moved without thinking about Mae Edna's habit, which lasted about two seconds. I wondered later about the odds of Adam slipping on a banana peel. Not high considering Mae Edna's propensity of leaving banana peels all over the bank. He hit the floor hard as The Boys came out at the vault and knocked over the trash can that was one peel short of a full day's bananas and a chair near the vault door. The Howards, running out, heard the commotion and saw Adam down on the floor from the night lights throughout the bank. They dropped the bags of loot taken and concentrated on getting out the front door. Not sure what was happening below, I ran back to the roof, careful not to drop my camera and possibly ruin my film. I went toward the front of the bank's roof overlooking Center Street. I saw Slim in the shadows on the corner of Center and Ninth Street. I looked over the edge, almost expecting my friend "The Shadow". But instead, I saw the Howards run out of the bank. And I wondered how did they get around Adam? The Howards were a good size, robust, and brutes, but Adam could have held his own with them, certainly long enough for Quirt to come behind the boys mere seconds later. The boys were hightailing it and were almost half a block down from the bank and approaching Tenth Street. Where's Adam? I thought. "Hey! Hey, stop!" I yelled at the Howards as if they would listen to me and stop on a dime at the corner of Tenth Street and Center Street. Would they heed my call? Probably not. Then I saw Quirt coming out of the bank.

Before Adam slipped on that banana peel, he stood in the dark, waiting and hoping he did not waste his night off and time away from Sue Ann. Even after hearing my idea of capturing John and Jake Howard, he still had doubts. Maybe the Howards were full of drink, braggadocio, and something else when telling Slim about their plan. When he had these thoughts, they ran out of the vault. Geesh, Hump was right. Adam rushed to the boys knowing Quirt would be behind them if all went right. But suddenly, Adam felt his feet go out from under him. Leaving his feet and on his way down, he thought two things in that millisecond: the Howards were getting away, and Mae Edna. He knew at once why his feet had left him.

Quirt, jumping down into the vault, went after the robbers. As he went out the vault door, he saw two things. The Howards, who were already out the bank's front door, and Adam rose to get off his feet. Without haste, Quirt jumped over Adam as he was getting up. Quirt was only about ten feet from the vault door to where Adam was, so he didn't have much of a start to jump over him. Quirt began running to the Howards and leaped over Adam, grazing Adam's head as he did so—quite a feat. Quirt claimed later that his adrenaline was sky-high. "I was ticked off that the boys might get away," he said later. Adam claimed later that it was not that high of a jump. He asserted that he saw a big bull approaching him and dropped to the floor as quickly as possible. Since it has always been this way with them, who will you believe?

Standing at the roof's edge, I see the Howards rush out and away from the bank. Neither one was carrying the bags.

I saw them with bags in the vault. They had to have dropped them. Did they throw them at Adam? Then I see Quirt running out. Where is Adam? The twins are almost at the Rexall Drug store on the corner of Center and Tenth Streets. At this point, I thought all my bets would be on Quirt catching them, and my second thought was that John and Jake did not have an escape plan. This was not going to end well for the Howards. Quirt was running as fast as I had ever seen him.

The boys had a good head start, but Quirt got to them quickly. I saw the boys get close to the drugstore, and if they had gotten there and turned left, they might have lost Quirt. Beside the Rexall and on the corner of the Center and Tenth Street stood the largest Magnolia tree in the county and possibly the state of North Carolina. It shaded part of that corner most times of the day. On the other side, it shadowed Jay Street just as well. At midnight it made for a dark, seemingly sinister place. A person could come off the Center Street sidewalk and be underneath it, and you could do the same if you came off the sidewalk at Jay Street.

If the Howards got to that corner, they only had to go about 10 feet off the sidewalk to be covered in complete darkness from the giant tree. And Quirt certainly knew this. He knew he had to catch them before they turned off Center

Street. I was yelling from above, "Quirt, get 'em! Get 'em!" About three steps from the corner, he did. Later that night, I told him it couldn't have been done without my loud exhortation. As the Howard boys were turning toward the ole Magnolia, Quirt made his game-saving tackle by leaping on the backs of both John and Jake Howard, changing the boys' lives forever. They would never recover from their capture by the strong hands of Quirt Eastman.

Before the boys could get up to make a challenge for Quirt, Adam was right behind to prevent any escape from them. Upon seeing Quirt lying on top of the boys, Adam said, "For a second there, I thought you might have missed them."

Quirt responded in his typical way to Adam, "What in the heck do you mean I might have missed them? I had those two idiots the second they left the bank. There's no way they are outrunning me. With a twenty-yard head start, I am still chasing them down and slamming them on the pavement."

Adam laughing, said, "It's not the running part I'm referring to, Quirt. It was bringing them down. You did miss some tackles in your day, ole man."

"What do you mean by missed tackles? And what is this old man stuff? I swear, Adam Eastman if you weren't blood,

I would bring you down on the sidewalk," Quirt said with a chuckle.

"You would have to catch me first," Adam responded.

"What?! You know I used to beat you in sprints and—"

Fortunately, I missed most of this banter between them and the brief family reunion they were undoubtedly enjoying. By the time I had gotten down from the roof and reached them, they had the Howards apprehended, and Adam had them handcuffed. Quirt was still going on about sprints and saying things I could not repeat when I approached him and Adam. The Howards were saying things I dare not to repeat, which were much worse than Quirt. The Howards were cussing and fussing so much that I thought a storm was coming up. By the time I had reached them on the sidewalk, Adam had called Bobby Matthews for assistance. Quirt and I could not legally watch John and Jake while Adam got his car. Being a small town, it took about a minute for Bobby to arrive for him and Adam to take the Howards to the station, ending The Boys' adventure or misadventure of the night.

Chapter Seven

The results of John and Jake's attempted caper and what I simply called the Howard case were that the twins received twelve months in prison, with six months suspended and probation for one year. It was for attempted robbery and stupidity. Their lawyer claimed it was attempted because the boys did not walk out with the money. They may have gotten less time had they not already had a history of misdeeds going back ten years. The Howards never recovered from their attempted heist. They never tried such a feat again. The pair's troubles were skirmishes or brawls down at the Stumbling Pig. Other police departments would have locked them up, so the Howards would violate their parole. It never happened. The worst thing for the Howards was the humiliation they received. They became the laughingstock of Melville, which was the major catalyst for their fights down at the Pig. The boys eventually stopped excursing to the Stumbling Pig as the humiliation continued. They began to get their libations from another source.

That source would be one Benjamin Braverman, known as "BB". In '77, he was fifty-five years old and 5'9 ft and 300 lbs. From the neck up; he was a dead ringer for the Country musician Charlie Daniels. While he resembled Daniels, he had no musical talent. He had a talent for making corn into one of the favorite drinks around the foothills. His stomach was so protruding it looked as if he drank more of his merchandise than sold it. He would have an ever-present wad of Redman tobacco in his mouth but also outside his mouth, on his shirt, pants, arms, wherever. He was not seen in town often but would be outside Davids's furniture factory every Friday at four o'clock, waiting for workers to leave. Even though he didn't have to, he would always ask as they came out the factory door, "Ya want some? Ya want some!?" Everyone knew that it meant, *"Would you like to partake in some nice exhilarating beverage?"*. Sometimes BB would be seen with Chief Wilson. I don't think they asked the other to Sunday dinner after attending the Melville First Baptist Church.

So, on a Friday evening in May of 1977, almost to the day when John and Jake Howard attempted to rob a bank three years earlier, the boys went to see BB for some of that famous homemade brew. However, that was pure speculation because the boys never made it. The Howard twins drove on Highway 91 at half past midnight after leaving the Stumbling Pig. Highway 91 goes through the town of Melville and ends at a crossroads about fifteen miles north of town. The stretch from town to the crossroads is the most dangerous and deadliest in the county. For the entire stretch, the speed limit is forty-five miles an hour. A lot of folks believe it should be thirty-five. It consists of curves and switchbacks like no one has ever seen, so bad that you must slow to twenty-five to get through. Most people avoid it if possible. Some residences are on the highway, but the homes only extend about three miles outside town. From that point on, it is desolate. The road then climbs up to the western edge of Stone Mountain. So treacherous and deadly, the highway department does not bother with snowplows in the wintertime. No one travels on it from December to March. There has been talk of closing the road altogether. It has no real purpose any longer, as some believe. It was constructed in the 1800s for people to travel across the Blue Ridge. The people of Melville call it Broke Neck Mountain, or simply "The Broke Neck". It is a mountain and not foothills.

That night the boys were most likely finishing off the corn liquor they had bought from BB the week before. As many witnesses claimed later, the Howards bought some of BB's finest outside the furniture factory the previous Friday. Fred March, a longtime employee at Davids, said, "Yeah, I saw them. They bought two jars of the stuff. More than they usually buy, I'll tell you that." And later, two jugs would be found in their car. Jake was driving when they left the Stumbling Pig at twelve-thirty early Saturday morning. An early time for the boys. No one knew where they were headed, but later all of Melville knew where the Howards ended up.

The Highway Patrol determined that the driver was driving at least sixty-five miles an hour on a curve that should have been taken at twenty-five. When John and Jake Howard were found, their bodies were out of the 1966 orange Chevy Bonneville. John's head was completely off, and Jake's was facing the other way. Since many people did not miss the boys that weekend, no one wondered where they were the following day or that Sunday. And since the boys did not work much, they had no employer looking for their whereabouts. They were discovered on Monday morning. Highway 91 is rarely used, but even less on Saturday or Sunday. No one saw the wreck and the small trees down on the curve until a truck driver arrived the following Monday. Since the boys were found several days after their crash, it was evident that wild animals had ravished their bodies. John's head was never found, most likely due to rolling down a hill or being carried off by a black bear. And that was the fate of the Howard boys.

Now, it is present-day in 1979. I am back to the question. Why the H file? Quirt and I are cleaning up his Minute Maid in my kitchen and trying to answer that question. Who would be interested in the simple case? Why now. The Howards are gone.

Suddenly, it came to me. I said, "The Shadow."

"What?" Quirt replied.

"The Shadow."

"Hump, what are you talking about?"

"Remember? I told you about it afterward."

"Oh, yeah. I forgot about him. Maybe you didn't see him; you called it the shadow for a reason Hump. Bad lighting or no lighting at the spot you said you saw it. Maybe you thought you saw something."

"I know what I saw, Quirt."

"Okay, let's say you did. But Hump, you've got to ask why now? The Howard boys have been dead for two years. They served their time before the crash. And nothing was taken from the bank. So why would anyone come looking?

If it was your guy from the alley who got the file, what makes this case so interesting to them? Our other cases have been much more mysterious than the Howard case."

"What if he thinks I have something interesting in the file? That must be it."

"But that's just it, Hump. I don't think anything is interesting in the file."

"But what if there is?"

"Like what? The case was simple. You don't have anything interesting. Do you?"

"No, I don't think so, but the person who came here doesn't know that. They might think that I have a good description of them. And that I would be able to identify the person.

"But why five years? You wouldn't sit on it for that long. You would have gone to the police."

"Our Police?"

"Point taken. But if the guy thought you had something, why wait so long to come looking for it?"

"That's the big question. Why now?"

"You are great at determining people's sizes immediately. How about this guy? You never said."

I never said because I figured I wouldn't have to; besides, the boys were caught, served their time, and killed. But I would say the guy was six feet tall if I remember correctly. The person was standing about twenty feet from John Howard at the time. John was no taller or shorter than the guy. So, I would say they were the same height.

"Amazing, Humphrey Larsen. I still don't know how you do that. Weight?"

"Weight is tougher to determine. People wear heavier clothes when it's cold, so determining their weight's a little more difficult. But I would say lighter than John Howard. Maybe 170 lbs. But what struck me was what he was wearing that night. I paused, thinking and relieving in my mind what I saw that night. It slowly came back to me."

"What did he have on?" Quirt asked.

"A jacket."

"What?"

"Yeah, it was cool that evening, especially for May, but one thing stood out. A hat. He's wearing a hat. Not just any hat, but a fedora. Just like you would have seen in the 1940s."

"You mean just like Bogie?" said Quirt.

"Just like Bogie," I said. "You would have thought you were looking at Humphrey Bogart himself."

Quirt said," With a glimpse of the guy, you could tell he had a jacket on?"

I replied, "I remembered he had the collar turned up. It was a cool night for May and cool enough for a jacket. I remember how our sweatshirts were worn so we would not be seen, your black Appalachian shirt, and my black Wake Forest. But also because of the coolness of the night. But there was something about him, Quirt. I don't know, but I had a feeling, even going back to that night, that maybe I had seen him before, well maybe not exactly him but just the way he stood, his body shape. I mean. I could not see a face."

"You mean you may have seen him here in Melville?"

"Maybe, maybe not, heck, I don't know."

"Well, where do we go from here?"

"Waiting for you to come over, I've been thinking of that. We need to get the guys together."

"Even Adam?"

"What do you mean, even Adam? Of course, Adam."

"Hump, He hasn't been with us on our cases."

Adam had not been with us on those cases because we did not need him in some of those cases. Mainly it was not to get Adam into trouble with the Chief of Police. Adam was highly reprimanded in 1974 when we caught the Howard boys. Since then, we have been extra careful not to get Adam involved. But Adam collaborated with us on this case. It would be hard to exclude him. Plus, he would want to be a part of it.

"Quirt, he helped us with the Howards. He will want to be a part of this. You call Adam, and I'll contact D and Slim. Maybe we missed something five years ago. Maybe I saw this so-called "Shadow" somewhere, and maybe the Howards told Slim something at the Stumbling Pig that didn't seem important at the time, but it is now."

"Do you think Slim will remember something from five years ago?"

I shrugged, "Maybe, but we won't know until we wrack his brain. It may be small, not worth noticing then, but it is now."

Later that night, we all met at my house. Slim skipped his end-of-the-week ritual at the Stumbling Pig. In return, I had to grill him hot dogs. In the same way, I kept Quirt's favorite beverage; I had Pabst Blue Ribbon beer for Slim. Unlike Quirt, I did not have to keep a boatload. Most of the time, it was just a six-pack for Slim.

In 1979 Adam didn't have to worry about a night without Sue Ann. They were now married. Adam could come over this Friday night because Sue Ann had some ladies over for card playing. I began the discussion by doing just the thing Quirt and I had talked about earlier, getting Slim to relive that night in the bar with the Howards five years ago and to see if there was anything else he could remember.

"Wow, Hump, that's been five years," said Slim.

I replied, "We know Slim, but anything you can recall. Think about the moment you went in, right up to when you left the bar. Were the Howards at the table the entire time? Did you see either one of them with someone else? Did either one or both step out at any time?"

"Why would they Hump?" Slim replied.

"We wouldn't know that, Slim," interjected Quirt, "But It could be important."

D said, "I've been thinking Hump since you talked about meeting. Suppose Slim got to my house later that night, later than usual. Do you remember Slim?"

"I've been thinking the same thing, D," Slim replied, "but I don't remember exactly. I was trying to get their scheme to rob the bank out of them. Wait a minute. I do remember leaving the Pig before the boys."

"Guys," I said, "hold on here. Let us not overthink. I distinctly remember that Slim may have had to stay later than usual, but he didn't. He got what he wanted from the boys earlier than we thought. Slim left his regular time. Slim, I'm talking about when you were at the bar after you left the Howards at the table. Anything after that. Did you see or hear anything odd?"

"Yeah, you're right, Hump. Now I remember the boys telling me early. I stayed around so I could leave at my regular time. I didn't want the boys to get suspicious."

"Hump is right, guys. You cannot overthink," said Adam. "Just relax, Slim, and let the memories return to you naturally."

"Does he need another hot dog? I can run to the grill if necessary," said Quirt.

"No," I said. "Here, Slim, let's do as Adam says: sit in the chair, lay your head back, close your eyes, and don't think of anything except going into the Stumbling Pig five years ago. If something hits you if you remember something you might think trivial tell us. It might be important."

"Okay." Said Slim.

I said, "Guys, let's give him about five minutes."

The rest of us stepped away from the den and into the kitchen. We whispered, anticipating and hoping for a recall from Slim.

"Do you think he needs another Blue Ribbon?" said Quirt.

"Hush!" I whispered back to Quirt. Then Slim called out,

"Hey! I remember something odd."

"What?!" We all ask in unison.

"When I was leaving that night, John was at the bar, and Jake was still in the back playing pool. We were all at the table, and I was antsy about leaving. I was anxious to tell you, Hump, about what I learned, and I didn't want to leave early, making them suspicious. John made it easy for me. Now I remember. Jake was bragging about fishing, and John got up from the table. He got up inconspicuously. He got up quietly, which is odd for the Howards. After listening to Jake for about ten minutes, enduring all I could stand, I left. I realized it was still too early and sat at the bar. I stayed there for about ten minutes and then decided to leave. As I was near the front door, Jake yelled, "*Say hey to the fat boy!*" He knew I was going to your house, D, so he referred to you."

"I know, Slim," said D.

"Now I remember right before I left The Pig. I turned and saw John at the other end of the bar talking to this guy. I would not have thought much about it, but the guy wore a jacket."

"What's odd about that, Slim?" said Adam. "A lot of guys don't take their jackets off. Plus, he may have just walked in."

Slim said, "That's true, Adam. But remember the night we caught them at the bank? It was cool; we all had sweatshirts on. But earlier that night, it was warm. It was odd to see someone with a jacket on and inside."

"Anything else?" I asked, almost knowing where this was going.

Slim said, "Yeah, he had the collar turned up as if he was trying to hide his face."

Adam must have thought like I was and asked, "Did he have a hat on, Slim?"

"Yeah, that's the strangest part. He was wearing a fedora."

"Wow," I exclaimed. Knowing that Quirt and I talked about the guy and his fedora earlier.

I said, "I told Quirt earlier about the man in the alley. He was wearing a fedora; it just came back to me. Now something else is coming back to me. I can't believe this. I didn't think about it then or have any reason to ponder it. But I may have seen this guy before that night of grabbing the Howards."

I think all the guys exclaimed in unison, "What?!"

"When I saw him in the alley beside the bank, it should have returned to me. I *had* seen him before. Remember the day of Howard's first attempt to rob the bank, and I chased after them?"

"Yeah, so?" said D.

"After my chase, I turned to come back toward our houses. I picked up the clown mask. As I returned, this guy walked up the sidewalk to Miss Johnson's house. Want to guess what he was wearing?"

Quirt and D said at the same time, "A fedora."

"You got it," I replied.

"Easy peasy, Miss Johnson?" asked Quirt.

"Be nice," growled D.

"Hey, I call it as I see it, D," replied Quirt.

I said, "Well like I said, I didn't think anything about it. He was walking up to her house. A man going into her house is not unusual. A man wearing a fedora is peculiar in this day and time. Maybe it should have rung a bell when I saw him in the alley. If it is the same guy."

"It has to be the same guy, Hump," said Adam. "How many guys wear fedoras these days? Maybe a few old guys, men in their 60s and 70s. I don't see them in an alley or near Miss Johnson's sidewalk. No disrespect intended."

"I know," I said. "A talk with her is called for, I believe."

"You're going to her house? Are you sure about that Hump? I mean Miss Rebecca Johnson—are you going to Miss Rebecca Johnson's house? You're kidding, right?" said a flabbergasted Quirt.

I replied, "To answer your questions, Quirt. Yes, yes, yes, and no. I am going to see Rebecca Johnson."

Miss Rebecca Johnson was forty-two years old. She had the features and face of Ava Gardner. And, I guess, the other features of Ava Gardner. Her rumored promiscuity was known in our little hamlet. For someone to see a stranger on the sidewalk leading up to her stately Victorian home was common. People would see men arriving at her house at odd times. That was just rumored because I never saw anyone after eight PM. At the time of day when I saw this stranger, possibly and most likely the "Shadow," it was shortly after nine AM. I think the earliest time I had seen anyone visiting Miss Johnson was after ten AM. Despite the rumors, I have never seen anyone sneak out before dawn. I jog past her house sometimes in the early morning and never see one person. No cars parked either.

Miss Johnson would not have been 'entertaining' her gentleman callers as the Howards were running up that hill on Seventh Street on the morning of their first attempted bank robbery. According to the May sisters, Rebecca Johnson usually hosted those men between four and five in the afternoon. I am sure the sisters watched from their front porch daily as if it were a TV show. From their front porch on Oak Street, the sisters could see between two houses on David Street and have a direct line of sight onto Miss Johnson's front door. I told the group, "I should have put more thought into it. No one goes to see Miss Johnson that early." I didn't think the guy was pretending, a feint to make me think he was going to her house.

Adam said, "You didn't think about it because you just saw them as a caller to Miss Johnson.

"Yeah, after seeing the dark figure in the alley, maybe I should have thought about it. It should have come back to me."

"But it was too late by then, Hump." Quirt said. "And we had captured the boys anyway. You didn't think twice because it wasn't significant."

"What did he look like, Hump?" asked Slim. "Maybe he was the guy that I saw at the Pig."

I said, "Well, another reason I should have thought more about it. I remembered his eyes."

"His eyes?" asked Adam.

I replied, "Yes, his eyes. They were a tint of blue that I had never seen before. They were almost purple. They were like the color of a Purple Martin."

"A what?" asked Quirt.

"A Purple Martin," I said.

"What in the heck is a Purple Martin?" replied a dumbfounded Quirt.

Slim said, "A Purple Martin is a bird found in eastern America and is blue, but a purplish blue."

Now, more astonished, Quirt said, "What?!"

I replied, "That is right. It is a Bluebird with a purple tint. That was the color of this guy's eyes. Again, I've never seen anyone with eyes that color."

D said, "Slim, did you notice the guy in the bar? His eye color?"

"No," said Slim. "He had his back turned, facing John. All I saw with his back and the collar of this jacket turned up."

"Now what?" said Quirt.

"We have more than we had before," I said.

Adam added, "That's right. It's something. Let us all ask around town to see if anyone remembers anything."

"The last five years?" asked Quirt.

"It's better than nothing," replied Adam.

"Yeah, it's all we have," I said.

"I'll look at the records of the last five years to see if anyone got arrested or was brought into the station, maybe someone I wasn't aware of," said Adam.

D asked, "You would not be aware of that, Adam?"

"No, not necessarily, D. With the Chief? What do you think?"

"No, I guess you might not look at that," replied D.

I said, "Let's get to it then. We'll start tomorrow. But for now, let us call it a night."

When everyone had left, it would just be Quirt and me. I knew why he was still hanging around. And I knew he would bring something up, something I didn't want to discuss.

"Have you talked to her?"

"Who?" I answered even though I knew who he was asking me about, someone I didn't want to discuss.

"C'mon Hump, you're so angry and upset with her you won't even acknowledge who I am referring to. Are you kidding me?"

"What would your answer be, Quirt? If you were me, huh?"

He replied, "Well, I guess you have a point, but you guys must get things straightened out. And I assumed you have talked to her. Well, maybe you haven't. Are you going to talk to her?"

"Okay, the answer to your first question is no. I haven't talked to her, and the answer to your second question is no. I do not plan on talking to her."

"But Hump, I—"

"Quirt," I replied in frustration, almost staring him down. And trying to get my point across that I was not too concerned about talking to her.

"I guess we better move on." He replied.

"You guess would be correct."

Chapter Eight

The Who he was asking me about was one Amy Anderson. Amy and I met in college while taking a creative writing class together. It was not love at first sight but more like friends at once. We reconnected when she got a teaching assignment at Northwest Community College, where I still teach part-time. She is 5'8 ft and 120 lbs with legs that run forever. I have always been a sucker for Ali McGraw, whom Amy is a dead ringer for, with her dark eyes and brunette hair. When she walks into a room, it seems that everything stops. It does for me, anyway. It would be an understatement to say that she is drop-dead gorgeous. Better yet, she is about perfect with her pleasant personality. She volunteers at the local animal shelter, where her greatest passion is cats. She also has a voice of an Angel when she sings in the Melville First Baptist Church choir. So, how does a fool like me be upset with such a person? As my Aunt Janice has repeatedly said, *"Humphrey, you just have to get over your jealousy."* I know she is right, as she is almost on all things. The reason for my jealousy? It's a long story, but here goes.

Amy went to a Boone seminar with some Community College colleagues. Mr. Frederick Edwards, or Freddie, as I affectionately call him, was most notable. Okay, not so affectionately. Petty, I know. I made it abundantly clear to her that I was none too enthused about her and old Frederick spending so much time together. She made it clear to me that he was just a colleague, that she could congregate with anyone she wanted and converse with anyone she wanted, and that if I could not handle these things, it was just too bad. Then we decided we needed a break from each other. Well, she decided that we needed a break from each other. It's been three weeks since we saw each other and two weeks since we talked. She called me exactly two weeks ago to tell me she left her coat at my house. She asked me if I could give it to Quirt, and she would drop by the grocery store to pick it up. My response to the conversation was "Yes" and a click from my telephone. Not very mature for a twenty-nine-year-old, I know. I never said I was very smart. She was probably calling to try to reconcile, right? Maybe. Maybe not. I don't think I helped things along. That has been two weeks and nothing since. It doesn't look good for the home team.

"Let's get back to our investigation," I told Quirt. "I think I'll go and have a talk tomorrow with Rebecca Johnson."

"So, you're still going to see her? Easy P—"

"Quirt, Yes, I'm going to see her," I said, interrupting him so he would not say what he said earlier about Miss Johnson.

"I'm going to see if she remembers the blue-eyed, dark figure from five years ago. Or maybe he was just one of her gentlemen callers. Maybe he was not "The Shadow", Quirt, why don't you go to the Stumbling Pig to talk to Wimpy Saunders? He might remember this guy. Something tells me he would be hard to forget."

The next morning, I walk down David St to the corner of Seventh St and then up the sidewalk to Miss Rebecca Johnson's old but restored house. I hope the May sisters are not watching me right now. I decided that eleven o'clock on a Saturday morning was a good time to come calling. Let me rephrase that. A good time to visit.

I approached the two-story house that could have been on the cover of any home magazine. There were two huge oak trees in the front and three maples on the left side of the house, parallel to Seventh Street and the hill the Howards had ascended five years before. In front of the house were azaleas and holly bushes on both sides. I wouldn't be surprised if her gardeners also worked at the Biltmore in Asheville; her grounds were so plush. Miss Rebecca Johnson may have been the scorn of Melville with all the rumors, but her house was the envy of all in Melville, including yours truly.

I didn't have to ring her doorbell. She must have been coming from another room when I saw her through the full glass storm door. She opened the door as I approached the steps leading to the long-covered porch. "Why Humphrey, I wondered if you would ever call." Seemingly yelling out to me as I stepped onto the porch, I was afraid the entire block of David Street could hear her. More importantly, I wondered if Ethel and Myrtle May heard her. I know my jaw must have dropped to the porch floor, not only what she had said to me but how she looked. She was stunning. Not only did she have Ava Gardner's facial features, but she also had the dark raven hair of Ava, which touched lightly on her bare shoulders. Yes, it was difficult not to notice. It was just enough to tease any red-blooded American male, which I was one. She smiled as she held the door for me as I entered, showing off her perfect white teeth. I think my heart melted.

I entered the foyer thinking I had never seen Rebecca Johnson that much, certainly not this close. She didn't get out much, seen sometimes walking around town to shop. She had been in this house for six years. I don't think people in Melville knew where she came from. Entering her home for the first time, I felt ashamed that I did not know her well. Also, I should have been more neighborly and not worried about other people's thoughts.

I just knew she was about forty years old but, in a way, looked thirty. She had a youthfulness about her but was no doubt a mature woman. I also knew my heart was still melting. She was 5'8 ft and 130 lbs, with a mature figure. Again, think Ava Gardner.

I was glad she began the conversation since I was tongue-tied. She had to be the most beautiful woman I had ever seen. I was hoping I could get through this. Maybe I should have sent Quirt here and me to the Stumbling Pig. Well, maybe not. Standing in the foyer, Rebecca Johnson said in a manner that seemed like honey was coming out of her mouth, "Humphrey, so glad to see you. I don't believe you have ever been here before."

I wanted to say, don't you think I would have remembered it if I had? But instead, and with all the smoothness of a Cary Grant, I responded with, "Um, oh no, no, Ma'am, I, um, don't believe I have."

You smooth talker, you. Cary would be proud. I wondered if she had noticed and if a stuttering Mel Tillis type was a turn-off for her. Here I was, in the House of the most beautiful woman I have ever encountered, and I can't seem to talk.

Getting under control, I asked her, "I came by to ask you a few questions about the Howard case."

"The Howard case?" She replied.

You dope, I thought. She was not going to remember it that way. She was not one of my cohorts. Could she become one? Could I should I dare replace Miss Clara with Miss Rebecca Johnson? After a second or two, maybe five, of daydreaming, well, fantasizing about Miss Johnson joining our team, I responded.

"Oh, do you remember when the Howard twins tried to rob the First Union Bank five years ago?"

"Yes, Humphrey." She replied.

"I do remember." She continued. "I remember that very well. Let us go to the parlor."

The parlor? I thought. Who called it a parlor in 1979? We left from the foyer into what I would call a living room, which she called a parlor. A couch was set on the right wall, and to the right was a curio with China that could have come from, well, China. I am no expert, but the exquisiteness of it was astounding. Miss Johnson must have noticed my staring at the fine pieces and the Curio, a maple finish with a gleaning shine.

"Humphrey, are you a collector?" She asked. Assuming I am a big-time collector of fine China or fine furniture with my ogling? I have nice furniture, but I am not a collector. My biggest collection is probably Minute Maid, Pabst Blue Ribbon, and Chock Full of Nuts coffee.

"Me? Oh no, Ma'am, but they are beautiful."

"From my late husband. Please have a seat on the couch, Humphrey."

Husband? What?! While trying to comprehend that news, I looked across from the couch in front of the big pane window. In front of the window is a long table with a vase of freshly cut flowers. On both sides of the table were two wingback chairs. One could tell that they were antiques. Everything was arranged as if a professional had done it. At this point, I was guessing it probably was, along with the rest of the house. My mouth was wide open from Miss Johnson's and her house's beauty. Across from the room was the entrance to the dining room. I saw a large table with a vase of yellow roses on it. The table was dark cherry and polished to perfection. It looked as if it had just come out of a showroom. She noticed me staring again and, maybe reading my mind, said, "Also from my husband. Humphrey, would you like a tour of my home?"

With that question, I'm now thinking this could go several ways. It could only go two ways. She could give me a tour, which might lead to the bedroom. Then I might have a lot of explaining to do. The second scenario would be running out the front door and yelling, "Help me, Quirt. Help me!" While contemplating these scenarios, she looked at me with her beautiful, perfect smile. Waiting for me to answer, I saved myself by responding like Gary Cooper without the "Aw shucks." and "Nope."

"No, Ma'am," I replied. "I was just admiring everything. You have a beautiful home." Then I walked, without thinking, to the couch and sat down. She did ask me to sit down, right? Why didn't you sit in one of the chairs? Then, Miss Rebecca Johnson came to the couch and sat beside me, almost touching our knees. Close enough to smell her perfume. I'm now thinking, "HUMPHREY! WHY DIDN'T YOU SIT IN ANOTHER CHAIR?!"

"So. Miss Johnson. Um, Um, you remember the Howards?"

"Humphrey, call me Becky. And I do remember. I was in the dining room that day. I saw them run by. You don't see too many clowns going up a hill in the middle of the day. I saw one of the masks fall off."

I turned toward the dining room and saw a window that faced Seventh Street. She would have had a direct line of sight on the boys running up the hill. "How did you know it was John and Jake?" I asked.

"By their shoes. I am quite observant, Humphrey. So, I knew it was those two because I would see them around town with those colored sneakers."

"Okay, something else, Mrs. Johnson."

"Humphrey, there is no need to be so formal. It's Becky. My friends call me Becky."

"Well, Um, Becky," I said with a nervous smile. "Did you also see someone else standing at the front of your sidewalk?"

"I did. I remember because I saw you across the street. You turned to go back to your house and stopped for a second. You looked at a man on the sidewalk. You both looked at each other. At first, I thought you both knew each other. Neither you nor he waved, so I knew you didn't know each other."

Wow, she is observant. "Had you ever seen him before? I mean, seeing him on the sidewalk before that day?"

"Would I have seen him anywhere else, Humphrey?" She replied with a smile.

"I, um, well, I didn't know if he had been at your house before?" She knew exactly what I was implying. I wasn't too subtle about it.

"You mean one of my callers?"

I was caught off guard. I wasn't sure why because we both knew what I was referring to and all the rumors I'd heard over the years. "Becky, I wasn't implying that he—"

"Were you not, Humphrey? One of my gentlemen callers? As the May sisters refer them."

"Well, um, I—"

"I'm sorry to interrupt, Humphrey. But I had not seen that man since that day. Nor did I ever see him before that day." She was even polite and apologetic for interrupting me even though I was the one with the accusations. I was quickly learning how much class she had.

I was probably more blushed now than when I first entered her home. I regained my composure and asked her, "Did you get a good look at him?"

"No, I saw both of you briefly. I saw you and then turned to go back into the kitchen. Why the questions, Humphrey? Is this man dangerous? A friend of the Howards? I am under the assumption that it is yes to both questions. Do you think that? Otherwise, you would not have asked, correct?"

She looked at me with the green eyes of Ava. And we both knew that I knew she was right. "I don't know yet, Becky." I had the feeling she knew I was not completely honest.

I continued, "Sorry. I knew you lived alone and always figured you were not married."

She responded, "As most people in Melville believe, correct? According to the May sisters?"

"Well, um, I—"

"Humphrey, I am so glad you stopped by. I know we met when I first moved to Melville. But we don't know each other well. Well, maybe that will change."

How will it change? I met Rebecca Johnson about six years ago. I would see her around town, and we were kind enough to speak to each other. That was the only interaction. I never got close enough to her. Sitting on her couch, I was becoming fascinated by her every second. Not just in a sensual way; I mean, who wouldn't be? But also in an intellectual way.

"Becky, I'm glad I came by as well." I instinctively looked through the window facing the street, with a direct line to Oak Street. The street where the May sisters reside. Are they watching now?

I asked. "Maybe you could have seen the man around town?"

"No, but I would remember seeing that dark figure."

Odd that she would use that adjective. "Dark?" I replied.

"Oh definitely, a mysterious dark figure."

"Why would you say that?"

"Why Humphrey? He had a dark, sinister aura, of course."

"What do you mean?"

"Well, Humphrey. They are—"

"I know what they are, Becky. Sorry to interrupt. Do you mean he had a dark aura?"

"Humphrey, the darkest I have ever seen."

"You believe you saw this around him in some way."

"I know I did. Just like I see blue in you."

What! I would have run out the door if Mrs. Rebecca Johnson was an old hag and not the beauty she was. Being mesmerized by her beauty, I didn't move. But maybe she has me under a spell and will turn back into an old hag at any minute. Or will she wait until she has me in her clutches? Of course, I have heard of auras. I just have never met anyone who talks about them.

"Come in here, Humphrey."

We entered her kitchen with a similar entryway to the living and dining rooms. There was a breakfast nook off the kitchen in the back left corner, making it a cozy spot.

"Here, sit down, Humphrey. This is where I serve my friends, clients, or whatever the townspeople call them. However, I know the May sisters called them gentlemen callers."

I sat down and swore my heart skipped several beats. I was about to get into a situation for town gossip. The May sisters refrain. "Lawd, have mercy! Did ya hear bout Humphrey Larsen coming out of that woman's house? And he was there a long time too. I betcha ya he's been going there a while now. He musta been sneaking in because Myrtle and I haven't seen him go in there but one time. Ain't that right, Myrtle?"

Now, I am coming to my senses. "Becky, I must go. Thanks for your time. I—"

"Nonsense, I'm glad you came by. You are a different caller for me."

Yeah, a scared one.

She winked and turned towards the kitchen. "I'll make us some tea."

I saw a different person than what I was expecting to see. She was a down-to-earth person who was very comfortable with herself. She fascinated me by the going minute. I knew I had enough information on "The Shadow," and she couldn't give me anymore. I knew I could leave at any time. But I was captivated by her beauty, of course, and the gentle way about her. The more I was around her, I saw not just the beautiful woman she was but a lady.

As she prepared the tea, I sat at the table and looked around the kitchen. Each room had its uniqueness. I looked back to the dining room and saw what had to be antiques there, ones I had not noticed when we went into it earlier. Maybe my eyes were locked on something else. I knew the house was built in the 1920s for one of the David sons. And I knew the house had been vacant for several years. It was clear that a bit was spent refurbishing and renovating the house. Becky asked, "Sugar in your tea, Humphrey?"

"Yes, please," I answered tentatively. I don't know. I don't drink tea. Couldn't she have given me a big mug of Chock Full of Nuts coffee? Oh, the price of solving crimes.

She brought the tea over, just as I expected, with a tea kettle, cups, even cubes of sugar. Along with that was a small cup of cream and slices of lemon. "Lemon, dear?" she asked.

"Yes. Thank you." Maybe I have moved past my Jerry Lewis, with no more ums, and have finally reached the debonair suaveness of Cary Grant. Wow, have I come a long way or what?

As she sat the tea on the table, I saw something flash from the living room to the dining room. I looked again and saw the biggest cat I had ever seen. Then we both heard a cry from it. Or was it a meow? "Hey, pretty boy." called out Becky.

What? She's now calling me pretty boy. Well, maybe she is talking to the cat. She said again, "Hey, pretty boy. Come on in. Humphrey is delightful. You will like him."

"Are you sure?" I responded to her call to the cat.

"Come here, pretty boy. Humphrey is a little shy at first, but he will get to know you."

Am I coming back?

She walked to the kitchen and got a treat for the cat. The huge cat emerged from his hiding place under the dining room table. It was black and white with a huge head. It talked or meowed during his entire travel from one table to the next.

"That is a big cat," I said.

"Yes, indeed, Humphrey. It's a Maine Coon. The Maine Coon is the largest cat breed. Isn't he gorgeous? I've always had one and always will. They're beautiful, talkative, and very loving cats."

I knew I needed to be going. The investigation would go nowhere if I sat here all day listening to a cat and ogling Mrs. Rebecca Johnson.

"So, you sense the man was dark?" Returning to our earlier discussion. I knew we had been over this already, but I had nothing else to say. I am not a cat person, so I wasn't going to discuss cats.

"Yes, Humphrey. As I said earlier. But I could also tell by the way he stood on the sidewalk. It just seemed as if he was plotting something. I saw him, and then I went into the kitchen. I was there for about three minutes and returned to see if he was lurking around. He was not. Then I locked all my doors and windows immediately."

"You didn't report this to the police?"

Smiling and knowing as I knew that it would have been a waste of her time. She responded gently and rhetorically, "Really, dear Humphrey?"

With my inquisitive mind and putting the case on the back burner for a minute, I had to ask, "You said I was blue?"

"Yes, Humphrey, you are unique. The blue is quite rare. It shows up in people with strong personalities, who make excellent writers, good organizers, and can motivate others." That's me.

"They are highly intelligent people." She added.

That is me. I wish Quirt could hear this.

She went on. "The downside is that they can take on too much, become workaholics, and neglect their relationships."

Wait a minute. Is that me? Unfortunately, I believe it could be. How about jealousy?

She concluded, "So you have some of those traits, don't you, Humphrey?"

"Yeah, I guess I do."

"Fascinating, isn't it? It is accurate. Just like the man on the sidewalk. Just like the pink for your dear Amy."

What?! My what? My Amy? I must not have heard her correctly. Maybe I am in a trance, a spell she has put me under.

Being cool once again and trying to be indifferent, I replied, "My who?" Trying my best to pretend I had no clue who she was referring to.

"Oh Humphrey, don't be so coy. It is not very becoming of you."

I then relented, "How do you know Amy?"

With a small laugh, she replied, "Why Humphrey, like anyone. I met her. It was right in front of my house. It was April 1976. I remember because my azaleas were in splendid bloom. It was a Saturday. Amy was walking while you were taking a nap or watching a baseball game. She has come by several times since then, of course. She is a dear soul. Pink traits are giving, generous on their time, creative, strong-willed, romantic, and once they find their soulmate, they will be faithful and loyal for life."

I responded, "Yes, that's my Amy. She is all those things. But why has she never told me you two know each other?"

"What would you think about it?"

"Well, I um—"

"Would you think, like most of the town, why would Amy talk or befriend me?" Noticing that I was taken aback, she added calmly, as if she wasn't distracted or disturbed by our discussion, asked me, "How is your tea Humphrey?"

I responded, "It is fine, thank you. It is soothing. I feel relaxed."

She said, "And that is exactly what is intended. You just experienced what my callers partake when they enter my home."

Now taken back, once again, wondering why she would give me the same toxin she gave her "visitors". What is she trying to do to me?

"I'm not sure I understand."

"Well, Humphrey dear, do you remember when you first heard of me?"

"No, not exactly," I replied sheepishly.

"Maybe from the two gossips?" She said with a laugh. "Oh, those old fools! It doesn't take long for a rumor to spread, does it, Humphrey?"

"No, Ma'am," I replied.

"Humphrey, have you ever seen anyone from Melville, well, gentlemen callers, I should say, come to my house?"

Suddenly I realized I hadn't seen any man from Melville come to her house, but the ones I had seen were strangers. The concept of a revolving door at the Johnson house was a myth. And I, a college-educated, level-headed guy, bought that idea just like everyone else in Melville.

She said calmly, "I pay those gossips no mind at all. Or anyone else in Melville."

Was she referring to me?

She continued., "People are going to believe what they want to believe. Humphrey, I am a counselor for men. You could say in some ways that I am a marriage counselor. If my clients are dealing with marital or any other problems, I try my best to help them with anything they face. I use mediation as a step in their quest for happiness and reconciliation with a spouse or lover. I get them to relax with various herbal teas and sometimes meditation. Or simple talk."

Sitting here and listening to the "new" Rebecca Johnson, I felt like the biggest dope in town. How did I not know this?

She went on, "I wear my finest clothes. I know I am an attractive woman. So, I used that to my advantage and their gain. I want to be as attractive to them as much as possible. Not in a sexual way, but in a relaxing way."

Are you kidding me?!

"If they like what they see, they are more relaxed. Then they can open up to me. People are drawn to attractive people, which relaxes the other person. Humphrey, you do see me as an attractive woman, do you not?" She said with a pleased but mild giggle.

What?! I wanted to scream, are you kidding me?! I almost wanted to say. But instead, I just said, "Yes, Ma'am."

She replied, "And I dress like this every day."

With that, she got up from the table and reached down to pet the cat. "Hey, pretty boy."

She said, "Amy tells me you are not too much of a cat person."

I said, "No. I'm not Becky. I tolerate them, I guess."

"Maybe that will come in time." She replied with a smile.

We walked back to the living room, which I took as a signal for me to leave. And I needed to go anyway. We got to the front door.

"Becky, thanks for seeing me and your help."

"Oh, I'm afraid I wasn't much help. But come by any time, Humphrey."

Then she reached up, lightly touched my right cheek with her left hand, and kissed me on my left cheek. It was not sensual, and I did not feel it that way. It was a gentle caress, a touch that said I care for you. I stepped out of her door and walked up her sidewalk to go home. I turned to give her a wave. Then she said something more astounding than anything she had said to me on my visit. She said with strong implication but gently, "And Humphrey, do not lose that girl."

On the way back to my house, I thought about the last words that *Mrs.* Rebecca Johnson said to me. Why did she have to go and mess up a nice visit? Coming in my front door, I decided not to think of it if I could. I wondered how Quirt was making out at the Pig.

When I was leaving Becky's house, Quirt entered the Stumbling Pig. He left early on his lunch break to talk to Wimpy Saunders. The Pig's clientele would start to file in around noon. Quirt wanted to get there early to have some uninterrupted time with the owner. Quirt figured he had a good fifteen minutes. Quirt didn't learn much from Wimpy and was frustrated, thinking it was a waste of time. Wimpy didn't remember anyone talking to John Howard. It had been five years. He sees many people, most of whom are from Melville. Sometimes strangers come in, but Wimpy doesn't remember them all. He did not remember a strange guy on the night in question. Wimpy told Quirt he sees strange guys daily, leading to more frustration on Quirt's Day.

When Quirt was about to finish talking to Wimpy, the first two patrons of the day came into the bar. They were loud at their entrance, with one yelling, "We'll have two Schlitz buddies and pronto." They headed for a table. Quirt did not turn around at the bar, concentrating on his interview with Wimpy. He saw the look on Wimpy's face and knew the tavern owner did not take too kindly of the informal "buddy". The worst was the "pronto" part of the loudmouth. Quirt thought maybe the guy did not mean it disrespectfully, but before he could finish, he called out, "Did you hear me, Slick?"

Wimpy replied sternly, saying, "You'll get it in time, pal." Wimpy then turned to get the beers and continued his conversation with Quirt. Quirt knew that Wimpy had to deal with loudmouths every day. He turned to see who the early patrons were but did not recognize them.

"That's all I know, Quirt," said Wimpy, returning to the conversation at the counter bar and pouring the two drafts for his only two customers. Quirt turned again to look at the two guys. Focusing on them now, he sees that they are strangers. No regular customer gave Wimpy the monikers *Buddy* or *Slick*.

Looking at them, Quirt thought that if his buddy Hump were here, he would be stating their height and weight. He would say, "One is 6'2 ft and 200 lbs. And the other is 5'10 ft and 250 lbs. The muscular guy was the talker of the two."

Then the guy, talking to Wimpy but looking directly at Quirt, said, "How about pronto instead of in time, buddy?"

Before Wimpy could react, the man continued, "Hey, did you say Quirt? Why, I bet you're called Quirt, The Squirt."

"Why don't you guys take a hike?" Yelled out, Wimpy. Quirt rose from his bar stool during the interchange and was ready to slug the guy. Older and wiser now, he was not easy to provoke. Well, not exactly. It took a little longer now that he was much more mature than in high school. He would still get riled up, as he was at this very moment. But he also felt that the guy was doing just that. To get him heated up and into a confrontation. But he was not just going to do nothing. And if he hated anything in life, he hated being called "Quirt, The Squirt."

Quirt replied to the big mouth, "The ladies' bar is down the street. I think you girls must have entered here by mistake. So, why don't you and your boyfriend there leave as the man said."

Now the big mouth was red-faced and riled up, and his partner, the more robust guy, at least 250 lbs, said, "Why you little—"

"Little? Fat boy?" replied Quirt.

"Let me at 'em, Roy," said the fat guy now, totally red-faced, as if he stayed too long in the sun.

"Roy?" asked Quirt. "Well, Roy Rogers, why don't you take your girlfriend, Dale Evans, there with you and go?"

With that, Wimpy laughed behind the bar, almost bent completely over. And with the bent, his Red Man tobacco wad fell on the dust floor, making him laugh even harder.

"Why, you—" yelled the fat guy as he charged toward the bar at Quirt. Given Quirt's size, one would suppose that the guy knew that Quirt Eastman would be a formidable opponent. The thing the hard-charging but slow-charging obese man probably did not know was that the man he was charging was a quick big man.

The big man swung clumsily, and Quirt easily stopped it with his forearm and twisted the guy's arm behind his back. Quirt kept twisting the arm while the fat man yelled, "Let me go." Or it sounded a little bit like it. It may have been more of a grunt. The more the man yelled, the more Quirt twisted.

"Okay," said Quirt, pushing the man toward the loudmouth and kicking the fat man three times before pushing him over a table. With that, the talker was so taken aback that he just watched. It seemed to happen so fast to him. Wimpy was laughing so hard that he leaned over the bar, his head down on the counter, and slapped his hands several times.

As the fat guy flew, well, not flying, but it certainly looked like it, the big loudmouth rushed toward Quirt and swung a left-hand roundhouse. Quirt easily saw it coming, ducked slightly, came up with his left, and drilled the guy in the gut. The talker's talk was all gone, now groaning as he was bent over. Quirt straightened him up, looked at the guy, and said right into his eyes, "Squirt, uh?" He got close to him, and with a short jab inches away from the man's face, Quirt hit him with enough force that the only sound coming from the tavern was the bone from the talker's newly formed broken nose. Roy, the talker, staggered back, dazed but not knocked out. If Quirt had hit him with a wind-up instead of a jab, he would have killed the man.

Then Roy came at Quirt with blind fury. Quirt feinted another swing from Roy, this one half-heartedly, grabbed the man's arm, just like he did the fat guy, and put it behind Roy's back. He walked Roy to the bar, twisting his arms and saying, "You need a lesson here, Roy. So far, you haven't learned. Maybe this will help you." Quirt grabbed Roy by the hair. If Quirt had used all his force, he would have killed the big mouth. Instead, he used about one-third of his strength as he slammed Roy's head on the bar, knocking him out cold. Quirt turned, expecting to see the man's partner coming toward him in retaliation. His assumption was right because the bigger of the two men was charging toward Quirt like a bull. Quirt helped the man get to the bar, but not how he would have liked. Quirt grabbed Roy's partner by his belt buckle and was about to use enough force to throw the fat man into the bar between two stools. Quirt had enough of the two troublemakers. He wanted to ram the guy's head into the bar but heard Wimpy yelling, "Quirt! No! You'll kill him."

Quirt hesitated and, realizing he had almost gone too far, replied to Wimpy's exhortation, "You're right, Wimp."

Then Quirt held the guy by the belt buckle and threw him into the bar, enough to stagger him, repeating the throw with the man's forehead hitting the bar as before. Then it was hard enough to knock the man out on the last one.

Turning to Wimpy and seeming like he did not break a sweat dismantling the two men, Quirt said, "What now, Wimpy?"

"Nothing, Quirt. Do not worry about it. These guys won't run to the police. They would be too embarrassed."

"Will you be okay?"

"I'll be fine. Betsy is right here if they want to start something else again."

"Betsy?" replied a perplexed Quirt, thinking, who's Betsy?

"Betsy," smiled Wimpy, "is this old saw-offed shotgun I got from my Pappy back in '45." Wimpy reached under the bar counter and pulled out the old gun.

"You just run along," said Wimpy.

Surprised by the unprovoked attack, Quirt turned to Wimpy, "Wimpy, have you ever seen these guys before?

"Never. They have never been here. But they seemed to know you."

"Yeah, I guess they did," said Quirt. He was still surprised by the two strangers who seemed to want something to go down. But why? "Call me if these two become a nuisance again, Wimpy. Or call Adam."

"They won't," said Wimpy as he laid the shotgun on the counter. "This will be waiting for them," the bar owner grinned as Quirt smiled back and headed for the exit.

Later that night, Quirt returned to my house so we could report to each other about the other's interviews. There wasn't any doubt I got the better end of the deal.

"So, it seems you had more fun than I did," said Quirt after we both had finished telling our stories.

"I wouldn't describe it that way, it may have been more interesting, but it might not have been as exciting as yours," I said. "She is a fascinating character; there is no doubt about that."

"And she knows Amy?"

"Yeah. Can you believe it? Amy never mentioned her to me. And I don't know why. Maybe she feels she cannot confide in me and our other issues. But the important thing is that we found nothing today except you showing off your bravado. You said you didn't know those guys? Recognize them?"

"Never seen them before, Hump."

"But maybe they did know you, Quirt. Or knew of you. I said.

"You may be right. When they started on Wimpy, they seemed to look more at me than him. When I first turned, it seemed their faces were on me, hoping I would react. I didn't react at first because there was no doubt Wimpy could handle it. I mean, I haven't been in a fight since middle school. You know I don't take anything from anybody, Hump, but I try not to get mixed up with things like that. I just sensed that those two guys would come after me."

I said, "But they also knew maybe you would react; they were counting on it. And maybe there is something else."

"And what would that be?"

"Don't you think it odd that we start investigating the break-in and something like this occurs? Maybe it was planned."

"C'mon, Hump. Your suspicious mind is getting to you."

"I don't think so, Quirt. Maybe these goons followed you in there."

"But why?"

"We'll have to figure that out and try to get the person or people who got into my house."

"Why follow me?" Quirt asked in an exasperated way.

"You're my friend, for one. They could have followed you because they knew what you were doing."

"But if they did Hump, they would have something to do with the Howard case. Unless, again, the missing H file is a coincidence.

"Quirt, I don't think it is a coincidence, but I don't think the Howards would have had others in the attempted robbery. I don't think they would rob the bank for someone else. Except for the "Shadow". I just don't see them partnering with more than one person. If you think about when you were at The Stumbling Pig, it was a time when the bar would be practically empty. They could have been there to work you over or worse. Of course, they don't know what they were getting into."

"What? Are you saying what I think you're saying, or am I being paranoid? You are saying they were not part of the robbery but were hired by someone to come after me?"

"Yes, that exactly."

"And do you know the logical suspect?" asked Quirt in a way that he knew the answer already.

"Yes. I do," I answered.

"Who?"

"The Shadow."

"The Shadow", named per my leisure, was one Carl Neal. At the precise time Quirt and I were meeting, Neal was meeting with Roy and his partner, aptly named by Quirt as "Fat Boy." The three men were meeting in a dilapidated shack on Loop Road. The old York place was an old house on Highway 91, the same road on which the Howards met their demise.

Carl Neal was half-heartedly listening to Roy and Fat Boy discuss their altercation with Quirt. Neal didn't want to listen to the two idiots, obviously with no good news.

Another pair of idiots he had hired. He was none too happy. But it was hard to tell. Neal looked neither happy nor sad. He had an unemotional, cold look about him. It was as if he was detached from everything and everyone he had encountered in his lifetime, which was forty years. He was 6'0 ft and 160 lbs. And he was, as Becky Johnson said, Dark.

Dark was a description that Carl Neal had prided himself on. He was a deranged, methodical killer. He left a lot of bodies on his path, just like the two fools before him would soon be. With these two, they were alive longer than he wanted.

Carl Neal had never been caught in the murders that, according to him, he had to do. He would kill the two fools before him. At that moment, they were trying, without success, to explain what happened at the bar in Melville.

"We should have gone in and wasted them right away. I had a shotgun in my car," said Roy.

Fat Boy, aka Ricky, added, "That's what we were trying to tell ya. But no, ya didn't want it dat way. How did we git in dis mess, Roy?! Damn!"

Roy replied, "What do you mean we? You had to convince me, remember? I didn't want to get involved with this weirdo. Who in the hell wears black all the time? And the collar turned up. What is that? Geez, you're a freak, man."

Roy was so upset he was almost shaking. He knew he would regret it when Ricky Boy called him up, asking if he wanted an easy two-hundred bucks to harass a guy or beat him up. Roy had no problem wasting this Eastman guy or anyone else for two-hundred dollars. He did not even know Eastman. He did not play football against him in high school or had ever seen him before that day in the bar. The information he got, especially the "Quirt, The Squirt" part, was from his younger brother, who did remember playing against the guy.

Neal patiently listened to their rants, almost wishing he went on and killed them as soon as the fat one started with his mouth. Knowing what they didn't know, he would not have to hear them much longer. He was only listening because he wanted all the details. This Quirt guy might be a formidable foe. After he had had enough of their talking, he asked, "What exactly did the bar guy say to you after he picked you off the floor?"

Now, Roy was just about sick of this guy and perturbed that Neal emphasized "picked off the floor" and said, "We told you. The barman yelled for us to get out. And that was it."

"And where is our money?" said the larger man.

"Did you finish the job?" asked Neal. "I don't think you did."

Now with Neal talking, he had grown more impatient. Like his other victims, he would just burn with anger. A rage like no other, an everlasting evil. Something that was just there, a part of him. As the sun rises in the morning, Carl Neal will be the way he is, never changing, always dark. When he became angry and so enraged, his eyes would become darker. His eyes were more violet than blue. But when the rage came, the eyes would seem to evolve into a deep purple, almost black. They would grow darker as the rage increased, as dark as the night. As the anger grew, Carl Neal would begin to talk to his soon-to-be victims. More than he had talked about preceding their demise.

Neal would use the same kind of weapon on all his victims. A gun. No mess, no worries. He would dispose of the gun as soon as possible. He would search for the nearest lake or pond to get rid of it. No traces would lead back to him. Then he would buy another one at the next opportunity. That was never a problem. Like Mr. Humphrey Larsen, he was full of money. You never knew when another fool would come along and where he had to kill them. The only thing he could predict was that his anger was unpredictable.

It could come at any time, any place. He did have enough self-control not to shoot everyone around him. He would eliminate the inconsiderate person holding up the line in the DMV or store, especially if they were loudmouths. Or the guy in the bar who brushes him and then shouts at him to get out of the way. Or anyone who passes him on the highway then yells at him and gives him a one-finger salute. Neal would find that person if it took him a week. He would tell them what they had done before he put a bullet in their brain.

Before Roy and Ricky could answer Neal's question about finishing the job, he took out his current weapon of choice, a 357 magnum, which had grown popular due to Dirty Harry's fame. And like Harry Callahan, Carl Neal shot Ricky and almost took his head off. Before Roy could respond, Neal shot Roy's right thigh. Roy screamed, and Neal walked to him and saw that the big mouth was almost in shock.

"No! No!" Roy screamed. "Please, God! Please! No!"

"Now, you're polite," said Neal. "A simple job. You two big guys could not beat up one guy. With all your talk. Why was I so dumb to hire idiots like you and your dead friend here? Can you tell me that, big mouth?"

Roy looked over at Ricky for the first time since he saw his partner's brains leave his head just seconds before. He knew that this had to be a dream. A nightmare. This could not be happening. He felt so much pain and shock that he could not think straight. He knew he was going to die in this stupid old shack. But he had a 38 special in the right pocket of his jacket. If he could get to it—

Before Roy had any more thought about his pistol, or a chance to reach for it, Carl Neal came closer to Roy. "You want your money now, big mouth!" With that, the last words that Roy would ever hear, Neal stood over him, much closer than when he shot the fat man, shot Roy between the eyes, and almost removed his head.

Chapter Nine

Elmer Wilson, no relation to Chief Wilson, was hunting, and coincidentally, it was near Loop Road.

It was about noon on the day Elmer had been hunting when he decided to go sit on the back porch of the old York place on Loop Road. He sat down on the porch to eat his lunch. Elmer would hunt around the area often. And often, he would stop at the old home place of the York family. Mr. Orville York and his three sons built it way back in 1908. Now, it was an old, dilapidated house. Most of the Yorks from Orville's time have long passed, and the few left seemed unable to part from it. They cannot find in their heart to tear it down. It has never been condemned but should have been long ago. Elmer feels that the porch is still sturdy to sit down on. He had not had any luck finding a deer in the morning, so he decided to open his lunch of Vienna sausages and a sandwich with his wife's homemade pimento cheese. He always needed his sweets, so for today, his wife Gladys packed him a Royal oatmeal cookie. All washed down with her sweet tea. Elmer was opening his lunch bag when he saw something dash to the house from the corner of his eye. He turned just in time to see a rat go towards the back door. Elmer went to the door and saw it slightly ajar and how the rat disappeared so quickly. He had never been inside the old house. When he got close to the door, he picked up a foul odor. Elmer was taken aback, surprised that he did not pick up the smell when he sat down on the old porch. Having served as a medic in the Korean War, Elmer Wilson knew the source of the odor immediately. He opened the door and saw them. Two men lay shot, both with their heads almost gone. Roy and his accomplice Ricky, two days after being shot by Neal, were discovered.

Chief Wilson, Assistant Chief Jim Lucas, and Dummy Smith were now looking at the bodies of Roy and Ricky. The three didn't know them or had seen them around Melville.

"We need to get them out of here ASAP," said a tired Chief Wilson, who had a bad night of sleep, probably due to his gluttony. He came to the station at six in the morning and planned to leave at around two. That was before Elmer Wilson came rushing into the station at one past noon, yelling about the two bodies.

"Looks like they was shot, if ya ask me," said Dummy Wilson, as the three police officers looked down at the bodies in the old York house,

"I know they was shot, you idiot," replied an exasperated Chief Wilson. "We need to find out with what."

And tired from another late-night binge, Jim Lucas said, "Looks like it was powerful whatever it was."

"Ya think?!" Replied the Chief in a sarcastic manner. "We don't even know who these guys were; it's going to be hard to find out who shot them."

Lucas answered, "We'll ask all around town and see if we come up with anything."

"That's exactly what we're going to do," replied Wilson. "Call Eastman in, and you two ask around the north side while me and Dummy here will search the south. Somebody's got to know something."

For the rest of that Monday, the Melville Police Department asked about everyone in town. After about six hours of searching, no one knew anything. The only ones who had seen Roy and Ricky were Quirt and Wimpy. Adam knew this already. He convinced Jim Lucas that he would see Wimpy Saunders. The bar owner couldn't tell Adam much more than what Adam already learned from Quirt. Adam had to tell the Chief about the episode between Quirt and the two men. The worst part for Adam was bringing Quirt in for questioning. Quirt was not asked too much because the Chief knew Quirt would not need a powerful weapon to dispose of the two men.

The next afternoon Quirt, Adam, and I met at my house. Adam began, "Quirt, I think you and Wimpy were the only ones in Melville who saw these two guys."

"Someone else had to have seen them. How could they not?" I said.

"But they didn't, Hump. I mean, I guess they could have, but no one remembered," replied Adam.

"Hump, they could have run out of Wimpy's, embarrassed and all. And since The Stumbling Pig is right on the street and on the corner, it would not take them long to get around that corner and be gone. And not be seen by anybody." added Quirt.

"Yeah, that's true," I said.

Quirt said, "But we probably know who hired these guys. The Purple Martin, Shadow guy. And we also know he is extremely dangerous."

I said, "Right, but we have got to dig and find out what it is about the Howards' case that intrigues this guy."

"If it is the Howards' case, Hump," said Adam.

"What do you mean if it has to be that?" Said Quirt.

"But like you two said, maybe it's a coincidence that the Howard case file is missing. Maybe the guy is just a nut job," said Adam.

I said, "I don't think so. My gut just tells me it is something dealing with the Howards. It must be."

"Hump, you must have had something in that file that could implicate him," said Quirt.

I replied, "That's true, but he has the file. So, what motivates him to get rid of you and, more likely me? Or anyone else he thinks might have been involved in catching the Howards, including Adam. There was something in that file that I recorded that put him there. There are all kinds of questions. Did he see me see him at the bank that night? I am sure I recorded that. Did he see Becky Johnson on the day of the first attempt at robbing the bank? If so, why hasn't he gone after her? Or is he planning on it? God, I would never forgive myself if something happened to her. Why? After five years? I have been wracking my brain about that. Adam, have you come across anything?"

Adam answered, "No, Hump. I vigilantly check if any strangers are around and if anyone remembers him from five years ago. I have gotten on the Chief's last nerve questioning him about anyone that fits that description in the last ten years. Nothing. And he knows we are asking around town. He says the case is closed, and that's it."

Carl Neal had been incredibly lucky the day he got the file from Larsen. No one saw him enter Larsen's house that morning. Neal began watching Larsen casually when he saw the man on the street in 1974. For two days, he watched the man's movements. Then Neal moved on; not worth his time. Then four years later, it hit him harder than a brick falling off a high rise. He realized that the man had something that would destroy Neal, whether the man knew it or not. He had to get it, no matter the cost.

He knew the amateur sleuth would be gone for the day because he had studied his routine for some time. An entire year, in fact. Neal began his spying in 1978. He went incognito many times through the town, not wanting to be recognized twice by anyone. But Neal knew he might have been seen by someone when he entered Larsen's home for the first and only time. In his lifetime of killing and evading the law, he knew anything unexpected could happen.

If he had been in the house and an unwanted visitor surprised him, he would have taken care of it. The door to the house was unlocked, and having all the files in alphabetical order made it easier for Neal. The day he entered the house, he knew all about the Sherlock Holmes of the small town. He knew from the two idiot Howards but also by observing and watching Larsen's movements. He also knew Humphrey Larsen's friends and girlfriend. Larsen may not remember what he put in that file, but Neal did not want to take a chance. He rampaged the Larsen house just for meanness, trashing the lemonade and making a mess in the house. Neal sneaked around Melville on and off for almost two years leading up to now. He would scurry behind the nearest shrub to keep from being detected by neighbors. Most of it was done in the dead of night. Sometimes his spying would be done in the daytime. After he looked at the file, Neal knew he would have to get rid of everyone involved. Maybe even friends or associates of Larsen. The two idiots, Roy and Ricky, made that more difficult now. Looking back, he wished he had gotten rid of their bodies, taking them five states away instead of leaving them in the shack.

Neal knew that Larsen, who he had to admit was a very bright guy, would solve the puzzle eventually. And the key to the puzzle is something the Howards dropped the night they were caught. A key. The key was to a safe deposit box. The box belonged to Neal. Fortunately for him, the two morons had not gotten the box. Since the key was deemed unimportant to the case, Neal's name never came up during the trial. If it had, the Howards would have met their end in a different way. And much sooner. Once Larsen began snooping around, he would come across the key and learn that it would be the solution and would lead to Neal.

Before Humphrey Larsen, Neal had come near the Melville area several years before. In 1970, driving on the Blue Ridge Parkway, Neal came across a male jogger. Jogging was not as popular as it became later. It just wasn't expected. Neal was perturbed, to put it mildly, when he came upon a curve at sixty miles an hour in his brand new '70 Chevy Cheville. He had to swerve to miss the lone runner. But in doing so, he overcompensated, turning left and flying over a ditch. He was lucky, along with his Cheville, to end up in a valley.

Neal did not have to be raving mad to kill someone, but on that summer day in 1970, he became a lunatic. When he got out of his car, he could not kill the jogger soon enough. Neal wanted to shoot him so badly in the open valley, but someone could see it.

"Hey man, didn't you see me running?! Are you ok? You were flying in that car," yelled the jogger as he ran toward Neal's car.

The jogger had not reached Neal but was talking the entire time coming. Neal had yet to answer. The closer the jogger got to Neal, the more obtuse Neal thought the man had become.

"Hey man, I said didn't you see me?" When the jogger got to Neal and looked at him, he slowed his talking. Something about the guy's eyes got to him. The jogger was a kid. No more than twenty or twenty-one. Now something stirred in the kid, frightened by the man that was now out of his car and glaring at him. "I mean, uh, joggers can run on the road, you know?"

Neal wanted to go ahead and shoot the kid right there. The boy, who was once running, but now berating Neal, was wearing red shorts, Adidas sneakers, and a yellow shirt with a peace sign on it. He had a white headband that supported his long hair. *Damned hippie*, thought Neal. Another reason to shoot him. Neal was standing beside his car door, and the hippie had just approached the passenger's side.

"Come look at my car," said Neal.

"What?!" said the young runner, a little frightened by the stranger but still indignant.

"Come look at my car," Repeated Neal.

The kid came around as ordered and looked at the front of Neal's car. Seeing no damage, the boy said, "Hey, man, it wasn't my fault. It wasn't my fault you ran off the road."

"Look," said Neal. He wanted to get the hippie close. Later, he would know that he would have to throw the hippie in the back seat instead of the trunk. The guy had gotten to the other side of the car, and Neal told him to look at the passenger door on the driver's side. Lucky for Neal, but not the kid, there was not a scratch on the door. "Look!" cried out Neal again.

"What! Where?!" replied the young jogger.

"Look closer," Neal said, "near the door handle."

The guy approached Neal's side of the car and got inches from the door. Before the kid knew it, Neal grabbed the boy by his hair and rammed the jogger headfirst into the door. It fazed him, and he staggered with arms reaching out to grab something. *Like that is going to help you,* Neal thought. Neal grabbed the kid again and rammed him again, but harder. He did not want to kill the boy right there. He wanted to savor the killing and relish in beating the snot-nose little brat. With the second ramming, the boy was out. Neal opened the back seat and was able to throw the hippie in the back seat. He looked around to see if a car was coming around the curve from the mountain. Luckily, no one was around.

Neal took the guy about a half mile off the Parkway. He waited until almost dusk so there would not be too many drivers out or hikers. He propped the kid against a tree and gave him a third eye with his weapon of choice at that time, a thirty-eight special. He did not know it at the time, but he made one of the biggest mistakes of his life that day. He thought the hippie would never be found, so he kept the gun instead of throwing it away as he would later on do after a killing.

Two days later, he was in Melville. A town he never thought about returning to. But after the hippie, he knew he would at some point. He was walking down Center Street when he saw a fat policeman who seemed to be the headman. Carl Neal realized that he had the gun he used at the jogger on him in his coat pocket. *Damn*, he thought. *What luck!* He got nervous and became afraid that the man might ask him questions. What if the boy's body had been found? What if the fat man suspected him because he was a stranger in town? What if the State Police is already searching for the killer? Or, in Neal's case, the man who relieved society of another hippie.

Neal had to get off the street as quickly as he could. As it so happened, he was standing directly in front of the First Union Bank. He slipped inside and looked back onto the street. The police officer kept walking, passed the bank, and went on his way. It seemed apparent the man was not looking for a stranger or did not notice him.

Unbeknownst to Carl Neal, the jogger was found by two college students at the precise time he was walking in the First Union Bank. The students had decided to go off the beaten path from a trail on the Parkway. The two young lovers wanted some private time. Private time, they did not get.

Neal, seeing the cops leave, was about to go out of the bank but was stopped by a big man in a three-piece suit. "May I help you?" said Mr. Griffith. Taken back at first, Neal regained his composure. He had an idea. He replied to the big man, "Yes, I think you can." Minutes later, Carl Neal was placing the 38 special into a safe deposit box. With a box comes a key. A key that would be around a few years later. The same key the Howards would have when Quirt Eastman tackled them on the street after the botched robbery. Neal gave it to the two idiots to get his gun out. Four years later, he did not get the key. Five years after that, in 1979, he still did not have the key.

Now, Neal needed to know if Larsen knew the importance of the key. Larsen would not know about the gun. However, Larsen might learn about the key. That was the reason for the break-in. Carl Neal, by this time, knew that Larsen had recorded in his so-called criminal case file about the key. Larsen recorded that the key was on the sidewalk and thought it was a mere coincidence the key was on the sidewalk. He did not record it as being especially important. Neal could try to get into Larsen's house at night, but it was lit up like a fortress; not that it would stop Neal, but it made it more difficult. He didn't want difficulty. Lights were everywhere, and Larsen stayed up late at night. The guy across the street, who Neal learned was Robert David, kept all kinds of hours. Neal could go to the bank and pay for another key but did not want to be seen. He could let it go and forget about it. What if something odd was to occur and the box and gun were discovered? Carl Neal had to get to Mr. Humphrey Larsen, an amateur sleuth and everyone's likable friend. He was the only one in that town who might figure it out.

Chapter Ten

After that Tuesday meeting with Quirt and Adam, there were no new developments, leads, or anything. It seemed everything had slowed down. Adam had not said anymore to the Chief. It would have been a waste of time anyway. Also, the Chief seemed not too eager to find the killers of Roy and Ricky. He did find out that they were from West Virginia. The Chief believes that they were traveling with another person or people and had a riff with them, and the result was two dead men. The culprit had probably moved on, and another case was closed for Chief Wilson and the Melville Police Department. It had been a frustrating week all around for me. It did not get any better on Sunday. A Redskin loss to the hated Philadelphia Eagles and things worse than that later that day.

Sunday morning was a wonderful fall morning in the piedmont near the foothills of North Carolina. The huge oak trees in front of Melville First Baptist Church, on the corner of Fifth and Elm Streets, were in prime fall color. The Elm trees beside the sidewalk on Elm Street *(it is named Elm Street for a reason)* were majestic. The Maples on the other side of the church were red and gold, with half their leaves lying in the churchyard. Approaching the church with the light fall breeze blowing those leaves and with a temperature of sixty-five degrees, it could almost be a perfect day. After my three-minute walk to church, I met Adam on the front sidewalk. Referring to the meeting on Tuesday, Adam said, "What are we missing, Hump?"

"I don't know," I replied. "But it's like I have it right on the tip of my brain, but I just can't come up with it. We missed something. With all of us together today watching the game, maybe we can figure it out."

We go inside and sit in our usual third pew from the back and on the left side. Quirt sings in the choir, or as we always say, he thinks he sings. Actually, he has a pretty good voice and has sung some solos in church. Slim does not attend church very often, but when he does, it is to Rock Hill United Methodist Church, two miles due South of Melville. Robert David claims he did not need to go to church and says he worships the Lord his own way. Whatever you say, big guy.

We had a spot on that pew for ourselves. Quirt would come to sit with us after the Choir sang the last hymn before the preaching began. Along with Quirt in the choir were Sue Ann and Amy, my used to be steady. They, like Quirt, would join us on 'our' pew. But unlike Sue Ann and Quirt, Amy has not joined us for several weeks. I wonder why. As Adam and I approached our usual seating spot, the choir was coming from the back of the church. Which meant it was close to eleven o'clock and that Adam and I were almost late. After the choir's last number, Amy goes and sits in the fourth pew on the right. I die a little each time she comes down the aisle and goes to her new seat. Each time I hope that she decides to sit with the old gang. But she does not. Maybe I should pray instead of hoping. I am in the right place for it, aren't I? At the beginning of our little spat, she would look pleadingly at me. That was several weeks ago. Now, she looks straight ahead and does not glance my way. Am I the stubborn one here? Quirt told me that Amy would ask about me before they came out at the beginning of the service. She had slowly veered away from that. The questions lessened, and the discussion about yours truly diminished as the Sundays went by. Quirt tried to talk to me about it later that afternoon while the guys were at my house watching the football game.

"I'm not talking about it, Quirt."

"But Hump, I'm your friend, and you know you and Amy are meant to—"

"I know you're my friend. Do you have to tell me that? Do you think you know what is best for us? When did you get to be so smart?"

"Okay, Hump," replied Quirt, who by this time was tired of my rants, and probably tired of me. "You're right; let's just drop it," he said.

It was an uncomfortable moment that Sunday for Adam, Robert D, and Slim. After the end of the third quarter, Quirt gently and strategically made his exit. His excuse was that Redskins were losing. Our somewhat heated discussion was during halftime. It was uncomfortable in my house during the third quarter. At the end of that quarter, he decided to leave. He said, "Guys. I think I'm going to head on, the Skins are getting whipped anyway, and I have to be in the store early tomorrow. You know Monday morning is our busiest morning."

I did not say anything, not knowing at the time that I was the stubborn one.

"C'mon, Quirt, stay a little longer," said Adam, trying to ease the tension.

"Yeah, stay," said D and Slim in unison.

"Nah, I better go," said Quirt. "See you guys later."

"Okay, later," I replied and then turned back as Quirt headed out.

Quirt looked back before he got to the door. With my back turned, I did not see his hurt until later that night. And later that night, I learned who the biggest fool in Melville was. It wasn't Quirt, and it was not Amy.

Quirt and I had never really had an argument before. When we got to high school, we were inseparable. So, this was the first time we had anything like this. Later that night, I was moping and feeling sorry for myself. Not one look from Amy today. Again. The tension of today with Quirt and me. To add to that, no clue about the missing Howard file. Quirt and I have solved cases before, but this looks like a dead end. And which might be our most dangerous. I heard the old grandfather clock chime seven times. All the guys are long gone. Then I heard my front door ring. All the guys come by at all kinds of odd hours. Adam might come by in the middle of the night when he is working if he sees my lights on and knows I am working. But they come by less on a Sunday evening. But they have already been here. Usually, they step in and yell out to me that they are there. And they don't ring my doorbell.

I was on my third beer, drinking Slim's stash. I am not much of a beer drinker, but I feel sorry for myself, moping around like a lost soul. I get out of my Lazy Boy and go to my front door. Who would be coming by on a Sunday evening? I came around the corner of my den and stepped toward the foyer. Ten feet away, I look through the glass storm door and see the last person I would imagine seeing. It was Amy.

I almost fainted, but before that, I almost melted, just like I did when I first saw Mrs. Rebecca Johnson. I didn't think my feet would get to the door. I know I stopped, probably for two seconds, which seemed like two minutes. She was in a red and white sundress, showing off her light brown arms. Her skin always looked like someone who sunbathed every day. But she was someone who never did. Her dark hair seemed darker, and her Ali McGraw look was right on. Her brownish hazel eyes were almost golden. Her presence on my doorstep had me excited *(Hey, she did look like Ali McGraw),* flabbergasted, apprehensive, and intrigued at the same time. I opened the door and, with all the debonair and charm I could muster, said, "Um, um, Amy?"

"Hello, Humphrey," said Amy.

Humphrey? When did she ever call me Humphrey? I knew this was not going to be good when I first saw her. I knew it was going to be worse when she called me that. For I knew she would not grovel, nor was she coming to apologize. She did not have anything to apologize for. Then with more ease, I replied, "Hey." And I was still standing at the threshold, holding the door halfway open, as if she was a salesman standing on my porch. Invite her in, dummy!

She saved me by saying, "May I come in?" When did she ever ask to come into my house? Usually, she would just walk right in and yell for me. This is not looking good for the home team.

"Yeah, um, sure," I replied.

Then I opened the door, both of us now standing in the foyer. I may have had my fingers crossed behind my back, wishing I had a rabbit's foot in one pocket and a horseshoe in another, while thinking, *God, please don't let this be a "we are done" speech*. If it would not have been too embarrassing for the both of us, I would have gotten down on my knees and talked to the good Lord right then and there. So, I waited, expecting her to say, "Hump, since you are an idiot like no other, I have decided to date my ugly coworker and drop a handsome devil like yourself. Instead of that, she said, "I came over to discuss you and Quirt."

What?!

She comes in like my dream movie star, and she wants to talk about Quirt! Are you kidding me?! Surprised, I say,

"You what? You came over to talk about Quirt and me? Are you kidding me right now, Amy? Not you or me?"

"No, Hump, not you and me." At least she is back to calling me Hump.

"What do you mean not us? Why Quirt? What did he do? Come crying to you?"

"Humphrey Larsen, stop it right now. How can you say that about Quirt? He is trying to help you. He is trying to help us. He came over earlier and—"

"So, he came to tell you about our disagreement. He can't fight for himself?"

"You know good, and well, that is not it, Hump. He wants the best for us. Or what used to be us."

"And what is that supposed to mean?"

"You know what it exactly means. You have been childish from the start and—"

"Oh, me? Childish?! You're the one that seems to have the goo-goo eyes for—"

"I'm not getting through to you, am I Hump? I'm leaving."

And with that, she practically ran out the door. I said, "Amy, wait—"

But by that time, she was halfway down my sidewalk. I knew it would be useless to chase her down before she reached the street. We would just create a scene on David Street. She was done with me. I could only hope that it was not forever.

The next day I didn't hear from Quirt. And certainly not Amy. I hadn't heard from her on a Monday in a long time, so I did not expect her to call me up or come over and say, "Wasn't last night fun?" I was not in the mood for much of anything. I went across the street to D's. My plan was to vent a little or wait for the words of wisdom I sometimes got from him. In those times, I would listen and maybe heed his advice. Who needs a shrink when your neighbor and friend is across the street?

I walk into his house, just like my friends enter mine, without knocking but calling out to D.

"Hey, D! It's me," I say as I walk in his front door. There was a small foyer, and to the right, as I entered, was a living room. His living area, if you want to call that, was more of a library. Facing the street and almost in a direct line to my front door was a huge double-pane window. On both sides of the window were bookshelves that were completely full. The wall opposite the entry to the area was also full. The reason is the room is simply known as the library. D could not reach the books high up on the shelf but relied on his friends to get them. There were not many days when I had not been in his house, and he did not ask me to get him a book. The ones he uses often he keeps down low on the shelf. Also, the ones important to him. He likes to know that they are close by and that he can get to them whenever he wants. And scattered all over the room were books. They were beside chairs, on chairs, in corners, some on a coffee table, some stacked directly in the center of the room. And there were others stacked on the floor near the foyer as you entered the room. Then there were magazines and newspapers stacked onto those books. No one dared to say anything about the 'mess' in the room. There would be a tongue-lashing if you did.

"Hey, Hump." D replies as I walk into his living room/library/study room. He is sitting at his desk, with newspapers and magazines scattered all over it. I did not study the publications to see what he was researching. Again, not in the mood.

D said, "I was just about to make a pot of coffee. Ya want some? It's not your brand, but it's good. In fact, it's good to the last drop."

His reference to the Maxwell House commercial did not humor me. "Sure," I replied.

I followed him out of the room and then through the small passage to the back of the house and then into the kitchen. Sitting in his wheelchair, D began to pour water into his new percolator, one that was growing in popularity every day, a new Mr. Coffee. The kitchen was built by Quirt, Adam, and me to accommodate D's handicap. Everything was at his level. Unlike the library, the kitchen was as neat as a pen. We all ribbed him about the chaos in the other room, but no reason to do it here. I saw where he had already had the sugar bowl on his table, along with a small pitcher of milk. He knew that I liked my first cup of coffee with a small spoon of milk and sugar. Was he expecting me?

"I knew you would come by this morning." Robert D said.

Almost sheepishly, I replied, "I figured you would. I'm not sure I want to talk about it, but maybe I do. I don't know." D probably saw Amy last night at my house.

"Hump, you either do or you don't. I think you do; otherwise, you wouldn't be here. I know I'm not the best guy to talk to, but I'm the closest. And I'm okay with that. Sometimes it's good to get things off your chest to the person available and the nearest."

"Amy came by last night."

"Everything okay now?"

"They are worse. D. Can I bend down so you can knock some sense into me? When a person doesn't want to listen to his best friend, something is nutty about him. And if I weren't so stubborn, Amy would still be in my life."

"I've got news for you, big boy," D said.

D had a certain way of talking to me that other people could not.

"She is still in your life, and so is Quirt. You have to reach out to them both, and you are right. Stop being so blasted hard headed. Do you ever think about what she is going through? What is she thinking? I know you are a lot smarter than what you are showing. Don't lose her, Hump."

I think someone else told me the very same thing some time ago. D went on, "As far as you and Quirt are concerned, that was nothing. You got agitated by what you thought was pestering about Amy. He wants the best for you, Humphrey Larsen, just as we all do. He was hurt, obviously, because that's not like you. But it was about Amy, which you have been stubborn about. Don't lose that girl, Hump."

I made the coffee black for him and that little bit of sugar kick for me. We went into the room across from his library, which he always jokingly called "the parlor." We entered from the foyer as I had before when I walked into his home. The 'parlor' was furnished with a large, eight feet long desk, but only three feet tall. A short desk so Robert David, the heir to the David fortune, wealthy with friends, could do his research. He would do his work here and zip his wheelchair across the foyer and into his library to find things. It was like one room, except for the foyer separating both. He could glide his chair under the short desk for researching and writing. The desk sat in front of a large pane window, like the one in his library. He had a direct line of view to my front step from his desk. I wonder if he saw Amy come out of my house. He did not say, nor would he ever say. I know D did not spy on me, but he had the desk positioned just so he could see David Street. On the right of his desk sat the ham radio to listen to the happenings in Melville. The remainder of the room consisted of a sofa directly behind him on the back wall and two wingback chairs on both sides of the sofa. The other room was for research, but this room was where he put it all together. But it also could be used for entertaining a small group like the gang. He did not mix the two rooms. Once he got his material from the library, he would go into the parlor and finish. From the look of his desk, now almost covered with newspapers, I knew he had been putting something together. I briefly thought that it was the case he told me about last week, the one he was so excited about. I playback our one-sided conversation:

"I'm telling you, Hump, this doctor killed his family."

"What, doctor D?"

"What do you mean what, doctor?"

What?! Why do people say what do you mean when they know what you mean?

I replied, "D, What I mean is what I asked. What doctor?"

"Oh, yeah. The doctor in Fort Bragg."

"You mean Dr. Jeffrey MacDonald?" Now I'm kind of doing it. "The doctor was convicted of killing his family while living on the Army base in 1970. Of course."

"Yeah, of course, you do. I guess it is a rhetorical question. But I have been doing a lot of research on it. The guy claimed, as you know, of course, that hippies came in and did the killing. Tried to make it like a Manson-type killing. A lot of people believe he got shafted and is innocent of the crime. But I think he is where he exactly belongs. He was a doctor and knew where to stab himself so he could survive."

So, seeing his papers, I assumed it was the MacDonald case.

"Hump, I've been doing some digging."

"Again?" I chuckled, thinking that maybe D was now studying Jack the Ripper or who shot Kennedy.

"Don't I always?" he said.

"Yeah, I guess so. What is it this time?"

"What else?" asking in a way and tone that there would be no doubt I'd know the answer.

"You mean the Howards' case?" I asked excitedly.

He replied, "Well, something that may pertain to it. Your stranger, the 'Shadow', as you call him."

"What about him?" I asked in a way, not expecting much of a promising result. We had not found anything, and it seemed we had asked everyone in town.

"Boy, you sound excited, don't get so carried away, Hump," asked D in his infamous sarcastic way that no one else could duplicate.

"Maybe I will, D, if it is something."

"Maybe something or not. We have been figuring that the guy hired this Roy and Ricky to attack Quirt, right?"

"Yeah, so?"

"Alright, just listen. The guy blows them away. Remember the jogger killed on the Parkway in 1970?"

"Yeah, sure. What about it?"

"Hump. That's where I've been digging. That case is still unsolved. I've got a police dispatcher buddy in Mt. Airy. It was closer to them than anybody. They have been working hard on it for nine years. Their department is as good as ours is bad. They have no leads, nothing. I've been hunting for similar cases around the south, close to here. There was a similar case in West Virginia and another in Charlottesville, Virginia. These people just got blown away, and no one has a clue. No feud with anyone, no lovers quarrel, nothing."

"Serial, maybe?"

Thinking quietly to himself, contemplating, D said, "Serial Killer? No. Too many differences. Some similarities, I guess, but not enough to say the person could be a serial killer."

"Similar to ours?" I asked.

"Well, the Parkway was just one guy. In West Virginia, two guys were killed outside a bar in a small town. Maybe like Roy and Ricky, but that's it. The one in Charlottesville was one guy, like the jogger."

"Jogging?" I asked.

"No. In 1968 a husband runs, I mean not jogging, but drives to the A&P for his wife. He is found a mile away at a country intersection. His car looked as if it had been involved in a fender bender. The authorities assumed he had a bump up with another car, and the other driver got ticked off and shot the husband. No clues whatsoever. It is just like the others, except for the Parkway shooting. They never gave up on that one."

Thinking that West Virginia was the only one like Roy and Ricky, I said, "Where in West Virginia?"

D began rummaging through the papers on his desk. He finds it much quicker than I expected. Talking more to himself, he says, "Let's see here, where did I put it?" Shuffling through the newspapers around until he comes across it. "Here it is. Yeah, I remember now. White Rock, West Virginia. Outside Beckley. Why? You got plans?"

"Yeah, I just might," I replied.

I went home and sat in my 'parlor', which was my den. I sat in my chair beside my filing cabinet and beside the back door of my little cottage. Where all of this started, and my Jack Higgins book lay in the same place on the table. I felt that nothing had happened since that day, that we got nowhere to find the person who came into my house. I thought of calling Adam to ask him to contact White Rock and see if there were any similarities between the killings there to the killing of Roy and Ricky. Better yet, maybe a road trip up there would be better. A week ago, I would have asked Quirt about going, but now I don't know. He may not want to hear from me. For the rest of the day, I did not do much. I read quite a bit of the Higgins novel, although my focus was not there as it normally would be. My mind drifted from the case to Quirt and certainly Amy. I did not know Adam's schedule for the week. I called him to see if he was interested in going up to White Rock. It would be a day trip.

A long day trip, but he would be back home and not be away from his family for a night.

I knew he was working the night shift, so I called him home before he went to the station. I told him about the killings in White Rock. We made plans to go to West Virginia on Wednesday, his day off from work. Since this was the only day we could go up, I had to cancel my volunteer work.

Later, I went to the Grill for a steak sandwich and decided to take it easy and watch the Monday Night Football Game between the Raiders and the Dolphins. Sometimes the guys would meet for a game, especially if the Redskins were playing. No one called about coming over tonight.

At about eight o'clock, my doorbell rang. The last time that occurred was yesterday when Amy came over. Surely it would not be her. Like the night before, when I went to answer the door and turned the corner to the foyer, I had another surprise. Unlike Amy, along with not looking as good as her, he had a bag in his hand. I opened the door, and unlike the night before, I did not stand there dumbfounded. "Since when did you feel like you had to ring the bell? C'mon in." I said.

Quirt replied, "I rang it because I was not sure you wanted to see me. I brought a peace offering." He handed me the bag. "Hump, I didn't mean to—"

I cut him off before he could finish. "Stop there, Quirt. No peace offering is needed. Nor an apology. If that's what you're about to say. I know you're trying to help. I'm the idiot here. If I were much smarter, I would have listened to you."

"I know, but I still probably crossed the line. I—"

"No, you didn't," I said. "You just wanted me to talk to Amy, which I did last night."

"That's good, Hump. That you reached out."

"No. It didn't happen that way. And it did not go too well. C'mon, let's go into the den."

We walked first into the kitchen, where he placed the bag on the counter and pulled out a fifth of Jack Daniels and a carton of Cokes. Quirt said, "I hope this makes amends."

Wow. Am I on my way to being a serious drinking man? Three beers the other night, and now this. The town might start talking, certainly the May sisters. I said, "Wow, we need to have more spats if this is what comes from them. I am glad you did not bring this after Amy's visit last night. There would not have been enough to share."

"That bad, uh?" Quirt asked.

"Yeah, that bad. Let me fix us one of these, and I'll tell you all about it."

I made us two large Jack & Cokes and told him about Amy. Then I told him about the case in West Virginia.

"So, you think maybe the Shadow could have killed those guys as well?" said Quirt.

"Oh, I don't know. It is probably not related at all. Just because two guys get killed, it does not mean it is the Shadow. I'm probably reaching here, hoping that it is something. Even if it was, it does not prove he killed Roy and Ricky. But Quirt, it might be more than something. It would tell us to be on our guard. I want to see if there has been a bank robbery or an attempted one in White Rock. If there was, it still would not prove that this guy was involved in either one. I just don't know. Do you think you could come with Adam and me?"

"I take every other Wednesday off, but I may have to go in early. What time do you plan on leaving?"

"I want to leave at eight."

Quirt contemplated before answering, "I can go in early, around six, and then you guys can pick me up at eight."

"Sounds like a plan," I said, excited about the prospect of hopefully finding something.

For the rest of the night, we sipped our drinks and watched the game. There was no talk of yesterday or talk of Amy. We just enjoyed each other's company. The way best friends are supposed to do. But occasionally, my mind would wander about Wednesday and those prospects. Will we find something in White Rock, West Virginia? Maybe this is the beginning of the end. But for who?

Chapter Eleven

Adam and I picked up Quirt on that Wednesday morning at eight. We set out for the big town of White Rock, West Virginia. We pulled into the police station there at 10:45. We were greeted by a young, nervous police officer, looking as if he had just graduated from middle school. He was 6'3 ft and 170 lbs. The young officer had coarse red hair and pale skin. The name on his uniform was Wilson. Adam had been in contact with Chief Clint Wilson. I hope he is not related to our Chief Wilson. I looked at the young man and hoped this wasn't the guy. Wet behind the ears is an understatement. We stood in a station that was half the size of the one in Melville. But unlike Melville, it looked as if it was built yesterday. The young officer stood as if he was eagerly anticipating someone to enter the station. The young man was nervous but, at the same time, confident. As some folks say of young men starting their way of life, they are full of piss and vinegar. I respected that totally because we all have been there at some point in our lives.

"Can I help you?" the young officer asked.

Adam answered for us with a slight weariness in his voice. *(Probably thinking and hoping that this cannot be Chief Wilson)* "Yes, we are here to see Chief Wilson."

The young man replied proudly, "Yeah, that's my dad. He's been Chief going on twenty-five years. Back when the station was in the back of the Fire Department. This station is new, well, kind of new. Been here for three years. Dad is proud of it. I've been helping him for six months; well, I'm training, I guess."

The young man was so excited he did not tell us his name. Maybe we are the only people he has seen all morning. Adam helped with it. "And you are?" asked Adam.

"Oh. I always forget to do that. Dad always says I need to introduce myself. I guess I forgot."

Oh boy. This young fella has a long way to go.

"I'm Clint, but most folks call me Lil Clint. My dad's Clint."

"Is he here?" asked Adam.

Before Lil Clint *(Clint Jr.)* could answer Adam's request, a man came out of a door near the back of the station.

"C? Who is it? Oh, there are people here. I thought so. Is C helping you?"

Apparently, this guy doesn't call the young man Officer Wilson, but C. And clearer is that this man must be Lil C's father, for he had the same blazing red hair, except for some gray trying to get in. The older Wilson, still assuming that it is, was much taller, coming in at 6'6 ft. Also heavier at 240 lbs. There wasn't much fat with twenty-five years of service. He seemed military-like. He was not as pale as the younger Clint, maybe from walking his beat in the town of just over eight hundred and fifty people. Robert D researched that for me.

Adam answered the tall man. "Well, he was right in the middle of it."

"Good. I'm Clint Wilson."

I knew it was him.

"Chief. I'm Adam Eastman."

The Chief replied, "Yeah, thought it might be you. We don't have too many folks coming to the station."

"These are my friends Humphrey Larsen and Quirt Eastman."

"Brothers?" asked the Chief, clearly focused on the introductions, while most people don't pick up people's names when they are introduced. Really, can most people say who they were introduced to five minutes after they met?

"Cousins," replied Adam.

"Well, no need to diddle, daddle. Let's go to the conference room," said Wilson. The bigger, older Wilson.

We went through the door he came out of minutes before. We walked into an office, and he led us to another door, which led to a conference room. A small room that had a small table with six chairs. I think Rebecca Johnson's dining room was bigger. Wilson sat at the end. Adam, being a policeman and the one who contacted Wilson, would be leading the conversation. We would put our brains together afterward, back in Melville. Quirt and I would ask questions if needed.

Adam began, "Well, Chief, like I said—"

"Call me Clint. Heck, most people do. They call me Clint one day and the next Chief."

Adam continued, "I told you on the phone about our case and just wanted to see if there are more similarities than we have already discussed."

Being the officer, Adam was a very good one. He knew not just to rely on one conversation. And not over the phone. Sometimes things come back to people if they talk in person. Adam was hoping for that, I was sure.

"Right," replied Wilson. "I don't think so. There were two males here, two males in your town. Both were shot in the head, which seems for no apparent reason. No suspects, nothing. And like yours, our victims were not from here. Let me go and get the file on it."

After Wilson goes into his office and rummages around his desk for two minutes, he returns with the file. The Chief says, "Here's what I'm going to do. Since you brought your friends with you, I will give you time to read over the case file if you don't walk out with it," he said with a wink, and a smile, which seemed directed at me. He said it with eyes that seemed to say, *"If you do, I will kill you"*. Maybe that was my wild imagination. I bet the worst we would get would be one night in the Clink. I did not want that either. I didn't want to wake up and see Opie staring through the bars of my cell. The Chief pulled out three copies. "I'll give you all the time you want," said Wilson. We opened the file. A summary by the Chief:

Bart Jefferson, 32, and James Thomas, 30, were shot with a 9mm Glock. Jefferson was shot twice, once in the thigh and once in the head. Thomas was shot once in the head. Thomas was in the back seat of a 1967 Pontiac GTO. Jefferson was in the driver's seat. After analysis by the coroner, it was determined they were shot at close range.

Close enough that the shooter was most likely in the front passenger seat. The car was on the street across from the bar.

I stopped reading and asked myself, What bar? I realized that this was not really an official document but a summary done just for the Chief himself. Later, I realized that it was not an official one but a very good summary by the Chief. I continued reading:

The car was in the side parking area. The trees and the bar's side brick wall could have lessened the sound of the shots. Later, bar patrons claimed to have heard what they assumed were backfires from a car. The most reliable witness was Jim Scruggs, who cracked open the front door. It was close to closing time, 1: 40 am, and he was sweeping. According to Jim, he heard several shots, not a backfire from a car. He knew gunshots when he heard them. There were three guys in the back of the bar, finishing their last hand of poker. One said he heard something but was not sure how many or if it was gunfire. Scruggs thought at first it might have been a backfire but knew that the only people out that late were the guys in the bar and himself. Then when he heard the rest, he knew it was gunfire. He told me later that it had to be from a gun. He heard the first, and then he heard the other two. I asked if the sounds were in succession. Jim had to think about it. He said it was probably a minute, a minute and a half at the most. When he heard the other two, it was "pop pop". He knew then it was a gun. And not backfire from a car.

I stopped reading again, impressed with the Chief, having asked Scruggs about the shot being fired in succession or a delay. This Police Chief was not a small-town bumpkin like Chief Wilson in Melville. I read on.

Jim said he thought it was someone's car at first. Then when he heard the "pop, pop", it had to be three gunshots. In all, he heard three. He thought it was teenagers goofing around, out late on a Saturday night.

The nearest house, a half block away, was Ralph and Nora Smith. They did not hear anything or see anything. No one saw the shooter. I interviewed Jim Scruggs after Jim came forward with some information. He said that the two victims had been seen with a third party about a week before in the side parking lot. All three were shadowed by another building in the back. It was hard to see them. Jim said it felt that the third guy was a stranger in town. I asked for a description, and he told me that he never got a good look at the person, but the only thing he remembered about the guy was that he had a jacket on, the collar turned up, and a fedora on his head. Jim said he remembered it well because it was in the high 70s that day. Who wears a hat and jacket on a day like that? Plus, who wears a fedora anymore?

I stopped reading and looked at Quirt and Adam. Seconds later, they both took a glance at me. We had all come to the part about the fedora-wearing man. Wow, not a coincidence. I continued reading.

I felt I had asked half the town about the stranger. No one remembered seeing anyone like that before or after the shooting. No one saw anyone fitting that description. There was no evidence left in the front passenger seat. After weeks of investigation, it was determined that the case was closed. Or unsolved.

After we finished reading, we all looked at each other and with our eyes saying *Wow!* Then Quirt said it aloud to all of us, "Wow. Holy Cow! That must be our guy."

The Chief, seeing our reaction, whom I had not realized had come back into the conference room, said, "Well, gentlemen. What do you think? I think with the reaction, I already know."

"Chief, no one saw this guy with the fedora, No one at all?" I asked.

"No, son, just Jim Scruggs. I talked to some regulars at the bar. Some remember a guy with the hat, but it seemed he kept his head down most of the time. They didn't think much of it at the time, but like me, they wondered if this guy was the shooter or had something to do with it. But that's how it is in most cases. Witnesses think they have seen or heard something, but they really do not. Their minds play tricks on them, or they want to see or hear something."

I ask Wilson, "Chief, were there any attempts to rob a bank in town about this time?"

"Well, it wasn't really an attempt. No one broke in or anything. I keep records. Hold on a minute."

The Chief retreated from the conference room and back into his office. We heard him rummaging through his files as before and returned a minute later holding a thick manila folder. He said, "Let's see here, for the year 1973. March 14. Here is what I recorded." He began to read:

"Checking the doors around town, I had just gotten to the front door of the bank."

I interrupted him. "Excuse me, Chief, which bank is that?"

"The only one we have. The White Rock Bank. I had just gotten to the front door of the bank. I heard something in the alley between the bank and Smith's Drug Store. I investigated and determined that it must have been a cat or a dog going through a trash can. I did see a ladder standing up on the bank's wall. I assumed it was there all the time. On March 15, I asked Mr. Apple from the bank and Mr. Smith from the drug store about the ladder. Neither remembered the ladder; they did not know what I was talking about. Both said the same thing, probably kids horsing around."

At this, Adam, Quirt, and I looked at each other again, no doubt thinking the same thing. Like Melville? Chief Wilson glanced up and saw us, probably with our mouths wide open and eyes bulging. The Chief said, "That sounds familiar to you boys?"

We all replied in unison, "Yes."

The Chief read on. "I discovered that the ladder belonged to Mr. Anderson of the hardware store. Mr. Anderson stated to me that there would be no reason that his ladder would be against the bank wall. He told me it was probably a kid. I tended to agree with him. There have been no incidents at the bank. No need to investigate any further."

Adam asked. "So, this was about two months before the killings?"

"Not quite two months." Said Wilson.

"And no one else saw this stranger?" asked Quirt.

"Nobody, and I asked about everyone here. You can tell our town is small. If a person saw him, they would have remembered it."

We all agreed with that. And with that, we had no more questions. But we got plenty of answers. I don't think there is much doubt, even if we don't have absolute proof, that the stranger here was our "Shadow". It was just too coincidental. Who else would wear a fedora and jacket in warm weather? Our guy would. Two killings here, two in Melville. Plus, an attempted bank robbery in Melville and maybe one here in White Rock? We just do not have the proof. The ladder here may have been kids and not the Shadow and two guys like the Howards. And besides, with all my investigating, the dark man with the fedora is probably long gone by now and has forgotten all about me. I was wrong, wasn't I?

Chapter Twelve

Even though we talked about White Rock all the way back to Melville, we decided to discuss it more when we got home. We drove to Davids Furniture to pick up Slim. Then we drove to D's.

"So, their guy is our guy," said D.

"Looks like it," I said. "There are just too many similarities. Even their guy and our guy have that evasiveness. How he goes around wearing that hat and not being seen by many people is beyond me. I don't know how he does it. He makes a point of not standing out. Whoever this guy is, he is good."

"What now?" asked Quirt.

Sounding dejected, I replied, "I don't know. This is the only lead we have if you can call it that. And it's not much."

After an hour of discussion and not really getting anywhere, we decided to call it a night. Before we broke up, I asked Adam, "I guess you go into the station tomorrow?"

A tired Adam said. "No. It's my two days off. I go in on Friday."

I replied in a disappointed tone, "Oh."

"Why, what do you need?" asked Adam.

Now I was hesitant to ask since it would be Adam's days off. Of course, that was not going to deter me from being selfish and not thinking about him enjoying his day off. I said, "I thought maybe you could look through your database and see if there have been any other bank robberies in the last five years that might be like ours. But you can do it on Friday; that's okay."

"No. I'll go in early in the morning. In fact, I can go in tonight."

Now I am feeling like a jerk for asking. This obsession with catching that man I saw that night. "No, you don't have to do that."

"No problem, Hump. The Chief will not be there to ask me questions."

"Yeah, I guess you're right."

"So, I will go in early tomorrow morning before he comes in, so he won't know."

The next week was uneventful. We did our routines, Quirt at the store, Slim at the factory, Adam and D doing their thing, and I did mine. On the days I was at Community,

I did not see Amy. Since our troubles, I had not seen her. I think we both had tried very hard to avoid each other. Thanksgiving was coming, and it would be difficult if we did not see each other then. It was always a special time. We would go to the Grill for breakfast and then go our separate ways, her to her family, and I would do my thing. I would spend some time with the guys watching football on the weekend, and I would spend a lot of time at Uncle Bill and Aunt Janice's house. They would prepare a large meal on Thanksgiving and would always have D and Slim over. As long as I can remember, Aunt Janice had made a point of including them since they had no family. D was the last David of the furniture family. He had no immediate family in town. No one really knew much about Slim's family, just that they were all gone as well. No one has a bigger heart than my Aunt Janice. This year will be different, I think. No Thanksgiving breakfast, no Amy coming over several times on the weekend.

The following week, I came out of my class for the day at Community. I literally bumped into Amy. I was looking down at some papers I was carrying. I believed she was doing the same thing. With our heads down and our minds elsewhere, we collided.

"Oh, Amy," I said.

"Hi, Hump."

"I'm sorry I didn't see you there."

"That's ok. My mind was on this paper I had begun reading in my class. It is so atrocious. I guess I was so focused on it I didn't see you."

"I was doing the same thing. But I was reading a good one. One of my best students. Hey, that was your last class, right? Would you like to go to the lounge to get a cup of coffee? Or whatever?"

I was pleasantly surprised that we were talking again so easily and casually that I felt comfortable asking her about coffee. Then I got nervous that I was being pushy, and I added with a hesitant *"or whatever"*. But with her answer, I did not have to worry about it.

"Well, I had just started these papers. And I have quite a few."

"Oh," I replied in a dejected way. I think I knew what was coming.

She said, "Maybe another time. I'm really busy."

Now, sounding more desperate than needed, I said, "Amy, can we just talk for a minute? Can we just step into my classroom?"

"Hump, I'm busy. I—"

"Amy, please. Just for a minute?" I don't think I had ever said please to her the entire time we had known each other. "It won't take long, I promise." I don't think I ever made a promise to her, either.

"Well, okay. Just for a minute."

"I just wanted to tell you that I know that I've been a jerk. I know that it was wrong to act like I did. Can we hit the restart button? I want us to go back where we were."

I just knew that Amy would start to tear up and tell me the same thing, let's get back where we were and that there was no way she could continue going through life without me. And I miss you so much Hump. I forgive you, and let's run away together. But that was not what she did.

"Hump, I appreciate you saying that. You are right. You were a childish jerk. I thought you were better than that. I am not sure hitting a restart button will fix it. It is not a cure-all. It may take a long time to get back to where we were. But if we do that, won't you be the same person? I don't want the same person, Hump. I don't want a person who gets jealous for no reason. A person who is insecure but sure of himself at the same time. A person who would do anything for anyone, a person who shows his love for all people, but a person who can't say I—"

"Amy, you know how I feel." Something told me I should not have interrupted her at this precise time.

"No Hump. I don't know how you feel. How do you feel?"

Something told me that I walked right into this one. "You know I adore you. You know—"

"I know nothing, Hump." Something else told me I should not have used the word adore. Adore? Really, Hump?!

Amy knows that I love her. I know she knew that. Right? So, why can't I say it? I feel certain that a psychiatrist would tell me why I haven't said that I love her.

There was a slight pause between us. We knew that the minute I had requested was longer than that and the next class would be starting soon. I had a feeling that we would not carry this conversation to a new location. This was not going the way I anticipated when I saw her—the way I wanted it to go.

"Humphrey, I think we need time apart. This is not a breakup, so don't think about that. My feelings have not changed. And they are not going to change. Unless Hump, there is a change in you."

Standing in shock, I didn't know what to say. I wanted to scream, *No! Amy, let's not do this. I will be a good boy from now on!* But I stood there, with my knees almost buckling, and not sure I could stand much longer. I knew that no matter what I said, at this point would not make any difference.

Then she came close to me. She reached up and, with both hands, held my face and kissed me on the cheek. "I love you, Humphrey." She whispered into my ear. And with that, she walked out the door.

Carl Neal, forever in the mind of Humphrey as "The Shadow", was laying low, as he generally did. A reason that he has never been caught. He was biding his time until he could get Larsen. And get him; he will.

He had followed Larsen and his crew to White Rock, West Virginia. He had thought about breaking into his house instead of following them to White Rock but changed his mind. He was now parked on the corner of Ninth Street and David Street. He knew Larsen was at the Community College and knew he had time to spy around. He didn't park his Chevy Malibu near the house. Larsen's friend, the wheelchair guy, as Neal called him, may be looking out. He was a busybody, always looking out at the street. Maybe he should get rid of him first. Neal had been all around Melville at night. He discovered during these excursions all the hiding places he could use during the day. A large tree, a row of hedges along a sleepy street, and certain buildings around the town. He could maneuver himself so that it would be difficult for someone to see him. He had learned all of these and knew the town almost as well as anyone who lived there.

But it was Larsen, the leader, the head of the snake. Neal thought to himself about Larsen and his cronies going to West Virginia. Who does that? Who goes to another state to investigate? And the amateur sleuth, wannabe detective may be getting close. Who does he think he is? It is going to be fun getting rid of him. Neal's method was putting bullet holes in his victims. Maybe that would be too fast for Larsen. Instead of getting rid of the weapon, he would get rid of the person. Neal chuckled at the thought, and Neal did not chuckle. He didn't laugh or smile. He could not remember when he did either. But when he thought of what could be, he could not help himself. He had a slight chuckle at the thought of Larsen. His other victims were just collateral damage. He had little (if any) emotion about killing his past victims. He did not get a kick in doing it. They were just in the way. Instead of getting rid of the weapon, as he would do in all the other killings, he would just get rid of the person. One Humphrey Larsen. Larsen would never be found; Neal would make sure of that. He will have a good time with Larsen. *Just bide your time,* he thought. *Just bide your time.*

Chapter Thirteen

Another week went by, and then another. No more clues, insights, or new developments. Until the Monday before Thanksgiving. The first was at the library, and the other was at my house.

I was volunteering at the library. I was working at the front desk. Miss Clara was putting books back on the shelf. She was very particular about placing books back on the shelf where they belonged. There were more returns on the weekend, and they would pile up on the carts in the back room. Miss Clara insisted on doing it on Mondays as if no one else knew the Dewey decimal system. Go at it, Miss Clara.

So, I was reading newspapers at the front desk. When I was not volunteering at the library, I would still come in and grab several newspapers. Being an English major and teacher, I am an avid reader and a voracious reader of newspapers. There isn't much in our weekly Melville

Gazette, but I read the Greensboro News and Record and the Winston-Salem Journal every day. Even though I am a sports guy, I do not read the Sports section first. I turn to the crime reports. If I find one interesting, I stay on the coverage of it until the case is closed. This Monday morning, I was reading the paper from Winston-Salem. I saw an article on two killings. I didn't think much of it at first but then almost yelled out, *What?*

Before I called out, I was halfway into the article. I continued reading:

Two Men Shot Saturday Night

Two men were found in a tobacco barn in Walnut Crove. They were identified as 42-year-old Robert Kellum and 44-year-old George Hampstead. The two men were not residents of Walnut Grove. The Walnut Grove Police state that it is still under investigation.

I called Adam. He contacted the police department in Walnut Grove and found out the two cases were similar. The two shootings were identical, and the two men were strangers in town.

"How about bank robberies or attempts like ours?" I asked.

Adam said, "Well, Hump, as a matter of fact, there may have been one last week."

"Really? When?"

"It was more like that of White Rock. The Assistant Chief was making his rounds and thought he heard something around the bank. When he went to look, trash cans from the store next door were toppled over. He thinks there was nothing to it. Probably some dogs."

I said, "It seems like we are going in circles. If something like this happens again, it will be no proof. The Shadow may not be involved in these. I mean, the disturbance in my house could have been done by Roy and Ricky."

"I don't think so, Hump. It could have been, but I think it was one guy; I still believe it was the Shadow. You said yourself he made it personal. He could have gotten those two to do it, but I don't think he did. It was like he was getting pleasure in coming into your house and trashing it."

"I know. I think so, too. I think it is him. But we have no proof. But it seems someone would have seen him."

"No. He's good, Hump. I think someone would have seen two guys come into your house. Especially as dumb as those two guys most likely were. This guy, the "Shadow", goes around and hires buffoons to do his dirty work."

"It doesn't seem as if he has been too successful," I said.

"That we know of. We or I should say I, need to investigate the bank robberies that were successful."

"But Adam. If this guy is so good, and I agree with you about him lurking around town without being seen, why is his method of hiring two idiots in banks smart?"

"Think about it, Hump. They would be easy prey for the guy afterward."

"You mean—"

"Yeah. I mean that he gets rid of them. Whether their bank robberies are successful or not."

I said, "Dead men tell no tales."

"Exactly."

"Wow." I thought of John and Jake Howard and how their fate was decided by their way of living and not by the hands of the Shadow. I added, "The Howard boys."

"That's right," Adam said. "They were doomed anyway. After it happened, it was my job to call the coroner over in Winston to get a report. I thought of the third man. The man you thought you saw the night we caught them—the Shadow. So, I was curious. I asked the coroner if the boys had been drugged, anything else in their system. Maybe this third man came back and did something to the Howards. I remember vividly his reply. *"Son, the only thing in their system was corn liquor and hard living"."*

The next morning, I got up earlier than usual. Thoughts jarred in my brain that I couldn't get out. The robberies and the killings, none that we had proof about. It did not seem to fall into our lap. Maybe Philip Marlow, aka Humphrey Bogart, was going to knock on my door, come in and say, *"Are you having trouble, kid?"*. Then he would proceed to tell me what I should do and how to do it while wearing his trench coat, fedora, and a half-smoked cigarette dangling from the side of his mouth. The last thing occupying my brain was Amy. Today would be the last of classes before Thanksgiving weekend. I had not seen her since last week when she kissed me and walked out of my classroom and probably my life. I knew that it was way too soon to force myself onto her. I also knew that we would not see each other this Thanksgiving, the first time in several years, Wouldn't the experts say give her some space, give her some time? Whatever.

I did not see her on the last day of classes. It was probably good for both of us. A time for her to think and time for me to try to think. And time to grow up? It would be an awkward setting each time we saw each other on a frequent basis, so it was good that it did not happen.

After my last class, I decided to see if Miss Clara needed help at the library. I helped her for an hour and then went to help Quirt and his dad at the grocery store. This was a busy time for them, so I tried to help because I was idle. With no steady girl, I am available. Coming home that day, I thought I saw something at the corner of my house. Or maybe someone. I pulled my 1978 Ford Mustang into the drive as quickly as I could. I almost treasure this car as much as my '68 Mustang. Well, maybe not. The '78 is customized with a black top and a yellow/gold exterior—the colors of Wake Forest University. I pulled into my drive and saw something on the right corner of the house, near the backyard. I jumped out of the car and ran to the corner. My house is situated on a corner lot on David Street, with three giant Oak trees in the front yard. In the back were two Maples and a row of Crape Myrtles on the left side of the yard, parallel to Eighth Street. But closer to the street beside the crape myrtles was a hedgerow of privet hedges, cut to perfection by my gardener. Yes, I have a gardener. He was more of a handyman than a gardener. Sometimes, I rake the leaves from those huge trees, and other times I get a handyman to do it. I have hired, along with many others in Melville, Mr. Raymond Tisdale. Since he can do a much better job at trimming those hedges than me, and since I can afford to pay him, I do it. The shrubs on the hedgerow were not planted by me but by the previous owner. They have been here a long time. They were about chest high on my 6'1 ft frame.

After getting out of my car, rushing to my house, and turning the corner in the back, I thought I heard someone at those shrubs. I could hear someone running toward the hedgerow. It was easy to detect because of the fallen leaves from the Maple trees. Mr. Tisdale was scheduled to get those leaves up the next day. I could hear the person running away due to them rustling through the leaves. If the leaves were raked up, I may not have heard the runner. I ran toward them. I knew that they would have to scale the five feet brick wall bordering my yard and Eighth Street. By the time I had reached it, they were gone. I jumped and grabbed the top, and my momentum was too much because when I went over it, I fell and almost rolled into a ditch on Eighth Street. Jumping up, I ran toward a car that was parked near the top of the hill on the street. A car I did not recognize. It was parked near the corner of Eighth and Oak Street—the street of the May Sisters. While falling and seeing the car, I wished I had come home earlier. After the grocery store, I went to Aunt Janice's house to discuss Thanksgiving. It was about five o'clock when I arrived home, enabling me not to have good daylight of the man now running toward that unrecognizable car. But, if I had come home earlier, would I have met the guy near my house? In my house? By the time I had gotten up from my fall, the runner was in the car. It would have been useless to give chase. By the time I could have gotten a view of the license plate, it would have been gone. I ran as fast as I could anyway to get a better look at the make of the car. It was a 77 Chevy Impala.

The next morning, I decided to have my morning coffee on the back patio. The same one that my intruder was running from the night before. It was a warm Wednesday morning. It was already sixty degrees at seven in the morning. It would be a high of seventy-five today and a steamy eighty-five on a Thanksgiving Day. Janice would say all weekend, "It just doesn't feel like Thanksgiving." She would prefer a more seasonal day. I guess I would too. But it was nice to sit and be comfortable this early in the morning. It was my second cup of Chock, and you just can't beat it to get your heart rate up. And to be awake enough to do some writing. Writing that I had been slacking on for a good while now. It's difficult to write a book when you don't do it. I have been preoccupied.

I did not call Quirt, Adam, and my other cohorts about last night. I did not go across the street to tell D. There would be time for that. I did not want to mess up Thanksgiving. I know Adam would have given me the "What the heck are you doing?" line that he has given me in the past. I would have told him that it was unlikely the intruder would come back the same night. And he would come back with a *'What!'* and explained to me that that is no guarantee. Unlike the last time, there was not anything disturbed; no lemonade on the floor. Maybe the intruder, "The Shadow", did not get into the house. My driving up scared him off? Quirt would be relieved that his Minute Maid was fully intact.

Sipping on my second cup, I had a jolt. Not from my coffee, but a noise from the front of my house. I knew no one would come invading me this early in the morning. Or would they? I jumped upright, startled by the noise. By the time I had jumped out of my chair, I had heard the distinctive and ever-present whistling of Mr. Raymond Tisdale. But he came from the opposite side of the house. And not from the side of the house; I had heard something seconds before. Oh well, probably just a rabbit or squirrel. Then the elderly black gentleman, a grandson of slaves from South Carolina, came around the corner. The word gentleman should be in bold letters, for there was no other man in Melville who was as cordial, nice, and courteous as Mr. Tisdale. He looked as tall as some of the small trees in the neighborhood. He was 6'7 ft but looked much taller with his trim 200 lbs frame. One of his hands would make two of mine. He might be in the range of sixty to seventy years. I think no one in Melville knew for sure. I can guess height and weight, but not too good at ages.

He worked at David's Furniture Factory until ten years ago. Mr. Tisdale was one of the few people of color in Melville, which made up only one percent of the population. The only explanation I can give is that Melville was settled in 1840 by whites, and the families have stayed and not moved to other areas or nearby large cities. Few Black people have come to Melville due to the Civil Rights policies, of course, but Melville is also not a major attraction to come to other than David's. And no minority would be hired at Davids in the early days. Unfortunately, the early days are not just the 1860s but the 1950s, as well. Not a thing that most people in Melville should be proud of. Robert D was one. He says it will perpetually be a blemish on the family name.

Mr. Tisdale did not see my startled look as he came around the corner. I was much relieved to see him instead of my visitor from the night before. He called out, "Why, hey, Mr. Larsen, good morning to ya. Beautiful morning aint it?"

Now, it was not deference to me that he called me Mr. Larsen. He calls everyone Mister except for the ladies, whom he addresses as Mrs. or Miss. I gave up long ago on trying to get him to call me by first name. No matter the race, religion, age, or anything else, Mr. Raymond Tisdale would say Mister.

"Good morning, Mr. Tisdale."

"Been warm, aint it?" he replied.

"Yes, it has. Too warm for November."

"Oh, I remember Thanksgivings warmer than this one. Way back in 55', it felt close to ninety. Of course, sometimes we have snow on the ground. I think we had two inches one year. I believe that was in 34'."

"Care for a cup of coffee?" I asked.

"No thanks, I got work at the May sisters after this. I'll go ahead and get busy".

"Okay, suit yourself, but I just put in some Pillsbury cinnamon rolls."

With a laugh that always seemed like a soft roar, he said, "Well, since you put it like that." But he still refused. "No, better not, maybe later."

I said, "Will do. I'll bring them out later."

Mr. Tisdale went on across the yard with his rake and other tools he needed for my yard. He raked more this time of year, of course, due to the falling leaves of November. This would be the last big raking of my yard he would have, but maybe a few in early December. It seemed he brought every tool he owned to my house, loaded in the back of his 1958 Ford Truck.

Thirty minutes later, I brought out the cinnamon rolls. I have a glass of milk with mine, and I yell out to Mr. Tisdale about his choice of drink.

"Well, Mr. Larsen, ya got anything cold?"

"I've got milk, Slim's beer, and Quirt's lemonade." He knew about my generosity and the pampering of my friends. He would always say that he would take Quirt's lemonade just to have a laugh or just think about getting some of Quirt's stash. But he always replied with, "No, No, I will take a cold glass of milk. Thank you." It was always milk. Mr. Tisdale would mow my yard in extreme heat, and when offered a drink, it would be milk. I would always try to give him some lemonade, but he would not be tempted. He would laugh and think about how Mr. Quirt would have a fit if he drank some of his lemonade. Quirt was the only person that Mr. Tisdale would call by their first name. It was always Mr. Quirt, and Quirt would call him Mr. Ray. And Mr. Tisdale would laugh each time Quirt did so.

Mr. Tisdale came across the yard toward the patio. He said, "Mr. Larsen, How am I going to do my work if I am eating your cinnamon rolls?" Then he stopped suddenly and looked down at the ground. He reached down and picked up something that was under one of the trees. He brought it over and asked, "This yours, Mr. Larsen?" He handed me a black fedora. My mouth must have looked as if I was once again in front of Mrs. Rebecca Johnson. But this time, without the drool. Mr. Tisdale noticed my look. "Are you okay, Mr. Larsen?"

"Uh, I'm fine." Hesitatingly, I said, "No, it's not mine, but can I see it?"

He handed me the hat. I looked inside and saw the label. Robin Litefelt. I don't know a thing about fedoras, but I could tell that this was a nice one. I don't think anyone in Melville sells these types of hats. But I had a strong feeling that it did not belong to anyone in Melville. Too pricy for around here. There was no doubt that this black Robin Litefelt fedora belonged to the "Shadow".

Chapter Fourteen

After telling a little lie to Mr. Tisdale, telling him that the hat must have blown into my yard, I had to inform my pals. First was D since he was only across the street, and then Quirt and Adam. I had D tell Slim. I got from Adam what I expected, "Why did you not tell me about the intruder?"

We decided to meet at my house at eight that night. Adam was off duty, and Quirt was working late since it was the day before Thanksgiving. It was around half past eight before we got settled. I told them about finding the fedora. They knew only about the guy running from my house the night before. We all knew that finding the fedora was almost proof that the Shadow was near. We couldn't go to Chief Wilson and say, "Hey, you see that stranger over there at the corner with the strange eyes and the new fedora he has on his head? He's a killer." Even if we had absolute proof, the Chief would still not be intelligent enough to believe it.

D said, "Hump, I don't like it. This guy has moxie; he's brazened as anything. We better be on the lookout. What do you think, Adam?"

Adam replied, "I think you're right. I don't believe he would try anything tonight. But like you said, D. He's brazened enough to do it. He was running from Hump, knowing he was caught sneaking around, and he lost his hat. He certainly knows we know and will think we will be on the lookout. He knows we are getting close to him."

Quirt said, "And him to us."

Slim said, "Why would he do all this in the first place? Why come here and get the file? I mean, Hump may not have looked at the file ever again or not look at it that often, right Hump?"

I said, "Right, Slim. I don't study the file. I go back sometimes and look again at our cases. But I think it had been about two years since I looked at the Howards."

Adam said, "But just in case he comes around tonight, I'll ask Bobby Matthews to keep a close lookout for anything odd or a stranger lurking around."

I said, "But Adam. This guy is good. I know Bobby is a police officer, but he's green."

"Hump, he's still green, I know. But not as green as you might think. Bobby has come a long way. He is smart and gutty but careful. He has a good head on his shoulders. And I plan on telling him not to stop the car at all. He will do that if I tell him to. Plus, I will be in the neighborhood."

"But it's your night off, Adam," I said.

"It's okay, Hump. I will tell Sue Ann. She will understand."

"Have you been in the holiday eggnog a little early, Adam? Sue Ann will give you what for. It's Thanksgiving, for goodness sake." said Quirt.

"But not tonight, Quirt." Said Adam.

"I have an idea," said Quirt. "Let me ride along with Bobby."

"Bad idea, "interjected Slim. "Let me ride with Bobby. Quirt, you are the muscle. You should stay with Hump."

"Wait a minute, guys, aren't we going overboard here?" I said. "Adam, you just said that he would not come back tonight."

Adam said, "True Hump, but better safe than sorry."

"I agree," said D.

"We all agree," said Quirt.

"Let's finalize our plans," said Adam. "Hump, when you called about the car he was driving, are you sure about the make of the guy's car?"

I said, "No, not a hundred percent. I think it was a '77 Chevy Impala, but I won't be able to swear under oath."

"You don't need to Hump," said Adam. "As long as it is close. If you see it again, you will know. We just need to keep a lookout for it."

Adam added, "He may have been following us. All of us."

"All of us?" I asked.

Adam replied, "He wants to come back and get his revenge."

"We must be guarded. And to guard you, Hump," said Quirt.

"And let us plan as if he is watching you, Hump," said Adam. "An ounce of prevention, right? So, here's what we will do, just as we discussed on the phone earlier. It's what I suggested. Hump and Quirt will stay here if Hump can tolerate Quirt all night."

"Is that your idea of being funny? Is that the best you can do? Wow. How does your wife live with you anyway?" Said Quirt. He always gave as good as he took, especially from Adam. He would come back harshly but always with a smile.

Adam said, "I will get Bobby to pick up Slim around midnight. Is that okay, Slim? It will give you time to rest up some."

"Sure," replied Slim.

Adam said with a huge grin, "And as you said, Slim, Quirt is the brawn, and you are the brains. We need brains to be with Bobby. Quirt would not do."

"What?!" shouted Quirt.

Adam added, "And D, you do your usual, staying up most of the night. We need to do the same as we would do ordinarily. For protection, I'll bring Buck to stay with you."

"Hey, how come D gets the best roommate?" I said with a laugh.

"Hey!" said an exasperated Quirt. "Thanks a lot!"

Buck was Adam's, Black German Shepherd. He was a gentle soul around all of us but would eat anyone alive if needed, especially if our guy broke into the house of D's. Buck was as much D's dog as he was Adam's.

Adam continued, "Hump and Quirt will be here, of course. I will roam the area until midnight. Bobby and Slim will take over then."

"But we can't do this every night, Adam," I said.

"If we must, Hump. We said this guy is smart and probably crazy enough to try at any time." Adam replied.

So that was our plan for the night before Thanksgiving. When we met the next day, at ten in the morning, and compared notes, everyone had the same kind of night. Quirt and I stayed up late. I went to bed about one and was out of bed at six. Quirt went to bed at twelve and was up at five. So, there was a four-hour window when we were both asleep and a chance for someone to invade my abode. We both went outside at seven and saw nothing abnormal. Bobby and Slim had patrolled the area and stayed on the move, as Adam requested. D stayed alert and listened to his ham radio. He said he may have slept for an hour. He stayed up guzzling huge mugs of Luzianne coffee with chicory. So, a quiet night for all of us. Adam said he got home around ten but out at four, helping Bobby and Slim, then sent them home.

Nothing from the man in the black fedora on that Wednesday before Thanksgiving. We didn't discuss it anymore on that day, trying to get it off our minds for at least a while. I think we all knew that this guy would be back. The question was, will we be ready? But we could not do it every night like we did last night. Quirt couldn't stay over every night. Adam has a family. I think we all knew that the guy would strike when we least expected.

Thanksgiving was what we all wanted it to be, with no talk about the Shadow. We all had our own rituals for the day. Uncle Bill and I had too much turkey and slept through the Detroit-Chicago game. The Lions won in a lopsided upset, 20-0. We got revved up later when we watched the

Houston Oilers beat the Cowboys 30–24. Anytime the Cowboys lose a game is an enjoyable day. It would have been a much better day if it had been spent with Amy. I had not seen her since that day at the Community College. The only good thing about Amy's absence is the chance that the Shadow has not seen her. I can only hope that he doesn't know she exists. What do they do in the movies? Grab the damsel in distress? I would never forgive myself if something happened to her. All because of my snooping. We don't know anything about this guy, and how can we find out about him? Where is he from? Close to Melville? And his fedora. It looked new. Who sells fedoras anymore? I knew that we could not wait for him. I needed to go look for him.

My search had to begin with the hat. If the Shadow was obsessed with fedoras, I had to go find a store where they were sold. So, my first look would begin right here in my hometown. The Village Store is owned and operated by Sam Peabody. I had a good idea that our man did not buy his hat there, but Mr. Peabody might know where the man could have bought a Robin Litefelt fedora.

So, I ventured out to The Village Store on the Friday after Thanksgiving to see Mr. Peabody. I wanted to use the rest of the weekend to spend on the case since I was freed up from my usual activities. If the "Shadow" bought another fedora, I wanted to know where he would buy it. Once again, no proof of anything. But catching him buying a hat, we would be closer. I'm not sure what we would do with that. Follow him around? Have a stakeout?

I walk into the Village Store, and I am immediately greeted by none other than Mr. Peabody himself. He is a heavy 6'0 ft and 240 lbs. Mr. Peabody had a gut that looked like most of his 240 lbs was there. Maybe from Mrs. Peabody's' famous Double Chocolate cake?

He is always congenial, talkative, and outgoing. Mr. Peabody was on Iwo Jima during the Second World War. Like many veterans of that era, he never talks about it. The best of men. In 1979, the business changed. They sold the fewest suits since they opened the store opened in 1946. However, through the years of wars, recessions, the opening of malls, and the changing times, they have strived and kept going. People still come to the store, not just for the clothes, but for Mr. Peabody. If he was a jerk, the store would have closed a long time ago. He is always friendly and not a pushy salesman. But if you walk in and say you are just looking around, odds are, before you leave, you will have something in your arms in front of the cash register. He could sell Henry

Ford a Chevrolet and Thomas Edison a light bulb, Clint Eastwood a tutu, and—Well, you get the idea.

Mr. Peabody greets me, "Well, Hello, young man." He always calls people young, whether they are or not. I have seen him greet the May sisters with, "Hello, young ladies." They must be eighty. Then he says to me, "How are you today, Humphrey? What can I do ya for? We have suits that just came in and just in time for Christmas. Come over here and see what I've got. I think you would look great in this three-piece suit with a pocket handkerchief and the works." I was not sure what Mr. Peabody meant by the 'works', but it had to be great, outstanding stuff. I had several suits, which I did not wear very often. Before I knew it, I was trying on a coat that fitted perfectly on me. In fact, it looked nice on me when I was looking in the mirror at myself, the same mirror that Mr. Peabody had gently coerced me in front of without me even realizing it. *WHAT?! Wait a minute. I'm not buying a suit!* I told you he's a good salesman. Before I could tell Mr. Peabody that I was not in the market for a suit today or any day soon, he had already slipped one on me.

"See how that looks on you, Humphrey. That looks sharp! Now, this is a display. We would have to take it up here and there."

He is pointing to places that he is talking about taking up, in which I am standing there taking it all in as if I am going to buy a suit. I must put a stop to this before I walk out of the store with two suits. He is that good. I continue looking in the mirror, thinking to myself, *Darn, I do look good in this coat. Wait! I am not buying a suit!*

"Mr. Peabody, first thing, I'm not buying a suit."

"But Humphrey, don't you like this one? We have others; come look at these."

Now, if Mr. Peabody was not a nice gentleman, and I cannot say nice old gentleman because he has the energy of a thirty-year-old, I would be screaming at him that I did not need a suit. Instead, I say, "Please, Mr. Peabody, I am not buying anything today." I may have crushed him a little because he answered in a slightly dejected way.

"You aren't?" he asked.

"No. I aren't. I mean, no, I'm not. But thanks anyway."

Seeming a little downcast, he responded with, "Oh, okay."

I knew that he did not need to sell another suit for his livelihood or to pay the bills. Mr. Peabody was one of the richest men in town. He was involved in other businesses in town and was not in need of money. His store was more of a need to please people. He got over my rejection quickly, however, with a laugh and said, "Well, what can I do ya for anyway, Humphrey?"

Before I could ask him about fedoras, the May sisters entered the store. Their brother George lived in Smithville and was not able to shop for himself, so the sisters did it for him. I knew that my chances of getting out of the store anytime soon were not looking particularly good. This may take longer than I anticipated.

"Well, Good morning, young ladies. What can I do ya for?"

Since Mr. Peabody now knew that I was not interested in the *"just-in-time Christmas suits"*, he focused his attention on the sisters. I knew that they would not say that they were just looking.

Ethel and Myrtle May responded with, "Oh, we need shirts for our brother George."

"Excuse me a minute, Humphrey." Mr. Peabody said to me.

While he waited on the sisters and I waited on Mr. Peabody waiting on the sisters, I decided to go look at hats. They had eight hats on display and about ten in boxes on the shelf. I had to be careful in case Mr. Peabody spotted me and thought I was in the market to buy a hat. That would take another ten minutes of my time. I looked at the eight on the shelf to see if any were Robin Litefelts. There were none, so I roamed the store haphazardly and tried patiently to wait on Mr. Peabody to finish with the May sisters.

In a near-miraculous way, the owner of the store was finished with the sisters in ten minutes. They were looking at more things for their brother, George, so I took it that Mr. Peabody figured they would be occupied for a while. He came up to me and said, "Okay, Humphrey, where were we?"

"Mr. Peabody. Have you ever sold Robin Litefelt fedoras?" I asked.

"Oh yes, we did. It was back in the sixties, but a little too pricey for around here, and we didn't sell a lot of them. In fact, I sold them to a store in Winston. They probably still sell Robin Litefelts."

"That was my next question. Do you know of any store in the state or in Virginia that may sell them?"

"Ya doing some research, Humphrey?" asked Mr. Peabody. Most people knew that I taught at a community college and that I was also a writer. Or, as I say, a novice writer.

I responded, "You could say that, Mr. Peabody."

"Well, the only one I know or could guess that may sell them would be the store I sold to almost twenty years ago.

The one in Winston-Salem. That would be Latimers. I would bet that they don't sell too many of them, just like we do not sell much at all. Men don't wear hats anymore, not like they used to. Have ya noticed that, Humphrey?"

"Yes, I have noticed that, Mr. Peabody. Anyone besides Latimers?"

"No, I don't think so. I mean, in Virginia, there might be a store in Roanoke, but here in our parts, there might be one in Raleigh or Greensboro. I know there used to be places everywhere that sold fedoras, but I don't keep up with it much now."

Mr. Peabody and I chatted a few minutes more. About the church, the town council, and everything in between, it seemed. Then it was time for me to leave, and I decided to go directly to Latimers in Winston Salem.

An hour after leaving Melville, Mr. Peabody, and the May sisters, I was in downtown Winston. I found Latimers easily. Being familiar with the city from my college days made it easy to locate. Even though I had heard of Latimers, I was not in need of a fedora during my college years. Nor am I now. Neither did I ever yearn to buy a suit from this store. I parked across the street from the store and made my way to it. Before crossing, I looked and admired the store from my car. It had a huge sign in the front, almost dead center of the building. The sign looked like an old movie marquee, which read: Latimers the Best Clothing Store in the piedmont. The store looked quite impressive with the three entries. All double doors. The store looked to have three levels. It had four display windows, showing off the latest fashion. There were suits in every window. What is this thing about suits? They were all on sale due to the holiday season.

When I entered the first door I came to, I saw a crowded store. It was the day after Thanksgiving, so what did I expect? It was filled with hustling and bustling shoppers and salesmen, the likes of which I had never seen. Nor do I want to see it again. I am not a shopping guy. If I want to be in a crowd, I want it to be at a football game, not at a mall or a Latimers. There were more shoppers here than I wanted. I wanted quality time with the boss and not having to fight a crowd to do so. I anticipated on entering the building that, I would receive a "Hello there, what can I do ya for?" Instead, I was greeted by a tall gentleman about 6'4 ft and 195 lbs. He looked to be close to sixty years old. He wore a suit that had to be the best-looking suit I had ever seen. Maybe it was the way he wore it. This guy could have passed for Cary Grant. He was trimmed and had a head full of salt and pepper hair. I was hoping that he would not give me a Mr. Peabody greeting because I think I would yell out, "Yeah, I want to buy a suit, so I can look like you." The suit the man wore was blue, the color of a blue jay with gray stripes. He wore a red and blue paisley tie which brought out the suit, and the suit brought out the tie. This guy was good.

He greeted me with a "Hi. May I help you?" I did not know if he was asking to help me find a suit or if I looked as if I was lost and in the wrong store. His greeting surprised me a little bit because I thought he would say, with a Cary Grant voice. "Judy, Judy, Judy." If you are a movie buff, you get the reference. You know about that. If not, oh, well.

I replied to the distinguished gentleman, "Yes. I would like to speak with the manager."

"Sir, I am the manager and the proprietor. I am James Latimer." He responded, "How may I help you?"

I said, "Is there anywhere we can talk privately?"

Noticing my urgency to talk and seeming lack of interest in buying a blue jay suit, He asked in a curious matter, "Concerning? And you are?"

Due to little sleep and my obsession with the "Shadow", my social skills and tact seemed to have declined. I should have opened with an introduction. I wondered if I could blame it on the company I keep.

"Oh, I am sorry, Mr. Latimer. My name is Humphrey Larsen from Melville." I knew that I had to be more professional while, at the same time, telling little lies.

"I am working on a criminal case with Officer Adam Eastman of the Melville Police Department." My first small lie, Adam did not know I was here, but it would have been no problem if James Latimer had called him to verify. If he calls the Police Chief of Melville, I am done. "Mr. Latimer, I know you are busy, but is there somewhere we can talk?"

Now, Latimer seems curious and intrigued. He must be wondering what he could talk to me about. "Yes. Let us go to my office."

He led me to the back of the store and up a flight of stairs. On my entrance to the store, I thought the second floor was also retail. However, it consisted of a lunchroom, restrooms, and Mr. Latimer's office.

"Have a seat, Mr. Larsen."

I sat down on a leather chair that seemed to swallow me whole. He sat behind the desk, which looked as long as my patio.

"Now, Mr. Larsen, what is it that I can help you with?"

I had seen enough Barnaby Jones episodes to have a system of asking questions concerning criminal activity, so I jumped right into it. "There is a person of interest in a case that wore a fedora. In fact, he left it behind one night while on a chase from the police." Another little lie, the only one chasing the criminal on his escape from my house was yours truly. I went on. "The brand was Robin Litefelt. I was wondering if you sold that brand. And if you did, maybe you sold our guy one."

"Yes, we do sell Robin Litefelts. We don't sell fedoras like we used to. The older clientele buys them, but the fashion is slowly dying along with that generation. In another ten to fifteen years, they will be extinct. But there is something about a fedora and the style it brings."

He and Mr. Peabody were right. I remembered, as a kid seeing men wearing hats. My dad wore one often. Like their generation, as Latimer just told me, both the generation and those hats are vanishing.

Latimer went on, "I can check with my staff. We don't have that many in the store. I think the only reason we sell so many fedoras is that we are the only one who sells them in a hundred-mile radius. Everyone comes to us."

Mr. Latimer led me back down to the sales floor, where James Latimer asked a salesman named Bob if he had a minute. Bob was 5'8 ft and 130 lbs. He looked as if he smoked four packs of cigarettes a day. His eyes were sunken back, and his teeth were so yellow-stained that I thought that all of them would pop right out of his mouth at any time. Without the pristine look of his teeth, I knew that he smoked on our approach to him. You could see the cloud of smoke that seemed to hover over him. Most likely, it came from the small butt still smoldering in the nearby ashtray on the counter and from the newly lit cigarette dangling from his lip. A chain smoker Bob was. When he turned to us, I saw he had black, slicked-back hair, part of it unkempt and greased with the smell of Vitalis. I knew the smell from long ago when Dad used it. Do they even make Vitalis anymore?

He had a tape measure around the neck of his faded white shirt. The shirt was almost hanging out of his wrinkled gray slacks. His sleeves were rolled up, and he looked as if he was coming off a three-night bender. With the gray streaks in his hair, I guessed that Bob was around fifty-five years old. But the rest of him looked as if he was seventy-five. His face was leather worn as if his trade was done outside roping cattle instead of being behind a sales counter. As immaculately dressed as James Latimer was, Bob was the opposite. Despite his aged looks, Bob had a look that screamed, "Hey, young man, want to buy a suit?" Fortunately for me, he didn't pursue it. Mr. Latimer asked him if he had time to talk to us.

"Bob, have you sold any Robin Litefelts lately?" asked Latimer.

Bob thought for a few seconds with a strained face as if he was asked what the circumference of the earth was. Then Bob leaned on the counter with both hands and held up his head and, with eyes closed, said, "Well, let me see, let me see, I think I sold one about six months ago." With the cigarette still dangling from his mouth, he spun around and ducked below the sales counter. With his diminutive size, it looked as if he was swallowed up by some unseen force that was about to take over the world. He stayed under the counter for about ten seconds and talked to himself in the process. He popped up from the counter like a rocket launching from Cape Canaveral. He had in his hand a ledger and placed it on the counter.

"Let me see, let me see," Bob softly said as if he was the only one there. The ledger was the size of a Family Bible. Written in bold black print on top was the year 1979. He opened it up, and there on the first page was written May in bold black print. Bob turned the pages until he got to a page that showed the third week of May, which was May fourteenth to the nineteenth.

Latimer spoke up. "Bob keeps meticulous and precise records."

"Yeah, I see that," I said.

"He has them going back to 1949 when he first started selling for us," said Latimer.

"Wow," I responded in a sincere way, thinking it was amazing that someone kept such records. Also impressed that Latimer did not say working for us but selling for us.

I could see that Mr. Latimer was right about Bob's records. He had written down every sale on each day of the week of May fourteenth to the nineteenth. Bob turned the ledger in our direction so we could see it much better. Bob said with a strain on his face, "I sold the fedora on Friday, the eighteenth. I remember it well."

"Why is that Bob?" asked Latimer.

Bob replied, "Well, this guy walked in and said he wanted a Robin." Bob looks at me as if I asked the question and says, "That's a Robin Litefelt. The one you are asking about." Bob continued, "I told him that the one he had on looked new to me. He seemed to take offense at that and told me with a threatening eye that he wanted a new one anyway. Boy, this guy was strange. And scary."

"Was he wearing a jacket?" I asked.

Bob hesitated as he got in deep thought again and said, "Yeah, that is what I remembered about him. It had to be eighty that day. I couldn't believe that he had a jacket on.

And with the collar up as if he had just come in from the cold." Bob hesitated again and looked at his ledger once again. "Yeah, right here. It was at one o'clock. I had just come back from lunch. But the thing I remembered the most was the guy's eyes."

Taken back a little but not surprised, I asked Bob, "His eyes?"

"Yeah, the bluest I have ever seen. Almost eerie looking."

You have no idea, Bob. "Anything else? I guess he paid cash and not by credit card."

Bob replied, "Yeah, he paid me cash. He gave me a fifty-dollar bill and left, not wanting his change back. The hat was forty-five dollars and seventy-five cents. It was like he wanted as little contact with me as possible. He did not want a box and took the old one off and left it on the counter. How rude is that?"

"Other than all the strangeness, anything else? I guess he did not talk much." I said.

"No, just said he wanted a Robin. Looked at the size and put it on the counter. Did not even try it on. I guess we had his size, and there was no need to try it. I gave him a few boxes to look through, and that was it. Did not say a word after that. Certainly not a thank you." said Bob.

I was not going to get any new information. Latimer did not remember seeing him. I was done here. I thanked Cary Grant, I mean Mr. James Latimer, manager and proprietor of Latimers. I told him to contact Adam if he or Bob sees the strange guy come back into his store. I explained to him the reason we were looking for this dangerous man. I told Mr. Latimer to explain to Bob in a subtle way that this guy is not someone to take lightly. They should contact the Winston Police ASAP if he comes back into the store. And then Adam. I was not certain why I told him this since we had no proof that this guy was a dangerous man.

I got back to Melville at about half past twelve. I decided to have some of Janice's turkey and dressing. Other folks may call it stuffing, but here in North Carolina, we say dressing. It is not cooked with the turkey, so it can't be called stuffing. After a turkey sandwich and a nap, I will meet my guys for an update. I hoped that my dreams if I have any, would be a girl who resembles Ali McGraw and not a strange, crazy, dangerous nut wearing a fedora.

We decided to meet at D's at fifteen past four, so Slim could get there after work. Quirt said he could leave the store for a while. Adam was on patrol, so he could easily swing by. I wanted everyone to stay in the loop. And not get things secondhand from one another. This is how we have always operated. Everyone knows or gets updated at the same time. And I arrive earlier than the rest to ask D about his ham radio buddies across the state. I had asked him to snoop around the state with his radio pals to see if they had strange guys in their town. I walked into D's and saw him hard at work researching.

"What's up this time, D?" I asked as I saw him from the foyer.

"Hey, Hump, I just got off the phone with one of my ham buddies. Ole JT Hart from Fayetteville way. He knows folks from Ft. Bragg, and they tell him that Jeffrey Macdonald needs to stay in prison. They say he did it. That is no news to me. No matter what the Doctor says about that night. I am like the folks down there. A doctor would know where to stab himself and survive it. I think that is exactly what he did."

I hated to interrupt D's excitement or fascination with that gruesome murder from nine years ago, but I had to get down to business. "Well, D. Have you found out anything?"

He replied, "Yeah, I've been in contact with all the guys from day one. You know me, Hump. I can't keep my mouth shut. But don't worry; they are as secretive as I am. Some have a police force like ours, so that makes it easy for them to keep everything on the low down. I told you about my buddy in Boone, right?"

Another town has a police force like ours?

"Right. You said he may have seen a guy with the description of the Shadow," I replied.

"Well, looks like the same guy is back in Boone."

"What?!"

"Yeah, Howard called me today and said he saw the guy today. He got a better look at him this time. Last time, his only description was a guy wearing a fedora and jacket in warm weather. But since Howard was on the lookout, he knew what to look out for. So, he sees this guy walk by his store. And—"

I interrupt D, "Store?"

"Yeah, store. I told you Howard owns a hardware store. Anyway, Howard tells me he was with a customer, and they were standing outside near the front of the store, and Howard saw a man walking on the street wearing a jacket and fedora. So, Howard excuses himself from this customer, and goes back into the store and runs as fast as he can to the back."

"What? Why would he?—"

"Wait, Hump. There are four other buildings on that street before you get to the corner. Howard's store is right in the middle of that street. So, he rushes out of the hardware store and goes in the back, and comes around to that main street, where the storefronts are located. He goes around the corner, so he can pretty much walk right up to the guy, to get a better look at him. Howard said ten seconds later, he would have missed the guy."

"But wouldn't the Shadow have recognized him from the front of your friend's store?"

"Howard does not think so. The guy had just turned the corner when Howard spotted him. When he saw the guy looking around, Howard said he had an idea, on a whim, mind you, by going out the back and around the opposite corner. So, he turns the corner and sees the guy coming in his direction. Now, Hump, Howard is a really sharp guy. And clever. So, he sees the Shadow, if it is the Shadow. After I am finished, you will believe that it was him. Anyway, Howard walks up, pulls out a pack of Lucky Strikes, and asks the guy for a light!"

D laughed for what seemed like thirty seconds and said, "Can you believe it? I tell ya, Howard is a hoot. And gutsy. Now, Howard knows the guy is dangerous. But that makes no difference to him. Howard is a cool customer, boy, let me tell ya." D laughs again, and this time seemed longer than before. After he had calmed down from laughter, he said, "Howard said the fedora guy said that he didn't have one and seemed in a hurry. Howard makes it hard for the man to walk away. He asks the guy about his hat. I am sure that Howard went on and on about the hat. About how nice it was, the color, I bet even the band around the hat. I can hear it now. Howard is a talker, I tell ya."

"Then what?" I asked impatiently.

"The guy almost ran away. Howard could tell the guy was getting impatient. But at the same time, he could not just run from Howard because he would look suspicious. When Howard got what he wanted, he let the guy go. Before that, though, Howard got a good look at him and his eyes."

"And?"

"Howard said that those eyes were the bluest he had ever seen."

"Did your buddy see him get into a car?"

"No. He watched the guy go down another block and then turned the corner. Did not see him anymore after that."

When the rest of the guys came over, we discussed our next move. We decided that D would stay in contact with his radio guys. Adam would go to Boone and investigate. He would ask every person he could to see if he could trace the Shadow's movements from the time he arrived in Boone to the time he departed. He would also call a friend in Raleigh to see if they could get any prints off the hat. I have been replaying the night I came home and saw him running. If I had arrived mere seconds before, could I have chased him down? Or would he have waited around the corner of my house and then clobbered me on the head? Quirt said he would stay at my house as he did before. We argued about that until Adam intervened.

"Hump, I think he will go on the attack. He may go after any of us. I like the idea of all of us staying close to one another. Slim can stay with D and Quirt with you, Hump. Not every day, of course. We don't want the Shadow to know what we are doing. I will ask all my buddies to keep a lookout."

Still frustrated, I said, "But with what, Adam? It's going to be hard to prove he has done anything."

"Hump, we can. Maybe other towns have seen him in suspicious circumstances. And maybe law enforcement is looking for him right now." replied Adam.

"But I think he's too smart. We all agree on that," I said.

"Hump, he slipped up at your house. You almost caught him," added D.

"Yeah, maybe so. I'm not sure that's something we should hope for," I said.

"I'm sure you don't want to hear this, Hump, but it might be something we should hope for," said Adam.

"What?! Do you want this nut to come after Hump? Are you crazy, Adam?" said a flabbergasted Quirt.

"I am with Quirt on that, Adam," I said.

"Guys, just hear me out. This guy is coming after Hump anyway. He's smart, but I think he is being a little too careless. As I said, he was almost caught by Hump. He wants you badly. Bad enough to take chances. And very careless in doing it. I think we need to be on guard. And it wouldn't surprise me if we do find something in his past. Maybe come across law enforcement who does know him."

"Yeah, maybe his emotions will get the better of him. His desire for revenge on Hump might just be his downfall," said D.

"And when he does, Hump, he will have to deal with more than just one of us," added Quirt.

Saturday was spent watching college football and grading papers from my class. There were not too many to grade, having graded quite a few earlier in the week. I had more free time because of the *"Amy Situation"*. I have been calling the problems with her the *"Amy Situation"* for quite some time now. I should have been calling it the "Humphrey Larsen is some dumb guy if he does not get his act together before he loses that girl, as he has been warned by many situation".

Adam called and said he decided to hold off on Quirt staying with me and Slim with D., But he was going to be on patrol. Bobby Mathews will do as well. He convinced Chief Wilson about the guy, and the Chief agreed to be on the lookout for him. Adam thinks the Shadow will not be focused on anything during the weekend, simply because I would be around family and friends anyway. Adam did not think the guy would try anything. There would be too many people around. I hope he is right.

After watching a game and having a quick nap, I decided to take a walk. I had to walk off the rest of Janice's sweet potato pie. I had no particular place to walk, as I usually do on my morning walk/run. I decided to go on a leisurely twenty-minute walk, about half of my normal routine. I went in the direction of Becky Johnson's house at the end of the street. Maybe my self-consciousness was telling me something. As I neared her house and was thinking about her, she stepped out of the house. I was almost near the spot where the Shadow was standing on the day the Howard boys were running up the street. When she came out, she spotted me. I couldn't very well keep walking or begin running when she greeted me. Could I? She called out cheerfully, "Well, Hello, Humphrey! How are you?" I hesitated, and by the time I could respond, we were both at her newspaper box.

She had her long black hair tied back and looked much fresher than me. In so many ways! She wore an orange dress with tints of brown on it. Then I realized the brown were leaves. Dressed for Autumn? If anyone could make brown look good, it was Mrs. Rebecca Johnson.

It took me a second or two to respond because of my deep admiration for her dress. Well, not the dress itself, but you know what I mean. She looked as beautiful as Ava Gardner herself. I think she may be more beautiful than Ms. Ava. Of course, I have not been close to any movie stars lately. Since I pulled off the suaveness of Cary Grant the last time we met, I thought I would try it again, "Well, uh, uh, I'm fine, Becky."

She asked about Amy, which by now, there wasn't much to discuss. Then she asked me about the fedora man, as she called him. Maybe I should call him that. He was just a shadow that one night. I hope one day we can call the creep by his name.

"Well, we are looking for him. We have the police looking out for him. He is an extremely dangerous man."

So far, I have been concerned about Quirt and the guys. I guess I haven't thought about others. Becky could very well cross his path.

"Becky, you need to be on the lookout as well. Please be careful and call me if you see anything suspicious. Then call the police. I am afraid he is unpredictable. I don't mean to scare you, Becky, but please be careful."

"Thank you for your concern, Humphrey. I will be fine. I have locked all the windows, and I keep my doors always locked. The streetlights should be a deterrent for him. And I keep both porch lights on all night."

"That's good. I will ask Adam Eastman. He's a policeman in town—"

"I know Adam, Humphrey," she said with a smile.

"Oh," I replied in my usual cool, suave way. Was Adam a client?

"I have known him for quite some time now. And Sue Ann is a delight. Humphrey, do you think I stay in my house all day?" she said with a laugh.

"Okay. No, I mean, I don't think you stay in your house all day. I guess I never thought about it much. But I do want you to be careful. Call me if you see or hear anything. I will ask Adam to get the guys on the force to patrol your house." Thanks to me, due to my investigation.

"I will do that very thing, Humphrey. Now, I will let you go on your walk." She got her newspaper out of her box; we said our goodbyes, and she began to walk back to her house.

She turned and gave me a wave as I began to continue my walk. I watched her go up the sidewalk. I observed the front of the dress; what is wrong with admiring it from the back?

I continued my leisurely and mindless walk, almost daydreaming up Seventh Street. Going up the hill on that street, thinking about the Howards running up it five years ago. When and where it all began. Making a turn on Oak Street, the May sister's street, again in a lackadaisical mind, I got near their house. The dear old ladies, I did not want to see them today. I was way too busy with my thoughts. With their love of talk, sometimes it is difficult to escape. But then again, maybe they know where the shadow is. They seemed to know everything else in town. I heard both call out in unison,

"Hello, Humphrey!"

"Oh, Hi, Ethel, Myrtle." I was hoping I would get past their house before they spotted me. What was I thinking? They are always on their rockers on their front porch. "How are you ladies today?" I asked.

"We are both fine today," answered Ethel.

Myrtle came back with her usual reply, "Fine and dandy, just fine and dandy."

"And how is Mr. Rockford today?" asked Ethel with a laugh.

"Now, don't even start that today, Ethel," Myrtle answered with a small chuckle.

Since the entire town knew about me and my gang solving big and not so big crimes around town the last five years, the May sisters like to compare me to James Garner of the TV show, "The Rockford Files". It is not from our comparable looks, with Garner with his black hair and my light brown hair and blue eyes, nor that he solves things in a big city and I in our small town. It is more of a gentle ribbing among the sisters. Myrtle has a big crush on James Garner. Ethel teases her sister endlessly. But Myrtle gives it right back.

"Besides, we know who your man is, right Humphrey?" Myrtle said with a laugh.

We had these same chats before if not every time I see them. But they do make me smile. Maybe this was what I needed today. A little pickup.

"Right," I replied.

Ethel's 'man' was Gregory Peck.

"Well, I can't help it," said Ethel with a big laugh.

The sisters kept on teasing each other, and I made my 'exit', leaving them to their razzing. I was almost halfway down the street before one called out, "Have a good day, Humphrey!"

"Okay, you too!" I replied with a half turn toward their house with a gentle wave. What gentle souls, even if they are gossip. I just hoped the 'Shadow' was not watching me at this very moment.

I spent the rest of the day watching football. Quirt came over at seven o'clock with the Grill's famous steak and cheese sandwiches and onion rings. I supplied the lemonade. The sandwiches were like Philly sandwiches that are made in Philadelphia. I know some folks who have been there and say those in Philadelphia are like the ones at the Grill. Or the other way around.

Quirt stayed until about midnight. I knew why. He felt he had to be my protector. I didn't push the issue. I think we talked the entire time, even though the TV was on. We talked about football and what may be coming to us or who may be coming to us. I knew we would come to another subject. He began, "Have you seen Amy? I mean, is it okay for me to ask?"

With a little smile, knowing Quirt was concerned about me, I said, "Sure, I can talk about it now. No, I haven't seen her. Not since I saw her that day at Community. I know I will see her at church tomorrow. After I saw her at school, I didn't want to see her. Quirt, I know it's my fault. I know I need to talk to her. I tried that day at school. She wanted some space. I'm afraid the more time goes by, she will just move on. I know she loves me. Maybe she doesn't know or think I love her."

"She does Hump. You just need to let her know that. If there is anyone meant for each other, it is you two. I know I am not telling you something you don't already know. It will work out. I know it will. Just give her time. Hey. You said Becky Johnson is some kind of shrink. Go to her. I wish I could think of an excuse to see her. I'm telling you, she is one fine-looking woman. She walked by me in the store last week. Hump, she had a red dress on, just above the knee. She was wearing a pearl necklace and white earrings. To top it off, she was wearing black high heels. I'm telling you, she is a fine-looking woman."

"So, you found time to observe everything she had on, just by her walking by?"

"Of course I did. I watched her coming towards me, and I had to watch her walk down the aisle. I don't know which side looked better." Quirt said with a laugh.

"And with that dark hair. Wow, you would have thought Ava Gardner was in the store. Hey, I wonder if she and the Duke were in any movies together. You know Hump, Ava is from North Carolina."

"Yes, I did know that." I didn't tell Quirt I, too, thought she resembled Ava. He might mistake my admiration for a crush.

"Just by walking by, huh?" I added.

"Well, I did kind of run to the front to help Nadine bag her groceries."

"Had a lot of groceries, did she?" I smiled, knowing the answer as much as Quirt did.

"Well, she had a couple of boxes of Triscuits, cheese, tea bags, and a carton of Pepsis." He said with a sheepish grin. Then he laughed a little.

"You observed all of that, did you?"

"Well, I did bag them." We both laughed and thought about him running around the store so he could ogle at Becky Johnson.

"Hey, and she asked me about you." Quirt said after we got control of our laughing. "If I didn't know better, you would think she—"

I jumped in, "Don't even think it. We are friends. She was just asking about me. In fact, I saw her this afternoon. She asked about Amy. If anything, she wants Amy and me back together. Maybe she sees that I'm hurt and that I am different without Amy. I'm telling you, Quirt; she's a sharp lady."

"And a fine-looking one too!"

"We all know that," I said as we began to laugh, not helping ourselves.

"I don't think she misses anything, Quirt. I guess, in her line of work, she has to be observant. I hope our guy doesn't observe us. I don't want her or Amy to be in danger if the Shadow is watching. Maybe it's good that Amy and I are not seeing each other right now. Hopefully, he has not seen her. I just don't know what I would do if something happened to her."

Chapter Fifteen

At the precise moment Hump and Quirt were enjoying the end of the Thanksgiving holiday, Carl Neal was in Greensboro, an hour-and-a-half drive from Melville. He was there to meet two men he had worked with in the past. They may have been the smartest crew he has worked with, even though it was only one time. It did not mean they were smart people, but they were not completely stupid like some other people Neal had used in the past, like the Howards. When people worked with him, it was usually their last time, period. Neal prefers to work with people only one time. However, there were times he collaborated with people more than once. But not often. If he felt that they did a decent job, he would 'keep' them around for another time.

He still cursed the Larsen guy. Neal knew he had to get him. Or someone close to him. Neal almost chuckled at the thought. He relished the thought. At the same time, it made him angry at himself. It irritated him because the Melville job was a small one. It was just spending money. Those fools! He thought again of the Howards. But he needed to relax and stop thinking of Melville. He laid back in the bed in the Holiday Inn. The next day he would meet the two guys to hear their plan.

This Sunday morning, I was out of bed later than usual. Not extremely late, but late, due to Quirt having stayed later than usual. I knew why, his thinking that the Shadow might come knocking. I only had time for coffee, figuring I could skip breakfast, anyway. I took my coffee out on the patio. As soon as I stepped outside, I heard a noise. Startled, initially, because it might be a visitor I did not want. Then I hear something scamming through my shrubs and going around the corner of my house toward the front yard. Probably a squirrel. It must have been a big one; it seemed louder than a squirrel.

I went to church, wanting to see Amy but not wanting to see Amy. After the service, we spoke to each other, but that was it. Had she really moved on? Calm down, Hump; she said she needed time, don't start thinking it is more than that. Still, I had not gotten used to not seeing her on Sundays. But this Sunday, I laid around and watched more football than usual. The guys came over, and we watched our team lose to the New York Giants 14–6. We did not talk about the

Shadow at all, even though I think it was on our minds. When the new week began, we all would get back at it, especially Adam, D, and I. But this day was for football and friends.

Carl Neal met with his coconspirators on the same Sunday. Neal was not a football fan, did not have an infatuation with a woman, had no gang of friends, and hated Thanksgiving. The men he was meeting had criminal records, which made them experienced and more dangerous, but also more expendable. He would get rid of them as soon as possible. That job might be more difficult, seeing they will try to do the same for him.

The first guy was one Bruno Bruning, a lifetime lawbreaker. He was charged with his first crime at eighteen. Before that, he was the epitome of a juvenile delinquent. At age fourteen, he used his father's pistol to scare girls in his Georgia neighborhood. It was discovered that the gun was not loaded when he squeezed the trigger four times. The town thought it was merely a kid playing around. The thing that they didn't know was that young Bruno thought that his father's pistol was loaded. At sixteen, he and some older boys almost beat a fourteen-year-old to death. So began his first stint in a juvenile center. After that, he went on a rampage of stealing all he could until he turned eighteen.

Then, he was charged with his first official crime and convicted.

In 1959, Bruning tried to rob a country store in his home state of Georgia. And with his cockiness, he did not feel the need to look over the place before he tried to rob it. He entered Clark's store on that hot 19th of July evening and, after seeing the old man behind the counter, immediately thought that it was going easy to rob the store. He will beat up the old man just for fun. But Bruning did not know that the old man behind the counter was not the only man there at the store. At the precise time that Bruning entered the store, the owner, John Clark, was coming from the side of the store. Clark saw Bruning, but Brunig did not see Clark. And Clark knows right off the bat, as he tells the law later, that he knew this kid was bad news.

Bruning enters the store and sees no other customers. The store is about to close. He looks around, just in case the old man is not alone. He looks outside and sees no one. Thinking he has time, he decides to go ahead and have fun. He did not see John Clark looking in the side window. So Bruning approaches the man at the counter. Before one old man, James Clark, the older brother of John Clark, finishes asking the new customer about helping him. Bruning cold cocks him, and the old man falls flat on the floor. He grabs what he can from the register and believes he has at least five hundred dollars. It must be the entire day's sales. He laughs, kicks the old man in the side of the head, and rushes out of the store.

The thing Bruning did not know and would not know was that the old man was only watching the counter while his younger brother John, the storeowner, the man who minded the store all day long, was outside putting things away for the night. And he certainly did not know that John Clark had just seen his older brother, ten years his senior, go down in a heap. Bruning rushed toward the door only to see John Clark enter. Bruning, shocked to see someone else, stops in his tracks. This man was younger and looked much like the other man he had just knocked down. But he was an old man, too. Or so he thought. This 'old' man would certainly have been considered old in 1959. But the man who now stood before Bruning was as tough as they came, and at the ripe old age of sixty-one, was a very fit 6'2 ft and 235 lbs. A former drill sergeant in World War One and former boxing champion, he had no trouble with the strange young man before him. John Clark would tell police later that all he could do was not kill the guy right there. Bruning sees Clark and, after getting over his surprise, chuckles and swings at this old man. Clark takes the blow with his forearm, swings at Bruning, and knocks the lights out of him.

After the court appearance of Bruning, he learns he gets off easy, with only a year in prison. After his release, and before he turns twenty, he is convicted of armed robbery and assault. He serves seven years, and then for the next three, he lies low. When he became an aged criminal at thirty, he was charged with assault, attempted robbery, serving another seven years. He had been out a year when Carl Neal contacted him. With Bruning's luck, Neal wondered if it was a good idea to use him at all.

Carl Neal's other accomplice was Larry Stanford, aka Lucky. He had a small record, being locked up for six months. He has committed many crimes but has not been caught. He seemed to have a rabbit's foot and a horseshoe stuffed somewhere in a part of his anatomy, as one of his crime buddies once said. Thus, the moniker Lucky. Growing up, he was called Runt due to his diminutive size. When he quit school at sixteen, he was only 5'4 ft and 110 lbs. When he became a teenager, some kids called him Peeping Runt because he was caught being a Peeping Tom. In the small town in New York where he grew up, he was caught five times in one night. He was fourteen years old. He would continue peeping and ogling girls for the rest of his life.

Besides his sleaziness, he was a person who looked for trouble. He was known as a sneaky coward who would stab you in the back with anything he could get his hands on. Most of his crime activity would take place in bars, where he would get in a fight with someone. At eighteen, he was locked up for six months for stabbing a man in the back. Another inch to the victim's left would have been murder. His luck would have run out. He was charged with rape at twenty-five but got off on a technicality. The girl was thirteen years old. The girl's father almost beat Stanford to a pulp when Stanford was being escorted to the courthouse. Lucky Larry laughs to the present time, having raped five women, never being caught. Nor with the rape of girls under sixteen.

So, Neal meets with them to discuss their plan. After this job, he will get rid of them. Sometimes, he would get rid of the idiots he used, but sometimes not. He did not want to leave bodies all over the country. The men he used never knew his name. They might give a fair description of him, but not a good one. Neal would have his fedora tipped down, his collar turned up on his jacket, and he would be in shadows the entire time. If he met with his conspirators in the daytime, he would wear aviator sunglasses to hide his distinguishable eyes.

Carl Neal met them in Greensboro. Neal was in the parking lot of the Kroger store on Wendover Avenue, waiting for the two. He was leaning against his car and had the sun at his back so Bruning and Stanford would have the glare right on their faces. Neal had no sun in his eyes but wore the aviators anyway. Walking up to Neal, Stanford yelled, "Hey, why in the hell do we have to meet at one o'clock in the afternoon? Huh?! I wanna watch some football. I've got two-hundred bucks on the games. I feel better if I'm watchin'! I gotta know what's happenin'!"

"Would ya shut up?" said a peeved Bruning. They were already five minutes late because Stanford had to go into the store to get some beer. He knew that Mr. Smith would not like it if they were late. Bruning knew that you did not want to agitate the "strange one", as he called Neal. He had heard stories about the guy. People who had worked with the guy had turned up missing. He did not want to be one of them. Bruning had decided this would be the last time he would work with him. Stanford can, *but I am out*, he thought to himself. It seemed to Bruning that the "strange one" was even more strange this time—stranger than five years ago when they worked on a job.

"We are not meeting on your terms, Lucky! If Mr. Smith wants to meet in the middle of the ocean, that's what we would do. Right, Mr. Smith?"

Neal never uses his real name, always using Smith, Jones, or any common name, even some Presidents' names. Neal did not reply, not talking when it was not necessary. It was one of those times. He spoke as little as he could, so no one would be able to recognize his voice.

Stanford was not really listening. He was staring at a cute brunette coming out of the store, wearing a red and white sundress, looking to be about twenty. She walks to her car and is about a hundred feet close to the men. She doesn't notice them as she reaches out to open her door. Stanford yells out, "Hey baby, ya wanna—" Lucky Larry does not get to finish his exhortation because he falls flat on the ground, not realizing what has happened. Then he felt a hard hit on his head.

Lucky was not lucky this day. He did not see Neal pull out a stick from his coat. Neal was wearing a trench coat this day. And Lucky did not get to see what Bruno saw. Bruno saw what looked like a walking stick being whipped out of the strange one's coat. To Bruno, it was like a flash. One second it looked like it was being whipped out of the coat, and another second, it was going across the back of Lucky's legs. Bruno saw Neal bring the thing out, flipped his wrist, and hit Stanford on the back of his ankles so hard that it brought the sleazy man down on his knees. Before Bruning and Stanford knew it, Neal whipped his wrist down on the back of Stanford's head.

"What the—?" cried out Stanford, who now was leaning over, still on his knees, until Neal pushed him down with Stanford's face down on the pavement.

"Shh, hush," whispered Neal to the man. Stanford began to talk until Neal stepped on the man's face, making it impossible for him to say a word. Lucky Larry was now kissing concrete. Neal had enough force on the man's face that it would come up with scrapes and burns.

"Look and see if anyone saw anything," Neal said to Bruning. Their vehicles were parked beneath some trees and on the side of the grocery store, where few cars would park.

Bruning looked and saw no one looking their way. The girl had already gotten in her car and driven away and probably did not hear Lucky Larry. Evidently, Lucky did not yell out that loudly. We are both lucky, thought Bruning. If the girl turned and saw them all, the strange one might have killed both right there. Now, the man had his foot down on Lucky's face.

"I don't think anyone saw," said Bruno.

"You think?" said Neal. "You do not know?"

"Look, I don't think anyone saw, okay," said Bruno. "The girl was the only one around. And Larry didn't yell out. He—"

"Enough!" hissed Neal. "I am here to listen to your amazing plan. So, let's hear it."

Neal looked around and saw no one looking their way. The trees and the cars blocked anyone's view. He was now pushing down on the man's face like someone rubbing out a cigarette butt. He was enjoying it much more than the other man. "Get up, you damn fool!" Neal hissed at Stanford.

Lucky Larry got up slowly. He was rubbing his face but took turns with his other hand on his head and the back of the ankles. He didn't know what hurt the most. The face was first, no doubt, but the head hurt as well. He couldn't understand the back of his legs. What in the hell happened? he thought to himself. And for the first time, Lucky Larry saw the man's eyes. Neal had pushed down the sunglasses, apparently to let the man see his eyes, and it probably did not matter to Neal if the man saw his eyes because soon, Stanford would not see anything.

Lucky Larry saw the man's eyes and was astonished at how blue they were but also menacing. Larry was now scared. He came to realize how dangerous the man was behind those eyes. Lucky believed he was looking right into the devil's own eyes.

"Get with it. What is the plan?" asked Neal to Bruning. He was still staring down the little pervert and wishing he could take the guy out right there.

"Okay. Here it is. There is a little town near here. Well, about thirty miles. It's called Cedar Crescent. A railroad track divides the town, just like it does in a lot of towns in the state. The police station is small, not many cops. The bank is on one side of the tracks, and the police are on the other. If someone was to hit the bank when a train came by, and the police were at the station, you'll be home free. Especially if the train was to stop". Bruning laughed with a gleam in his eye.

Neal said, "What if there are cops on the bank side? You would have to deal with that."

"We will stake it out," said Bruning. "And we would see if some cops went to lunch at a certain time. Or go home, or whatever. I'm telling you, it's easy if we are patient and just stake it out."

Having recovered somewhat, Stanford tried interjecting, "Sounds good to—"

"Shut up," said Neal. "No more from you today."

Again, he gave Stanford a glare that frightened Lucky once again. For Neal and his eyes, saying his looks could kill would be a huge understatement. *Man, was this guy a nut,* Stanford thought. Also, he thought he would love to cut him up. He had his knife in his jacket, thinking how much he would love to stab Neal right there.

Neal was not wearing his old fedora since he lost the other one in the backyard of Larsen's house. He was wearing a Trilby. He didn't like it as well as the other one. And it was very different, making it stand out more. And standing out was something he did not want. He planned on getting a new one, just like the one he had left at Larsen's house. He still kicked himself over that night. All because of the amateur detective.

"Why do you think this will work?" Neal asked Bruning.

"I've got a buddy from the area. He says he's been in that town and says the train even stops sometimes. We could rob the bank and get out before the cops know what hit 'em. We leave on the north side of town and go into the country, and then hit the interstate. I'm telling ya, it will be easy."

"We will meet again," said Neal abruptly. Then he began walking to his car.

"But when?" asked Bruning.

"Be patient," said Neal. With that, the man got in his car and drove off.

Bruning and Stanford stood there, almost flustered that nothing was planned.

"Damn it!" Bruning yelled out. He just knew that the man would plan and talk it over.

The only thing that Stanford could concentrate on was revenge. He said, "Im gonna get that guy if it's the last thing I do."

"Shut up, Stanford!" Bruning said as he walked away dejectedly, that nothing was finalized.

Chapter Sixteen

A Thanksgiving without Amy was not fun. But I got through it. I did it with the help of my friends and family, watching football and hanging out. Things got back to normal on that Monday. I fell into my regular routine of helping Miss Clara White, tutoring kids and classes at Community. I did not see Amy at all that week. The best part of the week was getting a break in the case. The Shadow had been spotted. Mr. James Latimer called me and said that Bob had seen the 'Shadow'.

That Wednesday, the 28th, Carl Neal walked into Latimers and bought a Robin Litefelt fedora from Bob. Neal bought this hat just like he did the last one. He gave Bob a fifty-dollar bill and then almost ran out the door. But Neal did not know that Bob, having been informed of the evil man, almost ran after him. Bob carefully watched the man while hiding behind a rack of sports coats near the front display window. He saw the strange man get into a red Impala. Bob saw the license plate. The tag was **SKV523**. I could not believe that we were closer to getting the guy. Of course, that proof thing is a big hindrance to that. The man driving away probably never thought that the one thing that would lead to his downfall would be his infatuation with a Robin Litefelt fedora on his head.

When I came to my house that morning to help Miss Clara, my phone rang. Mr. Latimer called and told me all about the man buying the hat.

"How long ago, Mr. Latimer?" I asked.

"About twenty minutes. Bob is pretty shaken up. He did not know what he would have done if the guy had been in the store any longer. I don't think he would have been able to keep it together. Thankfully, the guy just grabbed it and took off. I was upstairs and saw the whole thing. I'm pretty shaken up myself."

I looked at the clock. It was ten-thirty. The man had been away from the store for about thirty minutes. I thanked Latimer, hung up, and called Adam and filled him in.

"Can we track this guy down, Adam? Are we getting closer? We must be, since this new development. Right?" I sounded antsy and excited, like I had five cups of Chock instead of my regular dose.

"Calm down, Hump. We are getting closer. And yes, we can track him down. That is no problem. I'll contact the license bureau."

"Yeah, right. The license bureau. I knew that. What in the heck is wrong with me?"

"There is nothing wrong with you. You are just excited about this break in the case. This is huge. Just take a breath. I will call Raleigh about the tag. I've got to go. The chief is ranting about something. I'll call you."

After twenty minutes of pacing and thinking that Adam should have some info by now, I was on the verge of screaming. I knew it wouldn't do any good, of course. And if I did literally scream, the May sisters would tell the entire town about it. I looked at the clock again and saw eleven-fifteen. It had been thirty minutes since I got off the phone with Adam. I think I was warming up my voice box when Adam called.

"Hump, I got back as soon as I could. We've got a name. We have something in the process. There is a guy in Raleigh working on it as we speak. He said it's quite a bit. It may take a while. I want it to be right when I call you."

"Is it much?" I asked.

"The guy in Raleigh said it's a doozy. He said he would call me back and summarize it. I will write everything he gives me down on paper. I will come over when I get it. You have class today, right?"

"Yeah, but I will be out at two. I have nothing else this afternoon."

Adam arrived at my house at two-thirty. "I wrote everything down the agent told me. I typed it up so we could read it better," Adam said.

He had called D while he was driving to my house. He also picked up Quirt. It was convenient that Quirt was taking a two-hour break before going back to his father's store to close. We would have to fill Slim in later. Adam came in two minutes after D had arrived. Adam gave everyone a copy.

Adam said, "I got as much information as I could. The agent did a great job contacting people from the guy's past and all. I didn't tell you on the phone, Hump, I did not have time, but I talked to someone else about our strange guy. I'll let you all read what the agent gave me, and then I will tell you the rest."

We all began to read the summary:

Carl Neal—Age 46

Arrested in 1946 at age thirteen for assault and battery on a local barber. Neal had entered the shop and swung a baseball bat at the barber as the barber cut someone's hair.

Two men tackled Neal after Neal had swung the bat at the man for a second time. The two men testified that they believed that the boy would have killed the barber if they had not intervened. Neal, being the troublemaker that he was at school, and the Community, was the last straw. He was sent to a juvenile detention center. He was released in 1948 and was sent to live with his older brother Chester in Southern Virginia, his only living relative. He was with his brother from 1948 till 1952. In 1952, his brother Chester died in a fire under mysterious circumstances. He was in his bed when the authorities discovered his body. It was concluded that the fire was ruled arson. The Fire Marshall decided that the fire had started in the older brother's bedroom, under his bed. The accelerant was simply gasoline.

Carl Neal was brought in for questioning. He and his brother had a history of fighting each other. And in all kinds of places. In the rental where they lived, in the bars that his brother frequented. If a person saw the two Neals together, a fight was most likely about to break out. There was not enough evidence to hold the younger Neal for the murder of his older brother. Police never had enough evidence to arrest anyone else. The case was never solved. Neal left town for good a week after he was arrested and cleared of any wrongdoing. He has never been seen there again.

In 1954, after a confrontation in a bar, Neal was arrested for assault. The victim was attacked as he came out of the bar. Neal and the victim had words thirty minutes before the attack. Witnesses testified to the argument inside but could not testify about the event outside. Neal left town for good a week after he was arrested and cleared of any wrongdoing. Even though the people of the town never saw him, his name would come up after that, and a town police officer would see him later.

In 1956, the North Wilkesboro bank was robbed. Neal was identified as a friend of the two bank robbers. The two were Clem and Clarence Day of Stokes County. Two days after the bank robbery, the Day brothers were found dead of gunshot wounds. Even though the people of North Wilkesboro had not seen Carl Neal in two years, they claimed he had to be part of the gang. They knew that he knew the Day boys. The Days had relatives in the area and had been seen around Neal over the years. Neal was not considered a suspect by the law. The case was never solved.

Cash taken from the bank was ten thousand five hundred dollars.

In 1957, a bank nearby Elkin was robbed. A policeman, a former cop in North Wilkesboro in 1956, identified Neal as the getaway driver. He did not see Neal's face but saw the one thing that was only distinguishable to Neal—a hat. Neal began wearing a fedora about 1955, even though it was unfashionable for a twenty-three-year-old to wear. The policeman said it had to be Carl Neal. Since anyone could be wearing a fedora, that was not much proof that it was one Carl Neal. He was not brought in for questioning. Six months after the robbery, two bodies were found. The only thing determined were two bullet holes in each forehead. The bodies were never identified. One month to the day of the first robbery, a man entered the same bank and walked out with two thousand and forty dollars. The frightened bank teller said the man was wearing a black hat, later stated it was a black fedora, and asked for the money, threatening her with shooting her on the spot. He never said a word; he just showed her a large, printed note stating his intentions.

In 1960, a Vinton, Virginia, bank was robbed. Escaping in a 1957 Chevy, two of three bandits were shot in the getaway. Witnesses said that one of the robbers was wearing a fedora. The police officer who did the shooting was a friend of the police chief in North Wilkesboro. By chance, talking on the phone one evening, the two wondered if the guy in Vinton and the guy in North Wilkesboro were the same. A week after the robbery, two bodies were found off the Blue Ridge Parkway. There were wounds on the men from the policeman's weapon, but the fatal shots were to each man's head from another weapon. The policeman identified the two bodies as the men who were part of the robbery in Vinton. The third man was never found. The police officer stated that the driver of the getaway car was wearing a fedora. When he talked to the police chief in North Wilkesboro, and they discovered that they might have something similar, and maybe even the same culprit, they decided to investigate similar cases in their respective areas. In their findings, they believed that the "Fedora Guy", as they began to call him, might have been involved in bank robberies and missing persons. The years, along with the number of cases, were:

1962—1	*1973—3*
1963—2	*1975—4*
1964—3	*1976—1*
1967—4	*1977—2*
1970—1	*1978—3*
1972—2	*1979—4*

The officer in Vinton and the police chief in North Wilkesboro stay in constant touch. The chief believes that Carl Neal was part of all these crimes. He says that there is no doubt that Neal was the leader of all of them. The police chief was the chief when Neal was a boy. He said that Neal was always a strange kid. He began wearing a fedora when he was about seventeen. As a boy and as a teen, he was broody and stayed to himself unless he was up to no good. He was one of the sneakiest, most cunning people he had ever come across. The chief thought that there was no good in the boy at all. The local schools tried to help him, with little results. The chief said that Carl Neal was the most sociopathic person he had ever come across.

The two police officers are still investigating. They have sent out information to police departments across Southern Virginia and the northwest part of North Carolina.

I said, "Wow. Now I know why it took so long to get it back from the agent."

Quirt said, "Geez, this guy's nuts."

"But smart," added D. "Notice how he takes time off. I guess 1979 is his time to get back at it."

"Yeah, and he just had to choose Melville. Man, why couldn't we have captured him four years ago?" said Quirt. "If the Howards had ratted him out," he added.

I said, "They knew better. I think they were dumb but smart enough to see how dangerous it was".

Adam said, "After talking to Raleigh, I contacted North Wilkesboro police and talked to the chief there. We are lucky that the police chief knows Neal. He says it keeps him up at night. The guy is still out there and probably doing the things he has been doing for twenty years. The police chief, Robert Fowler, believes that Neal, without proof, of course, robbed the bank in Elkin in 1957, which is near North Wilkesboro, just to prove a point. He added that he thinks Neal knew he was seen.

"How does the chief know or believe that Neal knows he was seen?" I asked.

"The chief said the officer saw Neal look back in the rear-view mirror. He didn't see Neal's face, so he could not say a hundred percent it was Neal. Again, the fedora. It still gets Fowler's goat that, like us, he cannot prove that Neal helped with those robberies. Fowler believes that Neal wants to prove a point. The point would be, you might have seen me, know it was me, but can't prove it, and I will do it again to just stick it to you." Adam said. I wondered if the officer was still around. Adam answered it for me.

"The police chief said that the officer who believed it was Neal in Elkin in 1957 was killed in a car accident six months later," said Adam.

Quirt, D, and I looked at each other. All, without a doubt, are thinking the same thing. That Neal had to be part of that.

"And?" asked Quirt.

"No proof of foul play. The chief learned that there was no investigation. He said that he assumed it was just that, an accident. Elkin is a small town, and even smaller in 1957. Why investigate? They wouldn't think of putting the two together. Fowler believes differently now, seeing the missing persons through the years. He thinks Neal killed that officer," Adam explained.

We all looked at each other, knowing that this man was dangerous but now realizing the severity.

Adam said, "That is why Hump, as I have said before, will be back here."

I said, "But why four years later? Wouldn't he have done something sooner?"

"I can't answer that one, Hump. Maybe, biding his time. Maybe he was in no hurry. I don't know," Adam answered.

"Man, I would like to get my hands on this guy," said Quirt.

D said, "Guys, at least we know his name. We are closer than before. We need a plan."

"A plan?" asked Adam.

"Yeah, to capture the guy," said D.

"That's right, D. We do need a plan. We could get the guy," said Quirt.

"Now, wait a minute. Let's slow down now," said Adam.

I said, "I agree, D. We need to come up with a plan. I'm tired of looking over my shoulder."

Getting excited, D said, "Well, let's do it!" almost shouting.

"And we need everybody," I said.

"Oh yeah. Slim," said D.

"No. I mean everybody."

"Everybody?" Quirt asked, perplexed.

I said, "Everybody."

Carl Neal, in his new fedora, met with Bruing and Stanford one last time. This time the three met at Winn Dixie in Burlington, about twenty-five miles east of Greensboro. This was the third time the group met, and it was a different place each time on Neal's orders. Bruning and Stanford were waiting for Neal this time. Unlike the last time, this meeting was later, four-thirty in the evening, and almost dark.

This was by Neal's design as well. And It drove Bruning nuts. This was his plan from the get-go, and this crazy guy was taking over, deciding the time and place where they met. He could not figure out why he got this guy to help them. He knew the man was crazy the first time they worked together. Why again? For one, the man could drive a car as if he was born in it. The man could have been a NASCAR driver. And two, the thing that gave Bruning the creeps was the coldness of the man. He would kill in a blink of an eye. If anyone stood in their way, the man would drop them like he would smash a bug on the sidewalk. He was a dangerous, dangerous man. But no more. Bruning had decided after the second meeting that the first chance he got after robbing the bank, he would get rid of the so-called Mr. Smith. He could be a cold-blooded killer as well. Bruning smiled, not listening to Stanford jabbering about something. Yeah, I think I will get rid of Stanford, too, he thought.

"Why do we meet at a different place each time? Why um? Why do we, Bruno? Tell me that, will ya? I'm telling ya, I'm getting rid of him when this is over. You drive, and I'll sit in the back. He'll sit in front of you. And I'll gut him like a fish from behind." Said Stanford with a hearty laugh, relishing the thought.

"Would you just shut up? I've told ya, we will do it my way. I know what to do. We will get rid of him. You are the fool, Stanford. Smith will be driving. Damn, you're an idiot. Here he comes now."

As Neal approached the two, he saw something in both their eyes. Those eyes were plotting. They were going to get him; he knew that from the start. He knew they would turn on him. He had seen it before. These two fools did not know he would get rid of them long before they could do anything. He would kill them before they knew what hit them.

"I've got it all set up," Bruning told Neal as he came up.

"Let's hear it," said Neal.

"Okay, we hit the bank at four-forty-five. There is a train that comes through the town at about that time. It goes—"

"When exactly?" asked Neal.

Hesitating and wondering what Smith meant, Bruning thought maybe the man was hard of hearing. "Four-forty-five. Just like I said," said Bruning.

"You said about. It needs to be exact," said Neal.

Now getting agitated and wanting to choke the man, Bruning had to wait a second before he lost all control. "It's close, okay? You can ask anyone there in that town, and they can tell you that it comes by at four-forty-five."

"It needs to be," said Neal, now glaring at Bruning with cold dark eyes. Eyes that said that the person behind them would not hesitate to shoot him on the spot right there is what Bruning thought. Then Bruning was slightly frightened. He never remembered being frightened on a job before. He had worked with bad men before, but this guy was different. He looked into those eyes, and it seemed that he was looking at the man for the first time. He had never seen anything like it before. It was as if the man was possessed.

"It will be," said Bruning, trying to regain his bearings. Bruning went on, "Anyway, it goes east through town. We will get it stopped on the tracks at that time. The cops will have to go about a mile in either direction to get to the north side of the town. Remember, the police station is on the south side of the town. Even if the train is not stopped, and we hit the bank early, they would have to wait for the train to get us."

"How are you going to stop the train?" asked Neal.

Bruning said, "I've got a buddy that is—"

"Wait a minute," said Neal. "We don't want another person in this."

"But hear me out, okay? I'm going to pay my buddy two hundred bucks to help us. He doesn't know you. Neither of you. He will not see you. He will park an old jalopy on the track on the eastern end of the town. There are no cross rails so that it can be done. When we see the train stopped on the other end of the town, we will know that he stopped the train on the other end. This will be so easy. Even if the cops come to us, they will not be able to get to the other side of town. By the time they get to the bank, we will be long gone. It's so sweet, man. I'm telling ya, this will be so easy. So, are we good for it in a couple of days?"

Neal thought that Bruning's plan was not so bad. The plan would change, of course, because he would change it. He would go to the town on his own and look around for himself. To see where he could dispose of the two men when it came to that. He didn't want to drive two hundred miles with two bodies in the car.

"No," said Neal.

With exasperation, Bruning exclaimed, "What?! I thought that—"

"I've got to look at it," Neal said. What Bruning and Stanford did not know was that they would be in the bank alone. Neal would not be seen by anyone. That was something he never took a chance on. He would also have to see if the train would go through the town as Bruning said it did.

Dejectedly, Bruning asks, "Oh, okay."

"I will tell you when we hit it," Neal said. Then the man just walked away.

Bruning, standing there in almost shock, tried to say something. "But, but, wait!" he calls out. Neal ignored him. Bruning knew it would be a waste of his breath to try and call out louder to Neal. What a crazy, crazy man, he thought.

"I'm going to kill him, just wait and see," said Stanford.

Chapter Seventeen

On December 5th, we learned about a planned robbery in the small town of Cedar Crescent. A friend of D's informed him right away. D had alerted all his contacts about our situation in Melville.

I went to D's to begin planning on how to get Neal when he told me about Cedar Crescent. His friend in Mebane said he had heard about a guy and a fedora. And that it was tied into a planned bank robbery. D said his buddy Bill in Cedar Crescent called and said he might have a big-time lead in our search for Neal. Bill was in a beer joint the Saturday night after Thanksgiving. Bill was there that night at the bar and minding his own business when he heard a drunk nearby bragging about a 'heist.' Odd in the first place that someone called it a heist. That was when Bill took notice. He usually talked only to the bartender and stayed out of everyone else's way.

A drunk was bragging and telling the bartender about getting paid to do something to help in a robbery. The bartender seemed not to pay the drunk too much attention. Bill didn't either until the drunk mentioned a man in a fedora. Bill perked up and then gradually got into the conversation. It went like this:

Bill: To the drunk, "What did you say?"

Drunk: (Bruning's buddy) "I said my pal, Bruno, is going to pay me two hundred bucks."

At this, the bartender walked off, obviously thinking the drunk was drunk out of his mind, Bill thought. And he seemed not too interested in what the drunk was saying. But Bill certainly was.

Bill: "What did you say about a guy in a fedora?"

Drunk: "I said Bruno told me about this strange guy he is working with, always wearing this stupid hat, like out of an old movie or something, just a damn weird guy. Bruno said his eyes were weird. There was just something about those eyes. Bruno said they were freaky. Bruno called them devil eyes."

Bill: "Was the hat a fedora?"

Drunk: "What? Yeah, a fedora."

"Hump, this could just be a drunk talking in a bar. Or just a coincidence? It could be planned robbery, but not with Neal." said D.

"But the eyes, D. The eyes! And the fedora!" I exclaimed.

"Doesn't mean it's Neal," said D.

"Did Bill say when the robbery was going to happen?"

"He never got that from the drunk. He had just walked into the bar. But he had sensed that the conversation with the drunk and bartender had just begun."

"Has he tried to approach the guy again? To ask him about it?"

"No. Because he didn't know the guy, it was the first time he had seen him in the bar."

"Would your buddy recognize him if he saw him again?"

"I think so. He has a keen eye."

"Are you ready for a road trip?"

"You mean to that bar? Sure, why not? Let me check my schedule."

After about five seconds, D answered. "Yeah, I can work it in. When are we leaving?"

So, on Friday, December 7th, Pearl Harbor Day, Adam, D, and I went to Cedar Crescent. This day, we drove Adam's father-in-law's van. It was designed for D, having a folding ramp in it.

We left at noon. We met D's buddy Bill Johnson at a local barbecue restaurant in the town of Allentown, which was seven miles from Cedar Crescent. Bill was a big guy, about 6'5 ft and 260 lbs. He had little fat for 260 lbs, and I was guessing his age to be around fifty-five to sixty. D had said on the trip that Bill was an Army Captain during the Korean War. And no one messed with Bill. D introduced everyone, and after Bill swallowed my hand, shaking it, we decided to go inside and have a late lunch and plan a course of action for the bar.

We wanted to get to the bar a little before four before workers get there, and in case the drunk guy gets there early. The beer joint was a ten-minute drive from Cedar Crescent and in the middle of nowhere. The place was aptly named the Hideaway. We walked in and saw an L-shaped bar near the front door, two pool tables, and six small round tables.

Bill went up to the bar, spoke to the guy behind it briefly, and returned with our beers. I was full of lunch, but I had to keep up appearances. I hope we don't have to drink more than one. We were there to relax and have a beer or two, not to look like we were to interrogate anyone, which exactly is what I hope we get to do. Adam, D, and I were not big beer drinkers unless one had a broken heart. We waited for the drunk, hoping he would soon come in. At four-thirty, a man entered the bar and was immediately identified by Bill. It was our guy. Bill said, "There he is."

"Do you think he will remember you?" I asked.

Bill replied, "No. I don't think he will. He was drunk out of his mind. I don't think he'll remember it. It's been a while. We did not talk for long. But who knows?"

"Well, what's the plan?" I asked eagerly. "We will have to be careful and not scare him off," I added as if I knew about such clandestine matters.

D said, "Bill, he may not remember the conversation with you, but maybe he will remember your face. A friendly face."

"You might be right there, Big Guy," said Bill. Bill had the propensity to call D several names each time he spoke to him, from D to RD to Big Guy to Hoss.

Bill said, "We will have to bring him in gradually. I think he might have stopped talking to me that night because he told me too much. But I hope he just lost interest and started focusing on something else."

Adam said, "Well, I think the best thing is to get Bill close to him again. See if he talks."

"Yeah," D added. "Yeah, a great idea Adam. Bill, sit with him for a while. Buy him a beer, and get friendly with him. If he does not bring it up, you do it."

Adam said, "I don't think it will take long. Look at the guy. He has been drinking already."

Bill went to the bar. Adam and I went to a pool table, and D stayed behind to save our seats.

Adam and I played two games of pool. Before we began our third game, we saw Bill get up from the bar with the drunk and go to the table where D sat. I thought the drunk would now talk easily.

Adam whispered to me as we both headed for the table, "We have got to get him out of here. He's too loud."

But before we reached the table, Bill was thinking as we were. Getting near the table, Bill took a subtle turn away from it and reversed direction. Now, he was almost carrying the drunk to the door. By the time we reached them outside, Bill had the drunk on the other side of the van, away from the bar. No one else was on that side of the van. The van was parked between the bar and a line of trees on the left side of the van. Unless someone was in the trees, no one else could see that side of the vehicle.

Bill said, "Now here's my friends; tell them what you told me."

The drunk, shocked and almost in tears, said, "What? What? I don't know what you are talking about. Man. let me go!" It was obvious that Bill was not playing friendly with the loudmouth anymore.

Then I saw something I had never seen before or since. I knew Quirt was strong, but when the three of us saw Bill and heard the drunk say to Bill to let him go, it was an unbelievable sight what happened next. Bill picked the man up and just held him. I do not mean the guy was on his toes. I mean, he was in the air, literally off his feet! I know the guy was small, about 145 lbs, but Bill held him up, which seemed like a minute. The drunk tried to kick his feet, then stopped, obviously figuring it was a waste of time. He looked down and could not believe he was being held up for that long. The three of us could not believe it either. Bill, holding on to the guy, said, "Now, you are going to tell my friends what you told me in that bar, or you will not come down tonight." Bill said this with no strain from holding the guy up.

I believe that Bill could have held the man up another minute but gently and slowly lowered him to the ground. While lowering him down, Bill said, "Now, Artie, when I set you down, you are going to talk to my friends. If you refuse, I will lift you up again."

When Bill placed the terrified man on the ground, he introduced everyone. Which was comical. "Guys, this is Artie. Artie, these are my friends. My friends have come a long way to hear and see you. You have become an important person."

Bill told Adam, "Adam go inside and tell Jimmy, the bartender, that you need to call my buddy Dan Thompson. That is the police chief here. If he gives you any grief, tell him I sent you."

"Will do," Adam replied.

Adam went inside the bar and used his credentials to call Bill's friend Police Chief Dan Thompson of Cedar Crescent. Chief Thompson drove up mere moments after Adam had called him. I was expecting Deputy Barney Fife to step out of the vehicle since he drove up in an old black and white, as you see on the old Andy Griffith Show.

Thompson, with salt and pepper hair, looked to be about sixty and was trim but fit at 6'2 ft and 185 lbs. He asked Bill to help by sitting in the back of the squad car with Artie. It was clearly to intimidate Artie. I was an innocent bystander, and I was intimidated. Thompson seemed to be a man clearly in charge and a well-seasoned veteran of the police force. We learned later that he learned the trade on a ten-year beat on the streets of New York. After a fifteen-year career as a Desk Sergeant, he decided to move to small-town America.

At the Cedar Crescent police office, the interrogation of Artie, the loudmouth drunk, went something like this:

Artie: "Bruno told me to be on da railroad track when da train come through. Everybody knows it comes between four and four-thirty every Friday afternoon. You can almost figure it be dare round four-fifteen to four-twenty-five. If she comes after dat, it's late. I guarantee ya, if it comes before den, it's early. It happens but not much. I'm guessin' they gonna get the bank den; I don't know. Bruno told me dat ya gonna see it in da papers."

Chief Thompson: "Artie, but why only two hundred bucks? Didn't you wonder why so little and ask for more?"

Artie: "Two hundred is good. Most I ever got. Ask for more? No way, man, no way. Bruno is crazy, too, and mean. And for him to tell me how mean and crazy the fedora guy was, I mean, I was like, no, no way. I knew better."

"So, you thought Bruno would do harm to you?" asked Thompson.

Artie: "Look, I don't know if Bruno has ever killed anyone, but I wouldn't be surprised. I mean, the guy's psycho."

"Then why deal with him?"

"Da Money! Da money easy. This is an easy job compared to some. He leaves me alone after them. I know I ain't gonna git anymore. I stay away from him. I just know not to cross him. Would he kill me if I did? Damn right, he would."

"How many jobs, Artie?" asked Thompson.

"Uh, uh—"

"You said you do it for the money. So, how many times have you gotten paid for helping Bruno?"

With that, Artie knew he had stepped into it. He said he got paid for jobs. Now he must explain to the chief or dig himself a deeper hole than he was already in. It was brilliant what the chief had done. He made the man so comfortable and relaxed that the man thought he was among friends and could spill his guts and have no repercussions from it.

"How many Artie? And where?"

"It won't da many." Now the man was backtracking.

And the chief knew he had him.

We learned that there have been several robberies close to Cedar Crescent. One was in Hillsborough, and one in Roxboro, about forty miles away. And two more closer than those. Artie confessed that he was part of the robbery in Hillsborough in 1977. We also learned that the State Police had investigated these robberies for the last five years. Something that we, the amateur sleuths of Melville, did not know. And they have been looking, not just for a gang, but for a man. A man with a fedora, who had strange blue eyes and a dark disposition. One Carl Neal.

Chapter Eighteen

Returning from our trip, I had a restless night. Thinking about Carl Neal, learning that the State was involved and that this entire thing was not focused just on little ole Humphrey Larsen and Melville. We were getting closer to capturing the man. I got out of bed at seven-thirty and felt as if I had three hours of sleep. As I was making my coffee, I heard a noise right outside my kitchen window. If it had been seven-thirty at night, I would have thought it was Carl Neal paying me a visit. But would he do it this early in the morning? No. Well, maybe he would. I heard rustling below my kitchen window in the azaleas. It had to be a neighborhood dog. In my bare feet, I ran out my back door and onto the patio to catch the culprit. And hoping I would run into a mutt and not a killer. Whatever it was, it seemed to run around the corner of the house and toward the front. I dashed inside and out the front door, thinking I got you now, whoever you are. I would see it as it came around the left corner of the house. I went in that direction, to no avail, because the creature went once again to the back of the house. I reversed course and went back through the house and back onto my patio. I went to where I first heard it, to the azaleas below the kitchen window. To my surprise and chagrin, nothing! *What?!* By now, my peevishness had begun to grow. I go back inside to make coffee. The heck with it. It was probably nothing but my lack of sleep messing with my brain. When I poured the water into my new Mr. Coffee maker, I heard the rustling outside the window again. Have at it, I thought. It is way too early for such foolishness.

I was on my second cup and sitting in my chair, thinking about how I would spend my Saturday. I knew time with Amy was out of the question. I might go see Quirt at the grocery store and fill him in about the results of Cedar Crescent. Especially since he called my house about four or five times, probably wanting to know what happened. At that very thought, I heard a bang on my front door, and then someone entered, yelling out, "Anyone home?" I jumped up and saw Quirt coming in.

"Hey, I thought you were working."

Quirt replied, "Later. I'm going in at one. I had a long lunch yesterday and then had to work until midnight last night. I bet I didn't get into bed until one."

"We had a late night as well." Then I summarized the day I had with D and our findings.

"Wow," said Quirt.

"'Wow' is right," I said.

"What now?" asked Quirt.

"A waiting game now. Chief Thompson is hoping to catch them in the act. He is cooperating with the state to nab these guys at the precise moment they come into the bank."

Another slight knock on the door, and then Adam came in. My buddies would always knock and enter simultaneously—no need for formalities with them. Adam asked me, "Get enough sleep?"

"Probably not. I don't feel too bad right now."

"Well, Hump. I just got off the phone with Chief Thompson," said Adam.

"Wow. That soon?" I asked.

"Yeah. He contacted the State early this morning. They are taking this very seriously, and not just some drunk in a bar blabbing. They believe that this could be a part of the robberies of the last five years. Especially hearing about the man in the fedora. The chief said the state guys believe there is one mastermind. A guy who plans it all but doesn't directly participate in them."

I said, "Neal."

Adam replied, "That's what I'm thinking, Hump. I think he goes around and gets people who are dumb enough but brazen enough to do those jobs."

"And then he offs them," said Quirt.

Then another knock on my door. I moved about five feet toward the door and saw Slim and D entering my front foyer. It seemed I had a revolving door today. I did not have a ramp to my front door like D has to his front door, so Slim had to pull the chair on my front stoop. Lucky for us all, I have only two steps to my door. And my stoop and front door are low to the ground.

Slim called out as he turned D's chair around after he pushed the wheelchair into the foyer, "Hey, guys! D filled me in about your trip."

Then Adam repeated to them the exact details he had told Quirt and I minutes before.

"I think they are all connected," said D. I was looking into my files, the ones I keep of scanner calls and other records, like robberies, homicides, or whatever."

"You keep a record of your scanner calls?" asked Quirt.

"Yeah, and I match some of the calls with official records, just like when the Howards attempted their heist.

Going back to that case, something kept clicking in my brain. Something was familiar. In the last few weeks, I kept looking at my old files, trying to pinpoint what was similar in several cases. If we had not gone to Cedar Crescent, I don't know when it would have come to me. When Chief Thompson said the robberies had been going on for a while, really meaning the last five years, I decided to dig deeper because I believe it may have been going on for ten years, if not more. The men in those cases never named their accomplices. Do you know why? They were scared. Last week I called several Sheriff's offices throughout the state, and they all said that the guys caught were too frightened to say anything. And get this. Some suspects met a bad demise a week or two after the robberies. Makes you wonder, doesn't it?"

"Neal," said Quirt.

"That's my thinking," replied D.

"The Howards?" I asked, now thinking, did they meet their fateful end at the hands of Carl Neal?

"No, Hump. We said long ago that was just those boys being themselves. But they might have gotten it from Neal at some point," said Adam.

"I wished I had looked more into it five years ago. Maybe we would have caught him by now," said D.

"No, D. No need to rehash things. We are going to catch him. We are in a waiting game. We have done all we can now. Let's hope that Chief Dan Thompson and the State police catch him soon," I said.

Unbeknownst to Hump and the gang, at the precise time they were discussing the case, Carl Neal was directly across the street. To be more precise, Neal was in the backyard of one Robert David. The once-named 'Shadow' was hiding close to one of the giant Oak trees in D's yard. Neal knew he was taking a chance by coming back to Melville. He could not help himself. This Larsen guy was really getting to him, so much so that Neal feared that it would be his downfall. Still, Larsen had to know who Neal was, and Neal knew he had to get rid of the man once and for all. He was going to get him today. He knew that nightfall would be better, safer for him. But not for the little piss ant, a new name that Neal had given Larsen. "No more snooping, Mr. Larsen, No more Sherlock Holmes! I've grown mighty tired of you." Neal said out loud to himself. "Maybe I will just go charging in your house and shoot all of you up right now. Save you for last if I can. I'll get the policeman first; he might be armed. Then the big store clerk and the rest. Then you last, Mr. piss ant."

All the leaves of the old Oak had long fallen. Mr. Tisdale had raked all of them up the day before, but Neal still had a good hiding place. D's back property was bordered by high boxwoods that ran from the entire backyard to the side yard that was on Eighth Street. Neal could jump over there and hide in the shrubs. But if someone were standing on Humphrey Larsen's front porch, they would have a direct sight line to the oak tree that Larsen was behind. They would see him if they glanced in that direction and if he momentarily poked his head around the tree. And that was what exactly happened on December 8, 1979, in Melville.

After summing up the day before, the gang was going out the door. Adam said he was going home to take a nap. Quirt was hanging around a little longer in my kitchen, getting into my Fifth Avenue bars and one of his lemonades.

I called out to him as the other three guys were leaving, "Hey, since you are raiding my kitchen, can you find in your heart to put on a pot of Chock for me?"

He replied, "Sure. Does that mean I get another candy bar?"

"No."

Slim and D were now at my front door, headed to D's house. I promised Slim to fix him some hot dogs since he missed his regular Friday night supper. If I had known what he was about to do and the calm way he did it, I would have promised a supper of Caesar Salad, two T Bone steaks, a half bag of Ore-Ida Steak fries, and three Blue Ribbons. And some way to get him a slab of Aunt Janice's Chocolate cake. That was Slim's favorite meal. And he would have deserved every bit of it. Because of what Slim did as he stepped onto my porch, we were able to capture "The Shadow."

Slim stepped out onto the porch, holding the door for D while Adam was picking up D's wheelchair over the threshold. I was in the foyer, telling Quirt again about handing off any more of my candy. I saw Slim take an idle glance toward D's yard. Then he turned and came back to my front door. He came up to D's wheelchair and, almost in a whisper, said to Adam, D, and me. "It's Neal. Call me in ten minutes, Hump."

"What?" I almost yelled out.

Adam, shocked as I was, asked Slim quietly, "Where, Slim?"

"Shhh!" Slim whispered again. "Everyone, don't move! Just play along, okay? He is near, but do not look around. He will see you do it. D. Play along, okay?"

D, shocked like I was, said, "Slim, what are you talking about?"

Slim whispered again, "I said, Neal. Just play along."

D, now understanding, whispered back, "Okay."

Then Slim whispered again to me again, "Ten minutes Hump."

Remembering this entire episode later, I could not believe how cool and calm Slim was at that moment. One would have thought he would have yelled out, "Neal! Neal!". That would have been more like his persona. But something must have overcome him in the seconds he spotted Carl Neal. Later Slim would say that he knew he had to be calm and not excited because Neal would have seen it and taken off, screwing up our plans to get him.

But this day, Slim and D put on a performance that any Broadway actor might appreciate.

Slim went down the steps on my sidewalk and called out to D, "Get someone else to take you home, D! I'm tired of it!"

And Adam, in a supporting role, went down the sidewalk and called out to him, "C'mon Slim."

I pushed D onto the porch. D yelled back, "C'mon Slim, don't be like this."

"Like what?" Slim called out, by this time on the street sidewalk.

"What do you mean like what? Like a jerk, that's what! Like a moron!" D called back.

Adam, now beside Slim, added, "C'mon Slim, don't leave like this. D was just playing, ribbing you a little."

"Oh, let the crybaby go!" Yelled D.

"I am!" Slim yelled back. If I had not known better, I would have believed both were really ticked off with one another. It was truly a great performance. Slim and D have never had any disagreements or arguments. Never.

D turned and came back into the house, rolling his wheelchair as fast as he could. I saw Adam talking to Slim on the sidewalk, but this time quietly. And they were walking down the street in the direction of Becky Johnson's house. Neal should not be able to hear them that far away. I guess Adam was getting information about Neal. Adam turned away and came back to my house. Slim kept walking down David Street. Adam called back to Slim before he came up my sidewalk, "I wish you would consider it, Slim!" Adam was still performing, knowing that Neal must be close.

Adam entered the door, and D and I waited for him in the den. Quirt, still in the process of making my coffee, said, "What the heck is going on? What is all the yelling about?"s

Adam came in and said, "Neal is here."

"What?! Crap!" exclaimed Quirt.

"Where Adam?" asked D.

Adam replied, "In your yard, behind an Oak on the side of your house."

"Geez!" replied D.

"Is Slim sure?" I asked.

"Yes. I asked him. But obviously, we didn't have much time to discuss it. He said the guy had a hat on," replied Adam.

"But it could have been Mr. Tisdale," said Quirt.

"No. He finished my yard yesterday," said D.

"It's Neal. Slim is sure of it. I asked him. Though Slim saw him with his back turned in the bar, he was pretty certain that it could not be anyone else."

"It's been minutes. I'm going to call Slim," I said.

"Geez. What if Neal followed Slim? Oh no. Maybe you should go to Slim's house, Adam," said D.

Adam said, "No. We must be normal. If it is Neal, he might think I am leaving now for that reason. He may have seen Slim spot him. We don't want to scare him off. Hey, this is what we wanted, right? As scary as it is, Hump, this is what we all wanted. To catch this guy. Wait a minute before you call Slim. I'm going to check something out."

With that, Adam went down the hallway, turned right, and went into the bathroom, facing the street. I knew he was looking out the window towards D's house, looking for Neal. Quirt saw and knew the same thing, so he dashed to my front room, the living room, to do the same as Adam. Before I picked up the phone, it rang. We all looked at each other, maybe with the same thought. Would it be Neal calling from Slim's house? Dear God, don't let it be.

"Hello," I answered nervously.

"It's Neal," replied Slim.

"Are you sure, Slim?"

"It's him, Hump. I saw his fedora."

"Do you think he saw you?" I asked.

"I don't think so, but I couldn't swear to it."

"I see him," called out Quirt.

Adam came back to join the group. "Hey, Hump. Put Slim on speaker."

Adam called out to Quirt in the living room, "Quirt, you saw him. Where?"

Quirt replied, "At the tree. Just like Slim said, man, this guy is more brazen than we thought or just stupid. In daylight, no less."

Adam said, "Okay, Quirt. You stay there. Don't take your eyes off him."

"Got it! "Quirt answered.

Now we had Slim on speaker. We had to come up with a plan. "Well, I think we need to go on like nothing happened, meaning that we know Neal is over D's, and assuming he doesn't know that we know that he's there. "I said.

"I think you're right, Hump," said Adam. "Let's sit down and think about this for a while."

"But will Neal wonder why D is not going home now?" Asked Quirt.

I said, "I don't think so. He must be figuring that we are discussing Slim and D, But D can't stay too long, in case Neal does begin to think why D isn't going anywhere."

I thought a few seconds and wondered if we could set a trap for Neal. I almost didn't mention it, but I ventured anyway. "Do you think we could nab him, Adam?"

Adam and Quirt said in unison, and loudly, and so loud I was afraid Neal heard them." What!?"

"Hump, are you crazy?" Said Quirt.

"I believe he is Quirt," added Adam. "Hump, how are we going to do that? We can't just run across the street and chase him down."

I replied, "I know. I know. But Adam, you just said that this was what we wanted, right?"

"Right," answered Adam.

I said, " We all know why he is here, to get me. We knew that from the start. We can use me as bait. I bet he comes tonight."

Quirt yelled out from the living room, "Hump! Are you out of your mind? You have got to be kidding me. How in the heck are we going to use you as bait? Why don't you just go over to D's right now and yell out, 'Here I am, crazy man?!'"

I said to all of them, "I am not doing this alone. That's why we need to come up with a plan and quickly. This might be the best chance to get this guy. I don't know about you guys, but Carl Neal is getting a little tiresome."

Not realizing it, they all were thinking the same thing. That this was their best friend, who always had their backs, who had gone through this ordeal of worrying about Neal more than them, this should be his call.

Adam spoke up first. "Quirt, Hump is right. I am tired of this nut too."

"Yeah, I guess Hump is right. I agree," said Quirt.

"Me, too. One hundred percent," said D.

"Add me into the mix," said Slim.

Adam said, "Okay, let us come up with something. At this point, I don't think Neal cares if we saw him or not. He thinks he will still be able to surprise us. But I don't think he did see Slim spot him. And Hump, I think he is coming tonight."

We all became silent. Reality sank in, knowing that Adam was probably right. And with that, we began to conjure a plan to capture Carl Neal.

Chapter Nineteen

The first thing we had to do was to get D to his house. Neal might wonder why D had not gotten home. Adam pushed the wheelchair across the street. The ruse was for them to discuss Slim on D's front porch. To make it as real as possible and for Neal to hear them. We hoped Neal would not take off when he saw them come his way. Quirt and I looked out towards D's. I was in the dining room, and Quirt was in the front bathroom.

I knew that Neal had to be listening to the conversation that Adam and D were having. I think Quirt and I could hear it from our spots. They wanted to be loud enough for Neal to hear every word. I knew the man felt that he had not been spotted. He was still behind the tree. I still can't believe he was still there. He was taking a chance on his hiding. A chance that he had lost. Maybe he had become so psychotic that he was not thinking in an intelligent manner.

Adam pushed D up to the ramp and said, "Hey, when are you getting your wheelchair fixed?" There was nothing wrong with the chair. It was a ploy to get Adam over to D's and for them to have a conversation, hoping that Neal would hear them.

"Next week. Crazy thing is, Adam, sometimes it works, and sometimes it doesn't. "

They had to let Neal know this, just in case he saw D come into Humps' house unassisted earlier. Then D played with the reverse and forward on it as if the chair was halfway broken.

"See, Adam. This thing is crazy. Hey, what are your plans for the rest of the day?"

Adam replied, "Oh, we're going to the mall in Winston. Sue Ann wants to see the lights and decorations and Santa Claus. It's going to be a late night. I would be surprised if we don't get back until about eleven." Of course, this was for the benefit of Neal's listening. Adam had other plans.

"How about you, D?"

"An early night for me, I expect. I would not be surprised if I was not in bed by nine—a late night for me last night. I am worn out from yesterday. Man, it was a long day."

D added about the long day part just for Neal. In case the crazy man had followed them to Cedar Crescent. He would go to bed early when he went into the house. He was planning on a long nap, a restful afternoon, and coffee at five. Then the night, hoping to catch the crazed killer. But in case the madman had plans to come into D's house during the day, he would be surprised to see an armed Bobby Mathews waiting for him. Adam had already contacted Bobby, and he was on his way.

Adam had even convinced Chief Wilson of the situation. Telling Wilson that the State Police was looking for Neal made it easier to get the chief on board. Wilson was in all the way now. Adam stressed that, along with D's house being guarded, others had to be as well. They still feared that Neal might go after Hump's friends and their families. The entire gang believed that Neal would go to Hump's house, but they did not want to take any chances.

Their plan was to have Bobby sneak into D's house from the other side of it, away from Neal's side. Adam would go into the backyard of Hump's and stake it out. Adam's wife, Sue Ann, would still go to Winston but with her parents. Slim would come to D's house. Neal may not try to get into D's house if he knows two people are there. He would not be surprised by Slim's entry. He would just think he is coming over to patch things up. Bobby Mathews was stationed there to protect D and Slim, but also to be close to Hump's house if Adam called him on his police radio. Jim Lucas would stay with Becky Johnson. He would also be close to Hump's. Dummy Smith would stay with Hump's Uncle Bill and Aunt Janice, but if it came down to it, Bill Lewis would have been the one doing the protecting. It was decided that Neal would probably not make a move until late at night. They hoped they were right. So, the sneaking into all the houses began at five pm. No patrol cars were used, and all the officers came into the back doors of all the homes.

When Adam left D's, it was decided that Quirt would stay around for a while. This was normal. Periodically Quirt and I would see if Carl Neal had moved. For the next hour, he did not. Then he moved to the hedges that border David and Eight Streets. He did as we had exactly hoped. It was time for Quirt and me to put on our performance.

We went out and walked up the sidewalk toward Eight Street. We felt we were close enough to Neal for him to hear. I began, "So, you're going to your grandmother's house?"

Quirt replied, "Yeah, I thought I would go see her before I went back to the store."

"Another late night, huh?"

"Yeah. I bet I won't get home until midnight. We are trying to get ready for Monday. I will be very lucky if I get to leave by ten."

Quirt was going back to work, but not to Grandma Eastman's. But before he went to the store, he would go down the hill to Eighth Street, then turn left on Brown, go two blocks and turn left on Sixth Street, and circle back to my house. He would stay until one, then go back to work. Adam would relieve him. Then Quirt would come back at six, and Adam would hide out in my backyard in case Neal decided to come in that way.

"What are your plans?" asked Quirt.

"I need to catch up on my writing."

"Okay. I will catch up with you later."

As soon as I got back to my house, I began my lookout. I saw Neal near the hedges. If he decided to stay there all day, he was going to have a cool day. The high was only going to be fifty-two degrees. Either Neal was eager to get to me, or he had completely lost the smarts we had longed feared. Maybe his obsession with killing yours truly had gotten the better of him. I hoped so. Then he would be apt to make a mistake, which he is making right now.

I heard my back door open. I did not turn my head. I knew it wasn't Neal unless he had a twin. Perish the thought. And I knew it would be Quirt.

"Same place?" Quirt asked.

"Yeah," I replied.

"Wow. Did this guy buy lunch? Want me to go out and give this guy a knuckle sandwich? Hey, get it?" Quirt chuckled.

"Yeah. I get it." Then I thought, was Neal crazy enough to stay out there all day and half the night? I believe that he was.

Quirt said he would take over for me, looking out my dining room window. We did that all morning, and I was able to get a short nap in. Adam came in at exactly one pm.

"Here, take this," said Adam.

"What the—" I stammered.

"Just take it, and here is what Slim brought you. I'll explain later," said Adam.

Adam said that he had a short nap and was reasonably refreshed and would take over from Quirt. I read the newspaper, trying to focus the best I could. We alternated on the lookout every thirty minutes. At some point in the afternoon, we lost Neal. It was a cold and overcast day. By four, it was difficult to see across the street. He could have been behind my house at that time. Adam decided to have a look in my backyard. After ten minutes, he came back and said he saw nothing after a long scan of my property.

"Hump, have you checked your mail?"

Aware of why he was asking, I responded with, "I should have checked it already by now. Right."

"Right. Be normal as possible. In fact, it's probably time for you to take a walk."

"But what if he jumps me when I go around the block?"

"Don't go around the block; just walk back and forth on David. And DO NOT look in his direction one time. Be normal and go check your mail."

And that is what I exactly did. I checked my mail and took it back into my foyer, and then walked down David. Just like Adam said, I had a strong urge to look over at D's, so I could spot Neal. But the game and our cover would be blown. And besides, Neal might not even be there anymore. But where would he be? Becky's? Slims? I had no worries about Amy. She was spending the weekend with some friends from college, which I had heard someone say in church.

On my abbreviated walk, I thought of her. I still had hopes for things to work out. If they did not during Christmas, I would know that I'm toast. That the long courtship of Amy Anderson and Hump "Have You Lost Your Mind!" Larsen would be over.

Returning, I stepped back inside. Adam and I continued our reconnaissance, even though we believed Neal was gone. At five-thirty, Adam said he would look around my yard some and wait for Quirt. Adam said that I would be okay.

"The plan is going to work, Hump."

"Yeah," I said, not too confidently.

"It will," replied Adam.

I watched Adam go and hoped that maybe Quirt would get back here before his designated time of six o'clock.

At five forty-five, I heard something in the backyard. More specifically, it came from my kitchen window like it had this morning. Startled by the ruckus, which sounded as if someone was having a party in the shrubs, I tipped toed to my patio door. I'm not sure why I did that, but I did. Is Quirt coming back early? But I don't think Quirt would be playing below the kitchen window. Neal. It had to be. But it was too loud for him. It was like the one this morning. Using all my bravado, I opened the door and looked toward the azaleas below my kitchen window. There was enough light from my porch for me to see.

"Scat!" I yelled out. "Shoo! Get outta here!" Again, I yelled out, "Scat!" Don't you say that to cats? If it was a cat. I heard something scamper around the side of the house towards the front. Just like this morning! What the heck? Was this creature smarter than me? I saw the very end of the animal as it turned the corner. Literally, the end. The tail. I believed that it was a cat.

I went back in and locked the door, as Adam instructed. I hoped that Carl Neal had not sneaked into my house as I was chasing a cat. I could see and hear it now, "Man was killed by a Cat! Well, not really, but he was chasing a cat while a crazed maniac got into his house through an open patio door. Mourners at the funeral, weeping over the man's life, but also his stupidity, would be exclaiming, 'IF HE JUST HAD NOT CHASED THE CAT!'"

I turned back toward my den and heard the rap on the back door. I think I jumped five feet straight up. I turned slowly and hoped to see Quirt's face and not Neal's. I saw his ugly mug pressed to the window, almost mashed into it, like he was a ten-year-old. And with a stupid grin attached to it. Nothing looked better than to see my best friend waiting for me to open the door.

"Man. I'm glad to see you." I said, in an almost pant. I was almost breathless from the last two minutes.

"Of course you are. Do you know anyone who is never happy to see me?" laughed Quirt.

"I could think of a few people," I replied with a smile.

"And what are you doing with that bat?" I asked.

"Well, I hope I will not have to use it. I think if there is a one on one with this guy, I will not need it. Here, catch. But you might."

Quirt was right. He would not have trouble with Carl Neal face to face. But I like the idea of me having it. But a baseball bat would not stop a bullet.

Quirt said, "I saw Adam as I came through your backyard. I think he startled me more than I did you. I tell you, it will be hard to see Adam. I think I walked right by him. Neal won't see him either. He said that Bobby will call you from D's to tell you if they spot Neal over there. Like here, they have been looking out the windows for Neal too."

As soon as Quirt finished, the phone rang. If he had not just told me that, I might think it was Neal. But I had good hopes.

"Hello," I answered nervously.

D said, "Hey, Hump. Bobby just checked to see if Neal was still there. Bobby said he could barely see him with a little help from the streetlight on Eighth and the light from Mrs. Brown's backyard. Hump, there is no doubt that Neal will make his move tonight. For gosh sake, be careful."

"We will. Has Neal been there all day? Because we lost sight of him a long time ago."

"He has Hump. Bobby and Slim have taken turns keeping an eye out. The idiot has only moved from the tree, which was a blindside for us with the angle and all, to the hedges where we can see half of his body protruding out from them. I think he has lost it completely. "

"I might agree with you, D. Quirt just got back, and Adam is in the back. Call if you hear anything or if something happens. And I mean anything. He might still go to your house first."

"I will. Later," replied D, with his usual sign-off.

I did not have to relay the message to Quirt about Neal still being across the street.

"Hump. It's going to be tonight."

"I know. I know."

For the next four hours, Quirt and I watched TV, read at times, and even dozed. Just in case, our long night lasted until morning. We didn't have long or serious conversations because we wanted to stay alert. We took turns at the lookout, which was less often since we could not see much of anything. Or should I say we tried to do those things? It is difficult when you have a crazed killer who might storm your house at any moment.

I hoped that Neal heard me tell Quirt that I was going to bed early. So, at ten, we had the lights out. Adam came to check on us at eight and said that he would radio Bobby to remind D about going to bed early. At ten, it seemed that David Street was closed for the night. Adam, Quirt, and I decided that I would alternate being stationed at my bedroom window, which faced the backyard, and my chair at the backdoor. More about that in a moment. Adam would keep an eye out on the other corner of the house, along with the rest of the backyard, and Quirt would go from the bathroom and dining room windows which faced the front, and David Street.

The best way for Neal to come in would be from the front. Quirt would not be able to see Neal standing on my front porch from the bathroom window or the dining room window. The old house, designed differently from modern houses, had its quirks, one being that the front porch jutted out from the rest of the house. If you stood on my front porch, you would have a brick wall on both sides of you. On the other sides of those walls were the bathroom and the dining rooms. And with no porch light on, a person could almost hide on the porch, and he would not be seen from the street. Quirt would have to spot Neal before he got on the porch. If not, we would not know he was there. If Quirt did see him sneaking on it, he was to flash his light toward D's, and Bobby Mathews would come running. The porch configuration would benefit us with that; Neal would not be able to see the signal from the flashlight. Then Quirt would run to the bedroom facing the backyard and signal Adam, and he would rush to the house.

The most dangerous part of our plan, which we had all decided when we were all at my house earlier that morning, was to keep my front door unlocked. I had to do some convincing since it was my idea, I am afraid to admit. I said that we wanted to trap Neal, so what better way to just leave my door open, inviting him in? He will assume I left it unlocked by mistake. He will come in, and Quirt will jump him and beat him to smithereens. Well, maybe just jump him and keep him down on the floor, and I can beat him to smithereens. Well, maybe jump him, hold him down, and then Adam will come in and handcuff him. Darn it. That is the plan anyway. We all know about plans.

It would be a waiting game. We had no idea when he was coming. I had coffee again at about three o'clock, and Quirt had about three cans of lemonade since he came in. We wanted to be awake if Mr. Neal decided to enter my abode at two in the morning.

I sat in my chair, time slowly going by, and patiently expecting something that may not even happen. But I knew, along with my buddies, that it was going to happen tonight. But when? Midnight? Three in the morning? I took turns going to my bedroom window to my chair in my den. I had been in my chair now for the last hour. I looked at the old grandfather clock and saw that it was eleven-thirty. I will soon hear the clock chime twelve times for midnight. I began to think about the last few months. From me coming in and discovering the mess in my house, to Amy, to me meeting Becky Johnson, and discovering Carl Neal. A lot has changed in a brief period.

At twelve-twenty, we heard a step on the front porch. Quirt had just walked past the foyer on his way to the bathroom to watch from there. Neither one of us spoke because Adam told us to stay quiet as possible when we turned the lights off at ten. He explained that someone could possibly hear us from outside. There was to be little communication between Quirt and me. That was easy for me, not for him. With our eyes adjusted to the darkness and the streetlights streaming in, we could see each other. Quirt stopped right in his tracks. He walked gingerly down the hallway, leaving me alone in the den and alone with our soon-to-be guest. But that was our plan. Again, my bright idea.

I heard Neal turn the doorknob. I could tell that there was a slight hesitation on his part, as if Neal was surprised the door was unlocked. He turned it again, and I could hear the door come slightly open. I did not have a direct sight on my front door from my chair. When he steps in, I will not be able to see him in the foyer. Nor him seeing me in the den. Not until he walks about five steps and enters my den. If his eyes adjust to the dark, then he might be able to see me.

I hoped that Quirt would not come rushing into the den, which was only steps away, and clobbers Neal with the baseball bat and knock him unconscious, or worse. Neal is not breaking into my house. The door was unlocked, open for anyone. In court, he could claim anything for any reason he entered my house. We want, well, I wanted to catch Neal in the act. Not too much in the act, but in the process of it.

When I heard the door open, I could also hear Quirt coming back up the hall. I think he has signaled both Adam and Bobby. I hear the door open, hear Neal come in, and take a soft step into the foyer. Then he stops. Then nothing. A minute goes by. It is as if he knows that someone is nearby and that he senses something is going on. I can make out the clock enough to see that it is twelve twenty-four. I wait. Nothing. Is this what burglars do when they break into people's houses? Do they wait? I kept waiting for him to step from the foyer to my den. My eyes did not move away from that direction. I listen intently to any noise, any creak in the floor. I began to think in a panic. What if he is slithering on the floor like a serpent and comes out of nowhere and jumps me or comes from behind my Lazy Boy and chokes the life out of me, then slips out the front door, and Quirt finds me later? I glance back at the clock, afraid to take my eyes off the front hallway, even though the clock is near the passageway. The clock shows twelve-thirty. Where did six minutes go? Maybe in the class of Burglary 101, you are taught to wait ten minutes after your break-in.

I hear a creak from the floor. There were many creaks in the old house, and I knew where every one of them was located. And the sound of each one. I figured that he was just past the rug in the foyer. He is close. Another two steps, and I will see him.

It dawned on me. The reason for his wait. He was waiting for his eyes to take in the darkness, to get accustomed to the things around him. I see him step from the foyer into the den. He stopped and looked to his right toward the hall and left toward the kitchen and dining area. I could make out in the darkness that when the man had looked right, he did very slowly, like an animal searching for his prey. But when he had turned left, there was a slight hesitation. After he looked left toward my kitchen and once again to the right, he stopped and looked directly at me.

I was lying back in my recliner as if I was asleep, another dumb bright, super idea I had. I do not know if he bought it. But it didn't matter either way. Part of this plan was that I would turn the lamp on beside me. Then Quirt would come out of his hiding place and creep up the hallway, and Adam would see the light and be ready to come through my back door. Bobby Mathews, if he got Quirt's signal, would be at my front door and then sneak in when he sees my lamp come on. When I turned the light on, there was no going back. I just hoped his eyes had not adjusted quite yet to where he could see me turn the light on. I switched the lamp on.

Chapter Twenty

When the light came on, Neal jumped a little, startled by the surprise, which told me that he had not spotted me as I first thought. Adam had told me that I had to turn the light on as soon as I saw him because if I didn't, his eyes would adjust to the darkness. I was afraid that I would wait too late. I timed it right. So far, so good. Showing my bravado, or stupidity, I said to Neal, "Come on in, have a seat." Have a seat? What am I thinking?

The next step of the plan was for me to get out of my recliner. Adam said that I needed to get up and stand behind my lamp, which was positioned to the right of my chair. And to be at least twenty feet from the killer. Neal took a step toward me and stopped.

"You've been waiting on me? I didn't think you were that smart, Larsen. Or should I say that stupid? What are you going to do now?"

I felt assured that Neal thought that I was alone and that he hadn't heard the conversations that we set for him earlier in the day. Or he was going to come tonight whether he heard them or not.

"How many people, Neal?" I asked.

"You little—"

I went on, "How many people have you killed? How many people have you used to get what you wanted?"

"Well, I'm going to add one tonight," he said with an evil grin.

With his collar turned up and his fedora, he looked beyond menacing. I wasn't sure what I was getting into. If he pulled a gun out, I don't know if Quirt could get him before he shot me. We were hoping he would talk before he did. Again, a great plan.

"Did you kill the Howard boys?"

"Those idiots? I didn't have to. But it's funny. I was going to get rid of them that very night," he said with an evil snicker.

"The others," I said. "How many?"

"You know, Mr. Larsen, I usually blow people away at once. But since you have been a formidable foe, I will indulge you. But to let you know, I am going to kill you tonight. In fact, in fifteen minutes, you will be dead. Even though you look like you have a weapon on you."

I wore a Wake Forest hoodie and had my hands in my pocket. I guess that was a dead giveaway. No pun intended. But the giveaway was intentional. Slim had made me a wooden pistol, which I had in my pocket. Who brings a fake pistol to a gunfight? Adam had given it to me when he came back to my house to check in on me—the gift from Slim. I was to show the bulge to Neal, bluff him into thinking I had a real gun. This was the plan Adam had, and I didn't like it, but he convinced me. Hey, it was my idea to lure Neal in here in the first place, right?

I had to play this bluff to the hilt to act a heck of a lot tougher, braver, smarter, and meaner than I really was. He would probably see through the smarter part right away. I also hoped that he would not see the beads of sweat coming off my face, not due to the hoodie.

"Larsen, I could shoot you before you put your finger on the trigger."

Trying to be unshaken, calm, and cool, I asked, "How many?"

"Well, Larsen, I never really counted. But I would ascertain forty-five to fifty."

Dear God, I thought. This man was truly crazy. I just hoped he did not see the shocked look on my face. And the frightened look. "All your bank-robbing friends?" I asked.

"Oh no, no. I've killed people for getting under my skin. Joggers, people who have bumped into me. I came close to killing your buddy, Slim." He said with a smirky evil grin.

A shiver ran through me. It was as if Neal sensed it. I was not sure I could hold out much longer.

"Getting to you a little, Mr. Larsen?" Neal said with a laugh. "I will tell you some, but not all. I plan on leaving your peaceful little town and never to return."

Neal proceeded to tell me several of his heists. And what he did with his accomplices. Some of those he told me in detail. He bragged about how he would shoot them and then get rid of the weapon. I knew it would take him longer than fifteen minutes to tell me about his criminal career, but I wasn't complaining. I don't think I was going to tell him that he was a little off on the timing of my demise. I might just rub him the wrong way.

Then he told me that he had to come back to Melville to get his key to the bank deposit box. And the thing that he had in the box. If he had not put the weapon in the bank, we would not be here tonight. I would never have known Carl

Neal. If. The most-significant two-letter word in the English language.

When he had finished, he laughed the evilest laugh I had ever heard. And then he drew a pistol. A small pistol, which was good for me. If that makes sense, I mean, it was good for me that he did not come out with a 44 Magnum. I would have been thrown against the wall. Now mind you, I wasn't too excited about him having a little snub nose pistol near me. But I might have a chance if the gun went off. According to the plan, it was not supposed to go off. Quirt should be coming out any second.

There were several things Neal did not know about tonight. He didn't know Quirt was hiding in the hallway, that hopefully, by now, Bobby was right outside, and Adam was right outside my back door, which we left ajar so that he could come in quickly. We hoped that Neal would not see the door open. Adam would later testify that he had heard every word Carl Neal spoke in my house. And Neal did not know that I was wearing a brand spanking new bulletproof vest, thanks to Adam but also, unbelievably, Chief Stanley Wilson. That was the other gift I received earlier in the day from Adam.

It seemed like an eternity when Neal pulled the gun. I thought that Quirt would be seconds late. Before Neal could aim the gun at me, Quirt yelled out, "Hey!"

Neal turns, and before he can react or say anything, Quirt wildly swings the baseball bat and nails Neal square in the forehead. Neal's weapon drops to the floor, and his fedora goes flying. Instead of being knocked out cold, the man staggers and tries his best not to fall. I knew that Quirt did not swing as hard as he could because if he had, the man would be dead. When the man staggers, Adam rushes in from the back, and Bobby comes around the foyer. While Neal is trying to get his bearings, Quirt grabs him and turns him in his direction. Then Quirt cold cocks him with his fist, right on the base of Neal's nose. I hear two things; the cartilage of Neal's nose being shattered and the sound of Neal hitting the floor. Now, he is out cold.

Adam comes in from my back patio door when he hears Quirt yell out and reaches Neal right when he hits the floor after receiving the quick jab from Quirt's right fist. Adam runs to Neal and puts his foot on Neal's chest, with his weapon drawn and pointed at the fallen man.

Adam turns to Quirt. "Geez, Quirt. How hard did you hit him?"

"Hard enough," said Quirt.

Adam replied, "Yeah, I guess so. Everybody okay? Hump?"

Stunned, not by Quirt's right cross, but by how close I might have come to getting shot, I said. "Uh, yeah."

Still standing on Neal's chest, Adam said, "Quirt, hit the other lights."

Quirt turns the overhead light on, and now Adam sees for certain that Neal was completely knocked out. He checked to see if the man was still breathing and then turned him over and handcuffed him. He checked the man's face and saw that his nose was broken, and both eyes were already turning a deep purple. Adam calls out to Bobby, who is standing in Neal's original spot. "Bobby, radio the chief. I want to go over everything before we take Neal in. This must be done right. Then call Doc Wright. Neal is going to be seen by Doc before we haul him off to jail."

"Okay, Adam," Bobby replied excitedly, still energized by the current events.

Quirt walked up to me. "You okay, buddy?"

"Yeah, I guess so. Nice backhand. Just like John Wayne." I replied.

"Huh?"

"John Elder." I smiled.

"Oh, yeah," Quirt replied with a smile of his own. "Yeah, when Wayne takes that club and backhands George Kennedy in "The Sons of Katie Elder.""

"You got it," I said.

"Yeah, but let's not make a habit out of it," he said with a grin.

"I'm going to try my best not to; I'll tell you that," I replied with a relieved laugh.

The chief and Jim Lucas arrived quickly. Then the doctor. Adam, Quirt, and I give a summary of the events of the night. The official statement will be made later. Wilson and Lucas were in slight shock, not believing Adam to this point of the seriousness of the situation. They do now. I am still surprised that the Chief agreed to our plan.

Dr. Wright was examining Neal when he woke up—moaning, groaning, and cussing at the same time. Quirt stood over him, apparently just in case the killer got up. There was no getting up, at least not without help. Adam gave an unofficial summary to Chief Wilson.

I walked out my front door with Adam and Quirt to see them carry Neal off. The chief was ahead on the sidewalk. He turned and said, "Good job, Eastman." I think he was talking to Adam, but he certainly could have been speaking to Quirt.

"Thanks, chief," said Adam.

The chief rode off. We saw Slim and D on the sidewalk, along with some neighbors who had heard all the sirens.

We all went back inside my house. It was now close to two o'clock. We replayed the events of the night to D and Slim. Then we all discussed the last five years when it all began. With me seeing the man in the alley, calling him "The Shadow", Slim seeing Neal at "The Pig." The Howard boys, Cedar Crescent, and everything else that we did to try and get the man. We didn't discuss my infatuation with Becky Johnson.

Everyone left at three-thirty. I got to bed, finally at four. A restful and peaceful sleep. It could have been the best sleep I have had in over a year. It was over.

We learned later through Neal's trial that he had done more evil things in his lifetime than we had even thought. When he went to trial nine months later, he didn't have a chance. I turned over my file of the Howard Case to the authorities, the FBI. I never dreamed of turning anything to the FBI. The file was a summary of that night when the Howards tried to rob the bank. But the most important thing in my file was the deposit key of Carl Neal. It led to the gun that killed the jogger in 1977. I told the prosecutors that Neal mentioned, more like bragged about his killings and said something about joggers in doing so. The gun matched, and Neal was found guilty in that case and others that followed. There was no room for plea bargains or deals. Chief Dan Thomson caught Neal's cohorts, Bruno Bruning and Larry Stanford. They told of the planned bank robbery. It was their word against Neal's, but with other evidence, the court believed Bruning and Stanford. The other robberies in the area and other places matched that plan. He was sentenced more for his crimes throughout the state and not too much for Melville. But we did catch him. And my guys and I were just fine with that.

Five years into his sentence, Carl "The Shadow" Neal was found dead in his cell. It would be a mystery that would never be solved. I wondered if there was a huge effort to solve it. His moronic partners in the planned robbery in Allentown, Bruno Bruning and Larry Stanford, met their demise before Neal. Out on bail and before their trial date, Bruning, stoned on a lot of things, drove his car into a tree going eighty-five miles an hour. He was dead at the scene. Stanford had the worst luck. He was stabbed in the throat with a shiv in prison.

But in the present day, I woke up with my phone ringing. I reached for it without looking at the time. I just knew it was daylight. "Hello," I answered groggily.

"Humphrey?"

"Huh, what—" Again, no one calls me Humphrey often unless they are angry with me, or concerned about me, or they were Miss Clara. Well, also my new friend, Becky Johnson.

This was a concerned person. Amy.

"I, uh, oh, hey," I said, trying quickly to wake up.

"Are you okay? I just heard about last night."

"Uh, yeah. I'm okay. What time is it?"

"Nine-thirty," she said.

Seemly to be waking up, I got out of bed and answered more clearly. "Yes, I'm alright."

"What happened? I heard some of it, but not all, I'm sure."

"Well, Amy. Can I call you back? My head is throbbing. I need coffee."

"Oh, no, I mean, yes, you can call back. I shouldn't have called."

I could not tell if she was peeved about cutting her off or was genuinely sorry about walking me up. I probably messed up again. Or is it a disenchanted former boyfriend being paranoid?

I said, "No, that—it's just I'm worn out from everything. It's not that."

"No. I'll leave you alone."

"No, Amy. Please, I want to talk to you."

"Hump, I'm getting ready for church."

"Yeah, right. Listen, maybe later?"

"Yeah, sure."

"Call me later. Please. I'll—"

"Okay. Bye, Hump," she said.

"Amy? Amy?" I called out.

Well, that went great. She calls me, and I tell her basically to leave me alone. But then again, wouldn't she come to my house if she were that concerned? You dope. You are not dating. She has no obligations. You should have been nicer. Call her back. No. She is getting ready for church. Will she come by afterward?

I went and made a huge pot of coffee. After my first large mug, I decided to take a hot shower, followed by one lukewarm, and then ran the nozzle to almost all the way cold to help myself wake up. I had another mug of coffee and went to sit in my recliner. I replayed the scene from the night once again. Quirt swung the bat and then a fist to Neal's nose, then Adam busted in like Steve McGarrett from Hawaii Five-O.

When I poured my third cup of coffee, I sat and thought about nothing. Not the night before, not Amy, not anything. Nothing. I laid my head back, closed my eyes, and tried to get as relaxed as I could. Not to go to sleep, but just to be calm. But a noise from outside broke up my break. Then I realized that it was my other intruder, my backyard pest, the annoying thing that I had been hearing right outside my kitchen window for the last several weeks. I got up and went toward my patio door. I stepped out and heard something rustling around the shrubs right below my kitchen window. I did not move. I could still hear it. Instead of dashing off, it seems braver or brazen not to leave this time. I decided I would try to catch it or chase it off. Then I heard it come in my direction. I didn't move an inch, afraid that it would reverse course and take off around the house as before. I waited. It kept coming. What would it do when it saw me? What should I do? I heard it again. It was probably a squirrel. No, this was too predictable, coming to the same place each time. They knew where they were going. Too small for a dog. A puppy? I would have seen a puppy by now. I could now hear it as if it was creeping along slowly. Getting awfully close now. Then I saw something white, which was easy to spot through the green azalea. Then a speck of what looked like brown or beige. Then I saw it jump out from the shrub onto the patio. A kitten. What? What is a kitten doing here? Why my house? Why now? All questions I didn't have answers to. I don't think kittens have road maps to guide them. Nor do they plan on where they're going. Where did it come from?

I moved very gingerly and sat down in my lounge chair, mere feet from my patio door. The kitten was only about ten feet from me now. It was a beige and white kitten. It looked as if it had something sticking out of its mouth. I am not going to check. Then it took a step towards me. I could now see that it had a slither of a blade of grass in its mouth. Do cats eat grass? I don't know. I have never been much of a cat person. Then it spotted me. It stopped. It waited. Then it turned and ran and jumped into the azalea. I still did not move. I didn't want to scare it off. A minute passes and the kitten comes back out and gives me another look. He walks slowly toward me. I am hesitant to move and know it is wary of me. It might dash off, and I will never see it again. Then he comes to my feet. I move slightly, and it takes off again. At first, I thought I scared it off, and he would go running around the house. But it goes back to the azaleas. What is this cat doing? Playing? I waited again, even though I was thinking about going back inside the house to get my coffee, slowly getting cold. I waited for about five minutes for its possible return. I'm thinking, what am I doing?! I've got better things to do. Then I thought, no, I don't. I will not make church today. I don't have plans until football this afternoon. It was going to be a lazy morning anyway. So, I waited.

Then it returned. This time it comes slowly to my feet again. This time I tried to pick it up, and it ran off again. Look, cat! I am trying to help you. Instead of running back to the bushes, it goes a few feet away and looks back at me. Then it lays on my patio and rolls around several times, and then lays there. It looks at me and then its surroundings, seemly taking in everything. I call out quietly to it, "Here, Kitty Kitty!" I think that is what you do. The darn cat comes back several times, and several times I reach down and try to grab the cat to no avail. He runs off each time, but not as far each time. Eventually, it just goes two feet from me and then doesn't dash off but rolls around at my feet or lays there looking at me. It even jumped up in the air and did a few flips. Playing with me? I noticed for the first time how small the kitten was. I'm not sure where its energy came from since he looked malnourished.

Then it came up close enough for me to reach down and snatch him. Then he was not so playful. He wanted to get away, scratching me in the process. But the scratch was not too bad since the kitten was so small. I just laughed at it and said, "Tough guy, huh? Feisty, are you? Hey, I needed you last night. I didn't need Quirt, did I? Right? Huh? Huh?! I bet you would not have been afraid of "The Shadow"." I laughed again. What am I doing talking to a cat?!

I began to rub the back of his head. I think that is what you do with cats. He continued to fight some more, or was it playing? It was sometimes hard to tell. He calmed down, and I took a closer look at him. He had blue eyes and a light pink nose. I thought cats had green eyes and not blue. But what did I know? He got more comfortable with me but jumped down and started rolling on the patio once more. He was feeling at home, which made me tell him, "Don't get too comfortable, cat."

His answer was to come up and rub my legs, going to the front and back in a figure-eight motion, starting with the left leg and going to the right. "Don't even think about buttering me up, cat. We will find a home for you." Hey, just because I am not a lover of cats does not mean I hate them. "Do you want something to eat?" I asked him as if he was going to say, "Yes, please." I heard a small mew. "I will take that as a yes," I said with another laugh. I picked him up and went inside.

"Let's see what we have inside," as I opened the refrigerator. I remembered that I had a small Tupperware container that had some of Slim's leftovers from several days ago. They were Spaghetti-Os, which I keep on hand for him. Another food fetish that he has. I took the kitten outside and placed him and the container on the patio. He devoured it in a short time. I took him back inside and put him on the kitchen counter and didn't exactly know why I put him there. I hoped he would not take off running around the house. "You thirsty?" I asked. He answered with another mew. Smart cat. I grabbed a small bowl of water and placed it on the counter. He was lapping it like he was Lassie. "I wonder if you are still hungry." He didn't answer me on that one. I got some pimento cheese and put a big gob on a plate. I took him outside to eat. "No eating inside the house." He gobbled it as quickly as he had the Spaghetti-Os. Then he came and laid at my feet. I said to him, "Now look here, cat, you can't stay here. You need to go back to where you came from. I can't keep you here." He answered this time with a meow and not mew. I don't think he liked what he was hearing.

I sat down in my chair while he ate. "Now—" Suddenly, he ran and jumped in my lap. Astonished, I said, "Now see here, cat. You're not doing this." With that, I put him down on the patio and went back inside. I don't need a cat. Maybe he will leave and go look elsewhere for food. That is all he wants anyway. I ate a late breakfast and sat down in my recliner to read. I felt a little guilty about leaving the cat alone. Okay, a kitten. But he will go to another person's house. I felt better, thinking the kitten would be okay. I dozed off and woke up at one-thirty. I must have slept for three hours, catching up on my sleep.

I got up and showered again. I was ravished, having a piece of toast for breakfast when I came in earlier from dealing with the cat. About to make myself a sandwich, I heard scratching on the door. I look and see the kitten on its back legs and his front paws on the glass pane of my door. "Cat!" I called out as I went to open the door. He comes in and playfully runs several feet away from me. He jumps up several times as if he is doing a dance. I sat in my recliner and watched him. The kitten runs and jumps in my lap. I playfully tap his head and rub him and then ask him if he's feisty. I pretend as if I am going to grab his head, and he does the same thing to my hand. Then I let him grab my hand, and we played for a few minutes. Then it dawns on me that I will now have a feline at home. More specifically, a small kitten. I thought that maybe this was what I needed right now. After all that has gone on the last several months, with the case, with Amy, this may be what precisely I need right now.

"What am I going to name you? I don't know if you are a boy or a girl. We will worry about that later. Do you like the name Frank? You have blue eyes like Frank Sinatra. What do you think about that? Um?" This time he answered me with the biggest meow yet. "What's that?"

"Meow," he said again.

"Frank it will be then," I said with a laugh. Then pulling a Bogie, I said to him, "This is the beginning of a beautiful friendship." The kitten then looked at me as if he understood. I smile and say, "Here's looking at you, kid."

Acknowledgments

To my Lord and Savior. Baptized at the age of twelve, but finally seeing the light many years later, I try the very best I can every day to walk in the Spirit.

To my wife Marcy, who has been by my side since she walked into that small grocery store in the once-small town of Mebane, North Carolina, in May of 1980. And taking me to the Commonwealth of Virginia in 1985, one month after our wedding, to begin her teaching career. For sharing those years with me raising two sons in the beautiful Northern Neck of Virginia.

For her being the ever-faithful wife of a High School Basketball Coach for five decades and dealing with so many nights when her husband came in at midnight. Consoling me when we lost and keeping me grounded when we won. Going from small, loud gyms to big loud gyms on college campuses. And for listening. So many times.

And for her love of cats, because we might never have brought in that small lost kitten we rescued in August of 2006. He grabbed my heart and wouldn't let go. We grew old and curmudgeonly together for sixteen years. He may not have been the best cat ever, but he was the best one in Farnham, Virginia.

To my sons Grant and Stewart, one the apple of my eye, and the other my pride and joy. I will not say which is which. Both believed that their dad was the greatest basketball coach ever. And that was okay with me. I needed all the help I could get. I love them more than they will ever know.

To my parents, my dad, who brought to me the love of sports, and my mom, the love of reading. And for both, with seven mouths to feed, purchasing the 1964 set of World Book Encyclopedia and Childcraft books, which opened up my curiosity about historical events and adventures.

In honor of my small hometown of Mebane, which has changed so much. You will see familiar street names in this book or a facsimile of some, like David's Furniture for White's Furniture and Southern Yarns for Dixie Yarns. Instead of Clay, it is Jay. There is Center Street. And yes, there is the Stumbling Pig.

In honor of David Oakley, my cousin, you will find a little of him in this book.

Thanks to Amazon Publishing Pros for the editing of this book and the guidance they gave me to complete it. They certainly were pros at it. I sat down one-day several years ago and began writing. I don't remember the exact year because I would take a rest from it from time to time. When Marcy and I moved from Virginia to North Carolina, I took a year off from writing and finally completed it in 2023. It has been fun and hard work.